P9-CEZ-329

The SEPTEMBER SISTERS

Jillian Cantor

LAURA GERINGER BOOKS
HARPER TEEN
An Imprint of HarperCollins*Publishers*

HarperTeen is an imprint of HarperCollins Publishers.

The September Sisters

www.harperteen.com

Library of Congress Cataloging-in-Publication Data

Cantor, Jillian.

The September sisters / by Jillian Cantor. — 1st ed.

p. cm.

"Laura Geringer books."

Summary: A teenaged girl tries to keep her family and herself together after the disappearance of her younger sister.

ISBN 978-0-06-168648-1 (trade bdg.)

[1. Missing children—Fiction. 2. Sisters—Fiction. 3. Family problems—Fiction.] I. Title.

PZ7.C173554Se 2009 2008007120

[Fic]—dc22 CIP

AC

Typography by Jennifer Rozbruch

1 2 3 4 5 6 7 8 9 10

❖

First Edition

For Gregg

And in loving memory of my grandfather

Milton J. Schechter

Chapter 1

WHEN I'M CALLED OUT of my tenth-grade advanced English class at nine-thirty in the morning on a Thursday to come down to the office, I know immediately that something has happened. As I round the corner, I see my father standing there, and I'm suddenly afraid.

"What's the matter, Dad? Are you all right?" I whisper. There's a sinking feeling in my chest because I know he's not all right. He should be at work.

He shakes his head. And I'm not sure if I want to hear what he's about to say, but I know I need to hear it. "They've found her," he says.

His words are an ending, a relief and a heartbreak all at once, because I know that everything that happened over the last two years, everything that has led me right here, right to this moment, is finally over.

The night before Becky disappeared was amazingly normal; it could've been any night in my life, any night the summer before my thirteenth birthday. Becky and I fought, but this was nothing unusual.

It was a particularly humid night, even for July. There was a certain heaviness, an unbearable, budding sweat that refused to go away as we ate dinner in our bathing suits. The air in the house seemed to stand still, even as the paddle fans above us swung around and around.

We ate macaroni and cheese for dinner. It was my favorite meal and something my mother cooked for us often because it was easy and it was the one food Becky and I both could agree on. When we were eating, my mother disappeared into the bathroom. Becky and I chewed up the noodles and held them on our tongues, then stuck our tongues out to gross each other out. "*Ewww*," Becky kept saying. "Abby, don't show me." But I laughed and did it anyway. I knew she wasn't really annoyed, only pretending, but I wanted to push her to the edge, to make her angry.

Becky and I were at each other's throats—six weeks out

of school and somewhat bored. Our mother pretended we were friends and set us up with games and arts and crafts during the day, but we hated each other. Maybe hate is too strong a word; it was more like we were jealous and crazy for our mother's attention. I was two years and one day older than Becky, and I think that always drove her crazy. She didn't like being second, not in anything.

When my mother came back to the kitchen, her face was red and puffy, and we knew she'd been crying. She cried a lot then, though we didn't really know why. Ever since our grandmother had died the year before, my mother's sadness had become something we'd accepted, something we'd learned to live with, just like anything else, I guess. We usually tried to ignore it or make jokes. Becky chewed up more noodles, stuck out her tongue, and said, "Look, Mom."

"Oh, Becky, really. Behave yourself." And she went out on the back patio to have a cigarette. My mother didn't smoke inside the house. She said if she did it outside, it didn't count. And we believed her. We didn't see her cigarette as an indulgence, something sinful, but rather as an extension of her glamour, something a little dangerous that made her more than just our mother.

There was something about our mother that Becky and

I idolized. She's beautiful, but I don't think that just because she's my mother. She's medium height, but she's very thin, and she has this shiny blond hair that she usually pulls back in a ponytail against her neck. She doesn't wear a lot of makeup, but she wears enough to highlight her features, her enormous green eyes, her wide, toothy smile. Her bottom front tooth is slightly crooked, but this only adds to her charm, makes her not perfect, and to me makes her seem only more beautiful.

Our father was working late, something he does often. When he was home, she didn't smoke at all, and we all ate dinner together. This usually happened one or two nights a week. Most nights were like that night.

Our father is a stern man, unyielding. I'm both in awe and afraid of him. He's very tall and burly with this thick brown mustache and bushy eyebrows. He's a strange match for my mother's beauty, but somehow they seemed to fit perfectly, the way he put his hand on her leg as we rode in the car, the way he put his arm around her as they sat on the couch; it was almost like he was always protecting her from something.

He works as a controller for Velcor, a company that makes dishes, china, and just your normal everyday stuff.

That's why we always have very nice plates and little teacups and saucers and the like. That night we ate our macaroni and cheese out of these pink-flowered bowls. The bowls are white, and the pink flowers are stenciled around the edges in a little chain. It was Velcor's latest design, and Becky and I adored them. We loved pink; that was one thing we both could agree on.

After dinner I called my best friend, Jocelyn Redfern. We talked to each other at least once a day, and we usually saw each other on weekends. With Jocelyn, I was my grown-up self, the one who's interested in boys and clothes and makeup. It was an entirely different role from the one I played with Becky, chewing up noodles and displaying them as a gross-out technique.

The whole summer we'd been talking incessantly about James Harper, a boy we both had a crush on. Only we'd talk about him in secret code, so when Becky tried to listen in, she wouldn't understand what we were saying. We used names of food for people: Jam for James, Banana for Becky, Iced Tea for Jocelyn's mother, and so on.

"I think I'd like to have some jam," Jocelyn would say, and we would giggle. We thought it was a brilliant idea.

When I got off the phone, Becky was watching *Wheel of*

Fortune, and I sat on the couch and joined her. I don't like game shows very much, but I love Vanna White. In a certain way, she reminds me of my mother.

We argued over which one of us would grow up to look most like Vanna. It was something we talked about a lot. Becky said she would be the one, because her hair was almost blond. "It'll get lighter when I get older," she said. "That's what I've heard." Becky was always saying she heard things, which mainly I thought she made up.

"I'm taller," I told her. "You need to be tall for a job like that."

"You're too dumb to turn the letters."

"You'd probably trip," I told her. Becky was known for being the family klutz. Sometimes my father would call her Sticky Fingers Malone, just to be silly I guess, because it made Becky laugh, even though we had no idea who Malone was.

We didn't have air conditioning yet, so it was a nightly ritual in the summer for our mother to let us go into the pool to cool off before bed. That night in the pool we fought over an inner tube.

It boiled down to this: I was sitting in the tube that Becky wanted. We have two; one is pink and the other one is orange, but neither one of us ever wanted to use the orange one. I'm not sure why my mother decided to buy them in different colors, when both of us begged her to buy us pink tank tops and pink sparkly barrettes; but for some reason she had, and I was the one who always got stuck with the orange one. That's the way it was with Becky and me. She had a way of always getting what she wanted.

I'd gotten to the pink one first, something that rarely happened, and I'd pulled myself up through the center, so I was sitting on top of it like a queen on her throne. I sat there smirking as I watched Becky swimming ferociously toward me, breaststroking with her head above water, saying, "Abby, that's my tube. It's mine." I knew she was coming for me; I knew she was going to shove me off and take the tube from me even if she had to wrestle me. I wasn't a good physical fighter; I rarely won these battles, but for a moment I didn't care. I smiled.

"Girls, no fighting." My mother said it absentmindedly, as if she expected us to fight and there was nothing she could do to stop us. Our father was the one we listened to, the one we were afraid to fight in front of. From my spot in the tube, I could barely make out her shape, her long legs and torso stretched out as if she were sunbathing, as if she had failed to notice the darkness. She dangled her cigarette loosely from her hand, tip glowing red, tiny, like a firefly.

And then Becky jumped on top of the inner tube and knocked me off, so I was choking down water. She grabbed my hair and pushed my head under for a few seconds, just long enough for me to feel intensely suffocated, like I was going to drown. I tried to push up, to push her off me, but she wouldn't budge. Then she let go; I came up and sputtered for air, and she was already sitting on the inner tube, smiling at me. "The pink one is mine," she said.

"Mom." I protested even though I knew it was useless. My mother was really somewhere else: a tropical island, a cruise ship.

She took a puff from her cigarette and blew smoke into the air. "Girls, please. Abby, just sit in the other one."

She expected me to give in to Becky. She was always saying it: "Abby, you're older. You should act like the big sister. Abby, you're trying my patience." This was why I hated Becky, for being the younger one, the baby, for knowing how to take advantage of my mother's absentminded discipline.

If my father had been there, Becky never would've pushed me off. She would've taken the orange tube and kicked my legs discreetly under the water. If he'd been home and witnessed what happened, we both would've been out of the pool and punished in our rooms for the night. But Becky and I knew she could do what she wanted on my mother's watch.

I gave up and took the other inner tube, but I stuck my tongue out at Becky and told her that I hated her. "So?" She shrugged. "I hate you, too."

This was the last conversation we had before she disappeared.

The next morning I woke up to the sound of my father calling her name. I snuggled under the covers, feeling satisfied, knowing immediately that she was in trouble and that she deserved it after what she'd done to me the night before. So I allowed myself to lie in bed for a little while and bask in my victory.

By the time I got dressed and went downstairs, the police had already arrived. My father's friend Harry Baker is a policeman, and he and another guy were sitting on the couch in our family room. At first I wasn't frightened, not even when I saw Harry there or when I saw my mother staring out the kitchen window, her eyes looking glassy, or even when I saw the crease on my father's forehead, saw his lips twitching the way they do when he gets really angry.

"Abby," my father said, "have you seen your sister?" I shrugged. I didn't take him too seriously. I thought Becky was being Becky, trying to get attention again. "It's important," he said. And he grabbed my shoulders and shook me a little, maybe harder than he meant to, so I felt something small snap in the back of my neck.

"No," I whispered. I was frightened by my father's urgency, by the feel of his large hand gripping my shoulder so tightly. It wasn't the same as the anger I was used to, the way he would treat me when Becky and I fought, when we annoyed him. My father let go of me so suddenly that I thought I might fall, as if he'd been the only thing holding me up. He sat down on the couch and took shallow, rapid breaths. "Becky's missing," he said.

"What do you mean, missing?" I couldn't process what he'd said. Of course I'd heard about kidnappings. Our parents always warned us to stay away from strangers, not to go with anyone we didn't know. But until the moment when my father said the word "missing," I believed if you did everything right, if you followed my parents' rules, there was no way to disappear.

When I looked away from my father, I saw policemen

walking up and down the stairs, carrying things out of Becky's room. One of them had her sheets in a bag, her pink and white Barbie sheets crumpled up against the plastic. "What are they doing?" I asked.

"Evidence," Harry said.

"That's enough." My father stood up and grabbed me. He was trying to hug me, but his embrace was rough, and I squirmed. "Go sit with your mother."

My mother hummed quietly under her breath and stared out the window. When I sat down next to her, I realized that for the first time in as long as I could remember, I had her all to myself.

"You hungry?" Her voice sounded low, hollow. I shrugged. I didn't feel anything. I wasn't really afraid, certainly not hungry. I didn't think Becky was really missing. I figured she was outside, walking around the neighborhood. She would be back in an hour, and then my father would be really angry. "I'll make some eggs. Everyone could use eggs," she said.

We hardly ever had eggs for breakfast, something my mother reserved for special occasions, like Father's Day or our birthdays. She stood up and walked toward the refrigerator. She was humming again, something happy that I couldn't place. I looked out the window, toward the backyard, half expecting to see Becky in one of our favorite trees, waving and sticking her tongue out at me. The morning was bright and glaringly hazy. But the yard was empty.

When I turned back to face my mother, she was staring at me; only she had this blank look on her face. She was holding the eggs one minute, and then she let them drop to the floor the next. "Jesus." My father ran in from the other room. "Elaine."

"It's okay," she said. "I'll clean it up." My father stood there as if he were unsure, afraid to move.

The police questioned all of us over the course of the day. Harry Baker asked me questions about Becky, about my parents. He asked me if I thought Becky would run away or if I knew anyone who would take her. He asked me if I had heard anything suspicious in the night, if I had seen the slightest thing amiss.

I am an unusually sound sleeper; sometimes my mother would come into my room three or four times to get me up for school. I felt this sudden surge of guilt, as if I should've heard everything, should've heard Becky get out of bed. But I had heard nothing, and my answers to Harry were all empty, useless, something I saw reflected in the uneasy frown on his face.

I didn't know Harry Baker that well. He played on my father's community baseball team. My father is the pitcher, and Harry was the catcher. Before that morning I'd never spoken with him at any great length. My father is of the school of thought that children should be seen around their parents' friends, not necessarily heard. Harry is much smaller than my father and chubbier, with an oversize, balding head and feet that appear too large. There was almost this silliness about him, this clownlike quality that didn't disappear, even when he was wearing his stern police uniform.

Becky and I had secretly made fun of him, of his little roly-poly figure and extra-large square nose—the one reason, we were certain, that he wasn't married like everyone else on the baseball team. But I was no longer laughing at his appearance. I became serious; like everyone around me, I was suddenly in a whole new world.

The first day after Becky disappeared was filled with this strange sense of shock. None of us knew what had hit us, not me, not my parents, certainly not the police. Though I know this isn't entirely true, I feel as though we all sort of sat around, that we were afraid to move, unsure.

I know that the town we live in, Pinesboro, had never seen anything like this before. I overheard Harry Baker tell my father that the first twenty-four hours are crucial, that if a missing child isn't found on the first day, she's probably dead. But still, it felt like no one took any action, that even Harry Baker wasn't exactly sure what he was supposed to do in this situation.

It took my father until dinnertime to get a search together. He scoured the house for flashlights, pulling open every drawer in the kitchen and cursing when he couldn't find one. "Dammit, Elaine. Where do we keep the flashlights?"

My mother didn't answer. She'd already taken a Valium and fallen into a deep, silent sleep.

Chapter 2

MY HOUSE SITS on the corner of Shannon Drive and Sycamore Street. The house faces Sycamore, and we happen to be number six, giving us an address that seems to roll right off the tongue, 6 Sycamore Street. The three *S*'s make it an easy address to remember, something my parents have been drilling into me practically since I was born, our address and our phone number, two pieces of information that I must never forget.

It sounded funny, hearing our address on the news, listening to my father repeat it over and over again on the phone as he called everyone in his phone book and tried to enlist their help.

On the second day it was raining, but my father's entire

baseball team showed up, looking burly in green and yellow slickers, with flashlights and tangled umbrellas. They didn't look like the men I'd seen running around the dusty field, hollering at one another, or the men holding on to beers at a summer barbecue. These were different men, pitiful, soaking wet, and possibly afraid. My father told me they were going out in a search party, though it seemed strange to me, calling something like that a party.

I'm not sure exactly where they searched, but when my father came home, he left his shoes, a large white pair of Reeboks with blue stripes on the sides, in the foyer. They were so caked with mud that you couldn't even see the stripes anymore.

Before Becky disappeared, Pinesboro was a quiet place. We are only forty-five minutes from Philadelphia, but we might as well be an entire world away. The only time I've ever been to the city is on the occasional school field trip to the art museum or the Franklin Institute or to go to the airport the one time we went to Disney World. The city feels dirty, a little dangerous, crowded. But Pinesboro strikes me as the complete opposite. It's made up of treelined streets and colonial-style houses with nice green backyards and tall oaks and evergreens. Our neighborhood is like most others in Pinesboro, several winding, hilly streets, with two-story house after two-story house, each one strangely identical, yet slightly different in its color or style. It was the kind of place where people didn't always lock their doors, where we were allowed to play on the sidewalk, even at night.

The night Becky disappeared we'd been sleeping with the windows open. No one could be sure whether or not we'd locked the front door. My mother started crying when Harry Baker asked her, and my father said he hadn't checked, that it wasn't something he thought of. It may sound strange, but that's the way things were in Pinesboro.

One of the first things my father did the week after Becky disappeared was have air-conditioning units installed in all the bedrooms, so we could close the windows at night, and he had a new dead bolt installed on the front door. He also added a security system that he arms every time he enters or exits the house. Our house is like a prison, something that sometimes feels like it's keeping me in, locked away, not keeping other people out.

After Becky disappeared, my mother retreated to her bedroom, and she spent most of the first month in bed. I saw her only rarely when my father made me go in their bedroom and sit with her. But she wouldn't talk to me. She may have been sleeping, but I doubted it. She had done the same thing after my grandmother, her mother, had died the year before. She has this way of withdrawing, of folding herself up in her own sadness so no one can get through to her, not even my father.

When my father went out to search, Mrs. Ramirez, our next-door neighbor, came over to sit with me. I'd never liked her, even before Becky disappeared. She was old, and she smelled like cooked spinach, and she didn't speak English very well.

Before Becky disappeared, Mrs. Ramirez watched us occasionally if my parents went out to dinner, until I'd turned twelve the year before and insisted that we were too old for a babysitter. My father had relented, and we hadn't seen Mrs. Ramirez much over the past year except if she was in the backyard watering her rosebushes while we were out in the pool. Then she would come up to the wooden rail fence and lean over. "Hallo, girls," she would say, and wave. "How you doing?" Her accent was usually enough to send Becky and me into fits of giggles, so all we could do was dive under the water to try to suppress them and let my mother go over to the fence to chat.

"Abigail," she would say (only she pronounced it Ah-bee-hail) when she got up to go to the bathroom, "you no move."

I wondered what it would be like to be somewhere else, to have everyone out there looking for me, but then I was afraid. I didn't know exactly what to think about where Becky was, but I decided that bad people had her, that they were doing terrible things to her. I imagined her bound to a chair and gagged and being tortured with a hot poker. We'd seen something like that in a movie once. It was something we weren't supposed to be watching, and when my father walked in, he'd changed the channel and sent us to our rooms. I'd had nightmares about that movie sometimes, even before Becky disappeared.

When Mrs. Ramirez came back from the bathroom, she stared at me so intently that I wondered how it would feel to spit in her face. "Ah-bee-hail," she said, "we pray now for your *hermana*." This made me uncomfortable. We don't pray in my family. I don't even know how to pray. Mrs. Ramirez closed her eyes and whispered things that I didn't understand. I kept my eyes open and watched her, knowing that if Becky were here, she would kick me until we both started to giggle. Suddenly I began to miss her.

Across the street from us live the Petersons and the Olneys. Mr. and Mrs. Peterson are young and don't have any children. Both of them work in the city and are hardly home. Becky and I stole short glimpses of them sometimes on Saturdays, when they'd weed the front yard. We were strangely in awe of them, fascinated. Mrs. Peterson is beautiful, with long red hair halfway down her back, and she always wears high heels, even with jeans. Mr. Peterson is tall and muscular, and sometimes he takes his shirt off when he works outside in the summer, a sight I find both disturbing and enjoyable.

Mrs. Olney is a large, loud woman, and her husband, thin as a rail and quiet. In fact, even though he's lived across the street from me all my life, I'm not sure I've heard him talk more than once or twice. The Olneys have two boys. One was a junior in high school; the other one attended Pinesboro Community College and still lived at home. The one who was in high school, John Olney, is fat like his mother and quiet like his father. "Poor kid," my mother would say when we saw him. His older brother, Shawn, plays the guitar and aspires to be in a rock band. He dressed all in black and was the first person I'd ever seen wearing real leather pants.

Sometimes, before Becky disappeared, we'd hear his band rehearsing in their garage even though the door was closed and they were all the way across the street. It was a loud screeching sound that my mother hated, and she kept saying she couldn't wait until he moved out.

For a few weeks after Becky disappeared, Mrs. Olney brought over casseroles every night. They were delicious creations, better than anything my mother has ever cooked: tuna and noodles with cheddar cheese, chicken tetrazzini, turkey potpies. The food smelled amazing when she brought it to the door, and the whole house seemed to come alive when we warmed it in the oven.

One afternoon, while my father was out searching and Mrs. Ramirez was in the bathroom, I stole a glance out my front window, and I saw a police car in the Olneys' driveway. This was my first indication that my neighbors, people I'd known all my life, would become suspects.

Every day became startlingly the same, something like a routine. I watched television with Mrs. Ramirez while the world moved slowly all around me. My mother stayed immobile in her bedroom. My father searched and searched. There was no distinction among these days, something that set one apart from the others. Becky's absence began to feel like something normal, like something that had always been hanging over us.

One day, nearly three weeks after Becky disappeared, my mother left her bedroom for the first time and went out on the patio to smoke. Mrs. Ramirez and I were watching *Family Feud*, a show I can't stand but that Mrs. Ramirez loves. "Sur-bey says," she'd say over and over again, and chuckle. I heard my mother walk down the steps, but I didn't want to get up, didn't want to frighten her back into her room. Then I heard the patio door slam, and when I turned to look outside, I saw her sitting in the deck chair, white puffs of smoke swirling up above her head.

"I'm going outside," I said to Mrs. Ramirez.

"Where I can see you, Ah-bee-hail."

I opened the door to the patio as quietly as I could and snuck up and sat down next to her. "It's hot out here," I said.

She nodded. "It's hot in there too."

Mrs. Ramirez had a tiny personal fan that she sometimes blew on the back of my neck. But that fan gave me the creeps, and I hated it when she did that.

My mother took a drag on her cigarette, then took it out

of her mouth and tapped it in the ashtray. I inhaled deeply, intoxicated by the woodsy smell of the smoke, a smell so particular to my mother that I suddenly realized how much I loved it. She reached up and caressed the top of my head, ran her fingers through my hair. "We need to get you some school clothes," she said.

Every year we went school shopping in the middle of August. We waited until the big department stores had their back-to-school sales, and then we'd have a day at the mall—lunch and everything. The day usually ended early, with Becky and me fighting and my mother having a headache, but still, it was one of the best days of the year, something I always looked forward to. I was surprised my mother thought of it. I'd remembered that school started in a few weeks, but I didn't think she had.

She smashed out the cigarette in the ashtray, grinding it down to the butt. Then she turned to me and put her hand on my cheek. "As soon as Becky gets back," she said, "then we'll go." She sounded perfectly calm, normal almost.

"What if she doesn't come back?" I whispered. I couldn't help thinking it. The day before, I'd overheard Harry Baker say to my father that three weeks was a long time for these types of cases.

My mother took her hand from my cheek, then reached up and slapped me there, not hard but enough to surprise me. It was the first time she had ever hit me, had ever shown me more than indifference or love. She got up without saying a word and went back into the house.

I sat there for a few moments, staring longingly at the pool, which I hadn't been in since the night Becky disappeared. I began to wonder about those inner tubes, if they really mattered that much, pink or orange or whatever. I closed my eyes and did what Mrs. Ramirez was always trying to get me to, attempted to pray. I wasn't exactly sure how to do it, but I wondered if God made deals. If I told him that Becky could have the pink inner tube, if I promised to always be nice to her, I wondered if Becky would be allowed to come home. But I wasn't sure how to say it all, and then I felt silly sitting there all alone with my eyes closed, so I got up and went back in the house.

"Where's my mother?" I asked Mrs. Ramirez. She shushed me. It was the bonus round, and she was watching intently, but she pointed upstairs.

A few hours later my father came home, sweaty and dirty and carrying a pizza. "Did you find her?" I asked, the same way I asked him each night. I'd have the same feeling when I saw him walk in: It was hope that he'd have Becky with him, that she'd just been playing a game, hiding all along.

My father didn't answer. He put the pizza down on the table. "We have to eat," he said. My father isn't a cook; in fact I don't think I'd ever seen him make more than a can of chicken soup, and that was only one time, when my mother had the flu. My father is a numbers man, a bill payer, a straight-and-narrow arrow, as my grandma Jacobson used to call him.

I thought about telling him what had happened with my mother earlier on the patio, but I knew it would make him mad. He'd tell me I shouldn't bug her, that I should mind myself.

I took a piece of pizza, and we sat there together and ate in silence. There were a lot of things I wanted to ask him: where they were searching; what they'd found; if he, like my mother, truly believed that Becky would come home. But I wasn't sure how to ask him any of that without it sounding bad. Instead I asked him if he thought my mother was okay.

"Sure, Ab, she'll be fine. You know how she gets."

I nodded.

"Tomorrow morning I'm going back on TV," my father said. "We're going to offer a reward."

"What kind of reward?"

"Money, Ab. A hundred grand."

It suddenly seemed spectacular to me that Becky was worth that much money. We often talked about what we'd do if we had a lot of money, the things we'd buy. Becky always said she would buy her own horse, though I told her we wouldn't have anywhere to keep it. "It doesn't matter." She would shrug. "If I'm that rich, I'll buy my own stable."

"You'll come with me," he said. "Mrs. Ramirez has a doctor's appointment."

If Becky had been there, we would've spent the rest of the night looking through our closets for something to wear to the television station. We would've fought over the little makeup cases our mother bought us for our birthdays the year before. Becky would've insisted that she would somehow get on TV.

Instead, after we finished eating our pizza, my father sent me up to my room to go to bed. "We're getting up early tomorrow," he said.

In my room it was too hot to sleep. Though we had the new air conditioning, I wasn't allowed to turn down the temperature to cool the room off completely. My father had already told me about how expensive it was, about how we couldn't afford all the electric costs.

So I lay on the floor, under the fan, trying to follow a blade, around and around. For a moment I felt as if I could slow down time, make it move at my own pace, even make it go back.

Chapter 3

BECKY'S HAIR WAS straight, dirty blond, and just past her shoulders. She had green eyes and pinkish sunburned skin in the summer. She had dimples. She had some freckles on her nose. She had a two-inch scar just above her right elbow, from the time she fell off her bike. She was four feet eight inches tall, and she weighed seventy-three pounds. She was ten years old.

These were the things my parents told the police, the things my father said on the local news when he went on to make a plea for her safe return and to offer the reward.

There were other things that we didn't say. Becky's voice was high-pitched and scratchy, just like my grandmother's. Becky liked oranges but hated orange juice. Becky wanted to be an actress or a horse trainer when she grew up. Becky favored my mother in every way—the way she looked, the way she gestured even.

She hardly ever cried, even when she got upset. Instead her face turned bright red, and she scrunched it up real tight. When she smiled really wide, her forehead crinkled. When she did something spiteful, she got this mischievous half grin on her face.

Sometimes, after she disappeared, I'd imagine Becky as a superhero, Sticky Fingers Malone. I remembered this time when we all went ice-skating, and she couldn't stand up on her own two feet for more than a few seconds. She kept grabbing onto my shirt and pulling me down with her.

"Stop it, you little baby," I said to her. And then defiantly she held her head up high and tried to skate after me, but it was no use; she kept falling. I laughed at her then, even after she'd caught her balance, even after she'd skated once around the rink by herself. She may have been bruised and broken, but she kept on going until she could do it. That was Becky.

I, on the other hand, would've given up. I understood that there were some things I was never going to be good at, so I stopped trying at them almost right away.

At the TV station I thought about all those other things, while my father mechanically recounted what Harry Baker called the vital stats. I wondered if my father remembered these things, if he was thinking of Becky as more than her fifth-grade school picture, which he held up for the camera and which was also printed on posters in our neighborhood and the local Shop and Save and, I'd heard Harry Baker say, would soon be on milk cartons.

It is sometimes hard for me to think of her any other way, and I make myself remember the last night in the pool, Becky's face as she stole the inner tube from me, just so she is something else besides that school picture.

The TV station was boring, nothing like what Becky or I would've hoped. I got to sit in a chair back behind the cameras, so I was facing the anchorwoman and my father, who sat behind the news desk. Someone who seemed semi in charge gave me a cup of coffee, something I had never been allowed to have before. Before I drank it, I looked to my father to see if he was disapproving, but he didn't notice. He was talking animatedly to the anchorwoman, straightening his tie.

I took a sip, and I was surprised by how bitter and awful it tasted. But I kept drinking it, and I nodded at the guy who gave it to me, as if to say thanks, I drink this stuff all the time. No biggie. But he wasn't paying attention to me anymore. He'd already stopped noticing me, forgotten I was there.

I drank the whole cup, and then, almost immediately, I had to pee. My father was busy talking to the anchor-woman, so I asked the guy who'd given me the coffee where the bathroom was. He pointed down the hall and held his finger to his lips. They were about to go live.

After I peed, I stood in the bathroom and looked at myself in the mirror. I always thought that Becky was prettier than me. My hair is a mousy brown and has a frizzy sort of curl to it that never quite straightens, even when my mother used her straightening iron. But it doesn't curl right either, so it's just this useless, frizzy mop. My skin is darker than Becky's, and I don't have any freckles; my eyes are a dull sort of brown. I smiled at myself in the mirror and pinched my cheeks, trying to give them some color. I ran my fingers through my hair to try to straighten it, but it was no use.

I left the bathroom, and my father was standing right there. He grabbed me so fiercely that it frightened me. "Jesus, Ab. Don't wander off like that."

I shook him off. "I had to pee." I knew what he thought,

that I had disappeared too. I felt oddly satisfied that I'd frightened him in that way, that for a minute he'd been worried about me.

It was the first day I'd been out of the house in a while, and I didn't want it to end, so I was glad that my father said we were stopping at the police station on the way home. The police had become something of a permanent fixture around our neighborhood, but I had never been with my father to the station before.

"Don't wander off," my father said before we even got out of the car.

The inside of the station wasn't what I expected, nothing like it is on TV. It was more like an office, a series of cubicles with a receptionist and a small waiting area in the front. Some of the people walking around had police uniforms on, but some didn't. I was disappointed; I had imagined something exciting—a waiting room full of trash-talking hookers and drunks. But it was nothing like that. It was similar to my father's office, boring, only I let myself believe that there must be something exciting going on in some hidden interrogation room in the back.

Harry came out to the front area to meet us. He shook

my father's hand, but as usual he ignored me. It always bothered me the way Harry looked over me to my father. He never asked me how I was doing or if I was looking forward to going back to school, like most of the other adults who'd been hanging around our house. Though I can't stand when adults baby me like Mrs. Ramirez, I hate it more when they ignore me.

My father told me to have a seat in one of the waiting chairs, and he and Harry moved toward the row of cubicles to talk. I tried not to listen to what they were saying. Every time I overheard something Harry said to my father, it scared me.

It's not that I was clueless. Mrs. Ramirez kept me up on the gossip, and my father told me some of what went on. I already knew that there was a suspect. A few of our neighbors, including Mrs. Ramirez, had seen an unfamiliar blue van parked on the street the day before Becky disappeared. Somebody had seen a suspicious-looking man just sitting in there. We didn't know what he looked like or who he was, but I had my own image of him, my own theory.

This man was tall with blond hair, strikingly handsome. He just lost his wife and child in a terrible fire, and when he saw Becky walking down the street, he asked her to be his new daughter. He promised her all the toys that money could buy, a nice house in California. And now Becky was somewhere wonderful, having the time of her life.

The "evidence" the police had taken from Becky's room had turned up nothing, except a few drops of blood and my parents' fingerprints. It could be nothing, Harry had told my father of the blood. It could've been from an old cut. This was the last thing I'd overheard Harry tell my father, which was why I was trying not to listen this time.

But Harry talked loudly, expressively, and I couldn't help hearing him tell my father that it was "imperative for him to talk to Elaine."

"I'll see what I can do," my father said.

"Jim, if you don't get her to come down here to talk to us on her own, we're going to have to bring her in."

My father nodded. I could tell by the way his forehead looked tight, stretched, that he was angry.

I knew as well as my father did that there was no way my mother was getting out of bed to talk to Harry. I wondered what he meant by "bring her in"; when they said that on TV, they usually arrested someone.

In the car I asked my father why the police wanted to talk to my mother.

"Harry wants to ask her some questions, that's all."

My father turned up the radio, his usual cue that he doesn't want to talk anymore. That was how I knew immediately that he was lying to me. I reached over and turned it back down. "She wouldn't hurt Becky," I said.

"Of course she wouldn't. That's crazy."

But I could tell by the way my father said it, without even glancing at me, that my mother was a suspect.

Chapter 4

IN THE WEEK AFTER my father went on television to announce the reward, nearly 150 people called with "tips" about Becky's disappearance. Harry promised my father that each tip was being thoroughly examined by the police, but when each one of them led to nothing, my father shook his head in disgust and said, "Jesus, what some people won't do for money."

This week was also the week before school was about to start, and I hadn't talked to my mother again or heard another word about shopping. I'd had a growth spurt over the summer, and my body shape was so different that most of my clothes didn't fit anymore. Suddenly I had breasts, and I didn't even own a bra. In the beginning of the summer, before Becky had disappeared, my mother had mused about the two of us shopping for bras together "soon."

But it was my father, not my mother, who, to my dismay, finally noticed that I needed to go shopping. "I set it up with Mrs. Ramirez," he told me one evening that week. "She can take you to get all the girl things you need."

I felt my face turn red, and I hugged my arms around my chest. "I don't need to go with her," I said. The thought of bra shopping with smarmy Mrs. Ramirez made me want to die. "You can just drop me off. I can go by myself. "

My father shook his head.

"For Christ's sake, I'm almost thirteen."

He grabbed my shoulder. "Watch your mouth, Ab." We stared at each other fiercely, our eyes locked like two wild animals trying to decide if they should fight to the death. "While you're there, get some notebooks, pencils, whatever it is you need for school."

"Mom wanted to take me. She told me."

"Your mother's not feeling well."

"She's never feeling well. She has two daughters, you know. I'm still here." It was something I regretted saying out loud as soon as I said it, something so painfully obvious.

"That's enough." He let go suddenly. "Just be good

for Mrs. Ramirez." He went upstairs and left me sitting at the kitchen table all alone, the remnants of our half-eaten McDonald's on the table.

"Jesus Christ, I'm not a baby," I whispered under my breath after he left. "Shit, shit, shit." It felt good to curse, to say something so harsh out loud. If Becky had been there, she would've been laughing. *Ha-ha, you have to get a bra with Mrs. Ramee-rez.* "Go to hell," I whispered. "All of you can go to hell."

The next morning Mrs. Ramirez showed up promptly at nine. "We go girl shopping," she said when I got into the car. "Ah-bee-hail, you big woman now."

I nodded and looked out the window. I hoped that I wouldn't see any of my friends at the mall. I hadn't seen anyone since before Becky disappeared, and I'd talked to Jocelyn only twice. Both times we didn't mention Becky. We talked about what was going on on *General Hospital*, what we wanted to be wearing on the first day of school, and Jocelyn's birthday. I suspected that Jocelyn's mother, who was very prim and uptight, had warned her not to mention Becky. The fact that we didn't talk about her, though, made the conversations awkward. Becky was everywhere.

About two weeks after Becky disappeared, Jocelyn had a sleepover party for her thirteenth birthday, an event that I normally would've helped Jocelyn and her mother plan, to which I would've arrived early and left late, but to which this year my father said, "Absolutely not." Even though I'd told him how unfair he was being, he wouldn't budge. "You're sleeping in this house," he said, "where I can keep an eye on you." I reminded him that Becky had been sleeping in this house when she disappeared; that got me the rest of the night in my room and not being allowed even to go to the party, much less to sleep over. I hadn't talked to Jocelyn since the party, but deep down I sensed things were now different between us.

Mrs. Ramirez parked at Macy's, a store my mother hates. Usually we parked at Penney's and shopped there first, but I felt so weird shopping with Mrs. Ramirez that I didn't want to say anything. I think I'd been in Macy's only once or twice. My mother says it's overpriced and that the salesgirls are uppity. Mrs. Ramirez seemed to know the store well because she led me immediately to the lingerie section. "We need to get you measure," she said, and she started looking around for someone who worked there.

Jocelyn had told me about this earlier in the summer,

about the woman who wrapped the tape measure around your chest and told you what size you were. I thought it was creepy, and I didn't want anyone touching my chest, especially not in front of Mrs. Ramirez. "It's okay," I said. "I know my size."

She looked at me with disbelief and shook her head. "Uh-uh. We get you measure."

"No, really. They measured me earlier in the summer when I came with my mom."

She shook her head and pointed to my chest. "Then where you bra?"

I felt my face turning red as Mrs. Ramirez stared at my chest. But before I could protest anymore, the salesgirl was there, and Mrs. Ramirez pointed at my chest some more and said, "This her first bra!" excitedly. I wanted to die. I wished that I had been the one to disappear, who was somewhere else, anywhere but here.

"Thirty-two B," the salesgirl announced after thoroughly grabbing and pinching me.

"Oh, good size." Mrs. Ramirez patted my shoulder. "Not too big, not too small!"

"Whatever." I shrugged. I knew if my mother had been there, she would've been quiet, subdued. She wouldn't have embarrassed me; she wouldn't have commented about the size. She would have just handed me a bra over the dressing room door and smiled.

"I get the D," Mrs. Ramirez said. "Too much sometimes."

I couldn't look at her. I didn't want to hear her talk about her big, jiggly breasts. I don't know what size bra my mother wears, but I don't think it's a D.

I picked up the first 32B bra that I saw on the rack and told Mrs. Ramirez that was the one I wanted.

"You try on," she said.

I shook my head. "No, this is fine."

"No, you have to try on."

"I'm not trying it on." My teeth were clenched, and I was almost yelling. I knew I was practically having a tantrum, but I didn't care. I didn't want to get undressed in front of her, didn't want her to poke and prod and comment about my body.

"Okay." She shrugged. "You decision."

We paid for the bra, and Mrs. Ramirez asked me what else I needed for school.

"Nothing," I lied. "I already got everything else." I decided that I would rather start school with no clothes and supplies than be subjected to a whole day of Mrs. Ramirez in the mall and the possibility of seeing one of my friends in another store.

"Okey-doke," she said. "Have it your way, Ah-bee-hail."

When I got home, my mother was sitting out on the patio smoking and talking to Harry Baker and my father. It was the first time I'd seen her out of bed in so long that at first I was excited. But then I began to wonder, What was she doing up and why was she talking to Harry Baker? I wondered if they had found Becky.

I let myself out on the patio quietly, but my father turned and saw me right away. He gestured for me to go back in the house; I pretended not to understand what he was trying to tell me. I wanted to know what was going on.

"Abby." My mother stopped what she was saying to Harry, put her cigarette down, and motioned for me to come sit with her. Suddenly feeling shy, lost, I went.

"Abigail." Harry nodded in my direction but didn't meet my glare. I felt like my mother's shield, her only protector, so I kept on glaring at him for a minute or so.

I hugged my mother; she was so bony, much thinner

than usual. She'd lost weight spending so much time in bed. I was so happy to hug her, to have her there, that I almost deluded myself into believing that things would be okay again, that life could go back to normal. "Maybe we can go shopping later," I said to her.

"We'll see." She let go of me to pick up her cigarette, and as she took a long, slow drag, she stared off to nowhere.

"Ab, Mrs. Ramirez took you shopping already." My father sounded impatient, annoyed.

I didn't want to tell him that I hadn't gotten everything I needed, and I didn't have anything else to say, so all I said was: "I know."

I heard a steady tapping noise, and I realized the sound was Harry, tapping his ballpoint pen on one of chairs over and over again. "Ab, go watch TV or something," my father said. "We'll be in in a few minutes."

My mother smashed out her cigarette in the ashtray and coughed. "No." She held up her hand. "We're done here." She stood up. "I don't have anything else to tell you, Harry."

Harry stood up too. "Elaine," he said. But I noticed he seemed to be looking past my mother, as if he were fixated by the trellis of yellow roses that adorn the side of our fence. I wondered if he was trying to see into Mrs. Ramirez's yard, if she too was being questioned by the police.

My mother touched my cheek. "Be good, sweetie." Then she walked into the house.

Harry Baker and my father exchanged glances, so I knew something was going on. "What about the man in the blue van? " I asked Harry. "Have you found him yet?"

"Go inside, Ab. I'll be in in a minute," my father said. I felt the need to defend my mother, to tell Harry that she'd been sad long before Becky disappeared. But before I had a chance to say anything, my father added, "Go. Go ahead. What are you waiting for?"

He came inside a few minutes later, without Harry Baker.

"Where's Harry?" I asked.

"He left." He paused. "Did you get everything you needed at the mall?"

"Yes," I lied. I knew he would be angry if I told him the truth, and worse, he wouldn't understand.

"Good." He started to walk away, toward the stairs—toward my mother, I figured.

I was dying to ask him what was really going on, why he had wanted me out the house this morning, what exactly had gotten my mother out of bed. "Dad, wait."

"What is it, Ab?" He sounded exasperated, wound tight and just about ready to explode.

"Why did Mr. Baker want to talk to Mom?"

"Try not to make too much noise down here," he said. "Your mother is trying to sleep." Then he went upstairs and left me sitting there all alone.

Eventually I got sick of watching TV and went upstairs to my room to try on my new bra. It was nearly nighttime, and outside, it was cooling off, but in my room it was still stifling.

In winter months my room is my sanctuary. It's painted yellow and has ugly green shag carpeting that has been there since before my parents moved in, but I covered the walls with pictures of actors I like and hung pink and purple crepe paper flowers from the ceiling. My mother was always promising we would redecorate the room, but somehow we never got around to it. Becky's room had been the nursery, and it's painted a pale lilac with a border of little bunny rabbits. Becky complained that she was too old for such a babyish room, but I think she secretly didn't mind. It was just that if I was having my room redone, she wanted hers done too. I was always proud of the fact that my room was bigger than Becky's by two whole square feet, but I envied her purple walls and sleek hardwood floors.

I shut the door, turned the fan on high, and then took off all my clothes and stood in front of the mirror. I was surprised by the look of my body, by the new shape of it. I had actual breasts, and I turned sideways to see how I looked in profile. If Becky were there, she would've been laughing at me, but I think deep down she would have been jealous. We both always envied grown-ups—our mother especially—for their sheer grown-up-ness. My breasts would give me a big edge over Becky in that category.

I took the bra out of the bag and held it up to my chest. It was a plain bra, not like the ones I'd seen in my mother's room, which were sheer and lacy. This one was white and simple cotton. It had a tiny flowery bow in the center, in between the two cups. I wrapped it around my rib cage, then hooked it and spun it, the way I'd seen my mother do once after we'd gone to the beach and she was getting dressed in the public changing rooms. Then I pulled the straps up and turned to look at myself in the mirror head-on. The bra was a little small, constricting; it squeezed my rib cage funny and made it a little hard to breathe. I shifted it to try to adjust it, but one of my breasts hung out a little at the top. Mrs. Ramirez was right. I should've tried it on.

The next morning I woke up early. My parents were still asleep, and I decided to bring the paper in from the front porch. I had to disarm the security system to do it, but my father must've been sound asleep, because for the first time the little beeping noise of the alarm turning off didn't send him running down the stairs. I wondered if he'd taken one of my mother' s sleeping pills.

As soon as I opened up the paper, I saw the article about Becky. At first I was a little shocked, seeing her there, grainy and black and white, but then I realized this was probably not the first article. In fact she might have been in the paper frequently. The *Pinesboro Gazette* didn't have much else to report. But it was the first time I'd actually seen the paper since she'd disappeared. My father must have been hiding it, getting up early to read it and then throwing it out before I could see it.

On the front page was Becky's picture, the same school picture that had become Becky's image over the past few weeks. The headline read: POLICE SEARCH MORROW'S FIELD FOR MISSING GIRL'S BODY. It was the first time I'd ever thought of Becky as Becky's body, as something lifeless. It was the first time I'd ever thought that Becky might be dead.

Looking at the headline, at Becky's school picture and the word "body," I was astounded. Then I felt angry. Becky couldn't be dead.

I read the article quickly, afraid that my father would come downstairs and snatch the paper out of my hands before I had a chance to understand it. Mostly it said what I already knew, about when Becky had gone missing, about the reward. But it said two things that surprised me. The first was about the police searching Morrow's field.

Morrow's field is a big field that starts behind our neighborhood and separates us from Ford's Creek, a larger neighborhood of smaller houses and town houses. We played out there sometimes in the fall, softball and soccer. Every once in a while we had a neighborhood picnic or a birthday party there. In the winter we built snowmen and sledded there. The field is huge, grassy, and muddy. You could get to it if you walked through our backyard, went behind the pool, and let yourself out the back gate. The article mentioned how easily accessible it is from our house.

The other thing that surprised me was that the article said the police were questioning both my parents as well as some of the neighbors, whom the article didn't name. It said that the police hadn't officially named my parents as suspects, but I thought the article sort of implied that they were.

I already knew that they suspected my mother, that her weird behavior somehow made her seem suspicious, but to know that they suspected my father too was a shock. My father is such a straight arrow, always worrying about the rules.

I realized that I was going to have to do something. The adults all around me suddenly seemed so useless. I knew Becky had to be somewhere, maybe in Morrow's field, maybe not, but I knew for sure that my parents didn't have anything to do with it.

I felt disgusted as I folded the paper back up and put it back on the porch where I'd found it, and I tried to brainstorm possibilities for how I could find her. Though nothing came to me, I kept trying to think of something because I knew it was better than the alternative, thinking about her as a body buried in the field.

I reset the alarm. I didn't want my father to know I'd seen the newspaper, that I knew now what was going on. If he knew I'd gotten the paper, he'd yell at me. But worse, I was sure he wouldn't look at me the same, that he would somehow look guilty or ashamed.

ര

The last time I was in Morrow's field had been two weeks before Becky disappeared.

There was a barbecue at Harry Baker's house, in the Ford's Creek neighborhood, across the field from us. At the barbecue, Harry cooked hamburgers and hot dogs, and the men, my father included, stood in a circle around the grill, holding on tightly to their beer bottles. The men on my father's baseball team had a barbecue every summer, and it was something Becky and I dreaded being dragged to. This barbecue was even bigger and more boring than usual, with the baseball team and Harry's neighbors, none of whom we knew. We were instantly bored; we were the only children there over the age of five. We hung around my mother, listening to the women talk, but when the talk turned to gardening, Becky and I skipped away and plopped ourselves down in the middle of the yard.

We pulled out blades of grass in fistfuls and tried to whistle through the individual blades. It was a trick I could never quite master, and sick of the sweet taste of the grass, I gave up after a few tries. I started pulling petals off a dandelion, saying silently to myself: *James loves me, he loves me not, he loves me . . .*

Then Becky's grass whistled, a sound so clear and high-pitched that it cut through the noise of the crowd, a birdsong. "Hey, Ab, I did it. I did it." She clapped her hands.

"So what?" I shrugged. "That's stupid anyway."

"That's just because you can't do it."

"Can too."

"Cannot."

I reached over and yanked her pigtail so hard that her head bowed to the side. "Ow," she yelled. "I'm telling." And she jumped up and ran off in search of our mother. I pulled out clumps of grass and, frustrated, threw them around me.

Becky returned moments later with my mother in tow. "Abby," she whispered, but I could tell she was angry.

"What?"

"Really, you're embarrassing me. Behave yourself."

"I didn't do anything," I lied. When our mother turned around to walk back toward the women, I stuck my tongue out at Becky. *Tattletale*, I mouthed to her.

Maybe our mother had a sixth sense, or maybe she had witnessed this scene so many times that she'd known it by heart by then. "Abby, go home."

"What?" I was surprised that I was being banished, then strangely amused.

"Go home and wait for us in your room. Think about what you've done."

Now it was Becky's turn to smile, and smile she did, a large, toothy grin that made her whole face light up. "Well, fine then," I said. "This sucks anyway."

"Abby, mind yourself."

But I wasn't listening. I'd already stood up and started walking in the direction toward home, toward Morrow's field.

In the field there were a few boys in Becky's grade who were playing catch, and they seemed oddly lit up by the dusk, like shadows, throwing the ball and then chasing it. I could hear them yelling to one another, their voices high-pitched and mellow, like girls'. The grass was particularly green, a deep emerald shade that reminded me of *The Wizard of Oz* when it suddenly popped into color. We'd had an extraordinary amount of rain over the summer, and it showed. I skipped across the field, happy to be away from the party. I was free. Free at last.

After Becky disappeared, I tried to remember it the way it was then, emerald and amazing, nothing at all like a possible burial ground.

Chapter 5

I QUICKLY CAME to learn that everyone was a suspect. It wasn't just the steely glances or, worse, the people who refused to look at us as my father took me on our first trip to the supermarket, just the two of us. It was the lack of other things after a certain amount of time: condolences, well-wishers, offers to help, or even the missing space of something as simple as Mrs. Olney's tuna casserole on the top shelf of our fridge.

My father said to me, as we walked through the crowded market, feeling like lepers, "Well, you know, Ab, it's times like this when you learn who your real friends are." But it sounded like something mechanical, something he'd heard someone else say and decided he should believe. It did not sound like my father.

As luck would have it, we ran into Mrs. Olney in the pasta aisle. I saw her coming, but my father, who was sorting through brands of spaghetti, looking rather lost, didn't notice. "Dad," I whispered, trying to get his attention. But he didn't hear me. She might have been the first person to look directly at us, but seeing her didn't comfort me one bit. As soon as she saw the two of us, she sped up, all three hundred or so pounds of her bouncing in her pink floral muumuu, the sound of her pink flip-flops smacking the hard white tile, and her heavy breathing reminding me of this video I'd seen in school of a bull charging a matador.

"Despicable," she said. "You people." She shook her finger at my father, who suddenly looked up and frowned at her. "You sent those policemen after my son. My son wouldn't hurt anyone. And you parading around here like you didn't do anything wrong." I waited for my father to defend himself, but he didn't say anything. He just nodded his head slowly. "You can't just go around ruining people's lives," she said. "You just can't." She looked directly at me and shook her head. I noticed the mole she has above her left eye had a little hair growing out of it, and I had to suppress the urge to reach up and rip it out. "You tell them to leave Shawn alone," she said. "He hasn't done nothing to nobody!" Then she swung her cart around us and clacked down to the next aisle.

"Let's go." My father grabbed my arm.

"But we haven't gotten anything yet."

"I said let's go." He left the cart sitting there and pushed me toward the door.

The next week I had to go back to school, and for the first time since Becky disappeared, my father went back to work. I started to feel everything slow down, come to a sort of automatic halt. For the first time in weeks Becky became the background of our world.

On the first day of school my father dropped me off on his way to work. "Mrs. Ramirez will pick you up," he said. "Right out here. Three o'clock."

I nodded.

"Wait for her," he said. "Don't try to walk. Don't go with anyone else."

I was about to roll my eyes at him, but I didn't want to hear him yell at me, first thing in the morning, so instead I just promised to do what he said. "Ab," he said as I got out of the car. I turned back to look at him. "Have a good day."

When I walked into school on the first morning, people looked at me and looked away. People started whispering. At first I thought they were looking at my outfit. I wore the same jean shorts I'd been wearing all summer, my favorite pink shirt, which was now a little too tight, and my ratty pink flip-flops. It was my first first day of school ever without a new outfit to wear. But I hadn't mentioned that to anyone at home, not after that horrible trip to the mall with Mrs. Ramirez. It was also the first time in three years that Jocelyn and I hadn't coordinated our outfits over the phone the night before. I'd called her, but Mrs. Redfern told me Jocelyn was out with her father and would call me back if it wasn't too late. She never called.

It didn't take me long to realize that I was different, and it wasn't just the clothes or the new figure or the fact that Jocelyn wasn't waiting for me in our usual spot by the lockers. People stayed away from me like I was a disease, like something they might catch if they got too close, like they were afraid that they would disappear too.

The day began with homeroom, where I sat next to Jocelyn, just as I always had. Reed and Redfern—we were as close alphabetically as we had been friends for the past few years. "Hey." I tapped her on the shoulder.

She smiled, but I could tell it was fake. It was the smile she reserved for people we didn't like, for her mother's intrusive questions. We kind of stared at each other for a few minutes, and then it started to feel uncomfortable. For the first time in our friendship we weren't sure what to say to each other.

Finally she said, "Look what I got for my birthday." She pointed to her earrings, which were little pink stars, so delicate and perfect that they would've been exactly what I would've wished for most in the world six weeks ago.

"Nice." I was smiling so wide and so hard that I thought my face might crack. Usually Jocelyn and I had a lot to say to each other; we'd tell each other everything. But there was the huge, obvious gap between us, the difference between my summer and hers.

Mr. Halburt, our homeroom teacher, quieted us down and took roll. I watched Jocelyn out of the corner of my eye, and I noticed she was wearing makeup, blue eye shadow, to be exact, the palest shade of baby blue I've ever seen. We had never worn makeup to school before.

When the bell rang for first period, Mr. Halburt pulled me aside, so I didn't get to walk with Jocelyn. "Abigail," he said, "I have a note here from Mrs. Austin. She'd like you to go see her during first period."

"I have algebra," I said. "Math is my worst subject. I shouldn't miss it." Mrs. Austin is the school guidance counselor, and I knew immediately why she wanted to see me. She would want to know all about my summer and Becky and how I was handling it all. Mrs. Austin wears bright pink lipstick, and when she applies it, she must not use a mirror because it's always smudged down her chin. She was the last person I felt like talking to.

Mr. Halburt patted me on the shoulder, then looked me straight in the eye. I could tell he was trying to see if I was okay in that intrusive way that teachers have when they believe themselves to be gods who can fix everything. "It's the first day," he said. "You'll be fine." He said it like he was talking about the math class, but the way he looked at me, I wondered if he was trying to console me, to remind me that life goes on, that everything in junior high is a fad, here one week and gone the next. I might be a leper today, but by next month I would just be Abigail Reed again. Or so I hoped.

Mrs. Austin asked me a bunch of questions about how I felt, how things were at home, how my parents were. I told her everything was fine, that we were just fine, fine, fine. I thought about how annoyed my father would have been if he'd heard the questions Mrs. Austin asked me. *None of her damn business*, he would have said. But I guess she was just trying to do her job.

I suppose she was trying to help me, pulling me out of first period like that. But the truth of the matter was she only made things worse. I had to walk into algebra class in the middle, which meant that when I opened the door and walked in, everyone turned to stare at me. I felt my face turning red, and I slunk down into a seat in the back of the room.

The worst part of the day by far, though, was lunch. You have to understand the way the lunchroom worked. There were certain tables you sat at and certain ones you didn't. Each section of tables was reserved in a way: one for the popular kids, the ones who would be the homecoming queens and kings, the football players, and the cheerleaders in high school; one for the outcasts, nerds, geeks, computer whizzes, whatever you want to call them; one for the athletic kids; one for the brains who weren't quite nerds; and one for the up-and-coming populars, the people who are just on the brink of being cool but aren't quite there yet. This was the section Jocelyn and I and our other friends had sat in all last year.

When I walked into the lunchroom, Jocelyn was already there, but she wasn't sitting at our normal table. She was sitting at the popular table, and she was talking to Andrea Cass, her neighbor and also quite possibly the most snobbishly popular girl at our school. I debated walking up to them, asking them if I could sit there. Jocelyn and I had made a pact the year before. If one of us were to break into the popular crowd, we would bring the other one with us. But I suddenly knew that the pact was no longer good, that if I sat at that table, it would immediately get quiet, everyone would stare at me, and when I'd get up to put away my tray, they would giggle.

Instead I sat at my normal table, with some girls Jocelyn and I had been semifriends with the year before. These girls had been our lunch-table friends and nothing else. Jocelyn and I had aspirations to be in the popular crowd one day; these girls were perfectly content being behind them, always on the outside looking in.

"Hey," I said, and plopped my tray down.

"That seat's taken." This came from Katie Rainey, who is the plainest of the girls, too plain and boring to be popular, Jocelyn had always said. At first I thought she was lying, and I was ready to call her on it, about ready to punch someone in the face even. I felt this anger rush up inside me, like a violent thunderstorm that seems to come on suddenly but that you know has actually been welling up in the hot, hot atmosphere all day. But then I looked up and saw Katie Rainey's younger sister standing behind me. My seat was being taken by a stupid seventh grader.

"Sorry." Though I wasn't quite sure what I was apologizing for, I stood up, looked around the lunchroom, and decided there was nowhere for me to sit. I didn't belong anywhere. I dumped my tray without eating anything and spent the rest of my lunch in the library, pretending to read a book.

Mrs. Ramirez was late, and I ended up waiting out in front of the school for her for fifteen minutes. I was tempted to start walking home. I knew it would be quicker and less painful—the last thing I wanted to do was talk to her—but I knew she would tell my father, and he would be mad. Since Becky had disappeared, I'd had the constant craving for his acceptance, a need for him not to be disappointed in me. It was strange because before, I'd never really worried about what my father thought about me.

So I sat outside and waited. I watched Jocelyn and Andrea walk out together. I waved to Jocelyn as she walked by, and she gave me a little half smile. The year before, Jocelyn and Becky and I had walked to the corner together. The elementary school was next door to the junior high, and we all got out at the same time, so Jocelyn and I would meet Becky right outside.

When we got to the corner, Jocelyn turned one way toward her development, and Becky and I turned the other way toward ours. Sometimes Becky and I played a game when we were walking home, where we'd look at the people outside, our neighbors watering their plants or whatever, and make up stories about them. We said things like Mrs. Johnson, whom we often saw getting her mail, had killed her husband and buried him in the backyard, when really we both had overheard our mother say he'd left her.

I longed for that right then, for walking home after the first day of school, for someone to laugh with. I felt so desperately sad, suddenly, so empty.

By the time Mrs. Ramirez showed up, I was practically in tears, just sitting there, feeling sorry for myself. "How you day, Ah-bee-hail?" she asked as I got into the car.

"Fine," I lied. I guessed it was obvious from the tone of my voice that things weren't fine, that they would never be fine again.

Mrs. Ramirez patted my knee. "It get better," she said. "Tomorrow new day."

I wished for my mother right then, for a hug from her, for her to hold me against her and stroke my hair. Mrs. Ramirez was a poor substitute; her pat on the knee didn't console me at all.

The night after the first day of school was the first time I had the dream about the night Becky disappeared. I lay in bed, stuck on the idea of how she might have been lured out of our house, so I will never really know if the dream was a memory or a trick played on me by my overactive imagination.

In the dream, I saw a man standing at the door to my room. He was dressed in black pants, a black long-sleeved shirt, and a black woolen winter cap, and my first thought was how strange it was because it was summer and extraordinarily warm. I caught a glimpse of the man's face, and I knew I recognized him from somewhere, only I couldn't tell you from where. For a moment I thought he could be Harry

Baker; then he morphed into Shawn Olney, then maybe Mr. Peterson, because his handsomeness surprised me. In the dream he did not look like a monster, only a normal man.

The next day I was sick. I wasn't just pretending to get out of school either; I really was sick. It must've been something I ate, because I threw up three times before my father came in to get me up for school.

"I can't," I told him, and ran to the bathroom to puke again in the toilet.

"Ab," he said, "you've got to go back. There's no use pretending." I realized Mrs. Ramirez must have told him all about our moment in the car, because I hadn't mentioned my terrible day to him.

I shook my head. "I'm not."

I guess he noticed then that I really was a little green, because he let it go and felt my forehead with his hand. "You don't have a fever."

"I already threw up four times."

"Okay. I'll bring you up some tea before I go."

I nodded and crawled back into bed. I got under all the covers, even though I knew it must still be hot in there. I was shivering.

"You stay here today. Until I get home. If you're sick, you have to stay in bed."

Normally I would've argued. I don't have a TV in my room, and when Becky and I stayed home sick in the past, we'd gotten to take over the couch and the TV in the living room. But I was so happy that I didn't have to go back to school that I didn't even mind the churning in my stomach, the pulling at my insides like two hands twisting, the day without TV.

I fell back to sleep after my father left, but I woke up around noon when I heard the doorbell ringing. My stomach felt better, more settled somehow, and I was sweating. I got out of bed, turned on my fan, and debated if I should get the door. The doorbell rang again, and I decided to go downstairs and answer it.

I looked through the peephole and saw an unfamiliar man standing on the doorstep. "Who is it?" I yelled.

"Pinesboro Police, ma'am. Detective Kinney."

The man took his badge out of his coat pocket and held it up to the peephole, so I could see it. It looked authentic, similar to Harry Baker's, so I turned off the alarm, opened the door, and let him in.

He looked surprised when he saw me. After all, he had

called me ma'am, so I knew he'd been expecting my mother. This was the first time I ever saw Detective Kinney, but I instantly despised him. His nose protruded out over his mustache in a steep point in a way that made his whole face seem inaccurate, unreal. His eyes were a steely gray, and they shot right through me. If a look could burn your skin, Kinney had perfected it.

"Is your mother home?" he asked.

"She's sleeping," I said. "Anything to drink?" I was trying to act as grown up as I could, despite the fact that I was still in my pajamas, and my hair was sticking up in at least twenty different directions. I wanted him to talk to me, not my mother. If my mother came down, she would act crazy; this man would take that as guilty.

"Could you ask her to come down here, please?" Kinney was trying to baby me. I could tell, the way he made his voice all mushy, almost as if he were speaking in baby talk, but it didn't sound right coming from him

"Where's Harry Baker?" I asked. "Why isn't he with you?" I suddenly hated Harry Baker because I felt he'd sold us out, that he'd abandoned us. I could already tell this man was like the grown-up version of everyone in my school, who thought my parents were psychos who would kidnap their own child.

But I realized that here I was, all alone with him, and I knew it was my opportunity to plead my parents' case. "Look," I said, trying to use my best grown-up-sounding voice. "My parents would never do anything to hurt Becky." Kinney started squirming a little bit. I guess he didn't like being lectured by an almost-thirteen-year-old.

Normally I wouldn't speak to an adult like that. I would be quiet and respectful, but I felt so desperate that I wanted to scream until this detective listened to me, until someone listened to me. "I've lived with them all my life," I said, "and they're wonderful people. They really are. They love us. Both of us."

It may sound corny, but I believed it. Despite my mother's spacey, depressed episodes and my father's temper, I knew that they loved Becky and me. They used to seem just like everyone else's parents, distant, odd, adultish, but I always knew they wouldn't do anything to hurt us.

Then suddenly I knew I had to tell Kinney about my dream, an image that was still so fresh in my mind that it felt real. "I think there was a man here that night," I said.

He looked startled, as if he hadn't been expecting new information, new clues, and then he frowned. "A man?

What did he look like?"

"He was wearing all black, and he was very tall."

"Hmm?" Kinney didn't take out a notebook or anything the way detectives always do on TV, so I wondered how carefully he was listening. "Well, I'm afraid that doesn't help too much." He paused. "Why didn't you mention this earlier?"

"I didn't remember it before," I said. I didn't tell him the truth, that I wasn't sure if it was a memory or a nightmare, but I knew it couldn't hurt for the police to check it out.

Kinney frowned again, and I instantly knew that he didn't believe me, that he thought I was making the whole thing up. I felt my face turning red.

I heard a sound behind me, and when I turned around, my mother was standing there. She'd actually gotten dressed, put her lovely blond hair up in a twist, and was wearing some makeup, a little pink lipstick and some mascara.

She put her hand on my shoulder. "Abby, sweetie, get back into bed." Her voice was soft, subdued, without a trace of anger, craziness, irrationality. She turned to Kinney and smiled. "She was sick this morning, so my husband let her stay home from school."

"I'm feeling better now."

"You should rest, hon." She kissed the top of my head, which surprised me. Normally she was annoyed when I stayed home from school and felt better halfway through the day. Sometimes she'd threaten to send me in late.

"No," I said. "I'm fine." But the protest was useless. It was as if the adults had made a silent pact not to say another word until I left the room, because they didn't. And they started to stare at me so I began to feel uncomfortable.

"Come on," she said. "I'll tuck you in." She turned to Kinney. "If you'll excuse me for a minute."

My mother and I walked up the stairs together in silence. I didn't know why she was coming up to tuck me in, what exactly was going through her head. I wondered if she was putting on an act for Kinney, if she'd known that the only way to get me out of the room was to act like a real bona fide mother again.

But she did tuck me in, and she stroked my hair back from my forehead. "You feel warm," she said.

I shrugged. My body felt awkward again, off kilter. On the way up the steps I'd been slightly dizzy. "I'm okay," I said. "I'll be okay."

She kissed my forehead. "Sweet dreams," she whispered. "Sweet angel dreams."

I closed my eyes, and I heard her tiptoe out and shut the door behind her. For a second I felt a moment of safety, an odd sense that everything might be all right, but then I remembered what was waiting for her downstairs. So I lay there wide-awake, trying to think of a way to save her.

Chapter 6

ON SEPTEMBER 16th, exactly six weeks after Becky disappeared, I turned thirteen. Becky and I are two years and one day apart, which means her birthday is September 17th. My whole life my birthday has been reduced to the day before Becky's birthday, but never more so than on my thirteenth birthday.

In the days leading up to my birthday, I wasn't sure what to expect, really. I knew I wouldn't be having a party. That I just assumed without even asking my parents. But I wondered if they would ignore my birthday altogether. At school I was still something of an outcast, but I'd begun to blend in, to become this fixture that no one really noticed. People no longer stared and giggled at me, but they didn't talk to me either.

It's not like I had been everyone's friend before this year, but Jocelyn and I had been inseparable, and when we were best friends, it seemed like everyone liked us. Maybe it was just that everyone liked her, that without her I was semi-invisible. Even if my parents had given me a party, I'm not sure there would've been anyone to invite.

On the day of my birthday I begged my father to let me stay home from school. "You only become a teenager once," I told him.

"Ab, you already missed a day last week."

"But I was sick. That was different."

He shook his head. "Don't whine. You're too old to whine."

I wanted to tell him I wasn't whining, but he was right: I was. I'd never gotten to stay home from school on my birthday any other year, so I couldn't blame that on Becky's disappearance or my mother's strange behavior or any of it. I guess the thing was, in years past I'd always liked going to school on my birthday. Last year Jocelyn brought me a balloon, and I carried it through the hallways of the junior high, from class to class, and as I walked by, people I hardly knew said happy birthday.

I got to homeroom early, before Jocelyn arrived, and I

felt a small glimmer of hope. Maybe Jocelyn would come through for me. She couldn't forget my birthday, after all.

When she walked in without a balloon, I felt something small drop in my stomach, like I'd just swallowed a piece of gum and it'd got stuck going down. Jocelyn sat in her seat next to me, and she stared straight ahead to the front of the room, the same way she'd been doing every day since the first one. Then she reached down and pulled a card out of her bag.

"Here," she whispered, and sort of threw the card on my desk without really looking over.

"Thanks." I wanted her to look at me, to smile, to tell me that everything would be okay, that even though the rest of the world had collapsed everywhere all around me, she was still there for me. But the bell rang, and she didn't say anything, so I just picked up the card and put it in my bag.

All morning I imagined what the card might say, and I thought that Jocelyn must've written a secret cryptic note that only I could understand. I began thinking that Jocelyn still wanted to be my friend but her mother had suggested she stay away from me, or maybe she was just afraid of our talking in front of everyone at school. I couldn't blame her, really. I didn't want her to be an outcast just because of me.

I didn't get to open her card until lunch. The week before, I'd begun eating lunch at the nerd table, mainly because no one at that table cared who sat there; everyone left me alone, and I realized that it beat eating in the library. I was happy then, though, that no one talked to me or noticed me, because it gave me a chance to open Jocelyn's card with some sort of privacy.

The card had two red balloons on the front, and it said "Happy Birthday" in bright red bubbly letters. On the inside Jocelyn had written, "Happy 13th, Luv, Joce." I was disappointed, and I knew immediately that Jocelyn's mother had made her give me this card. I imagined Mrs. Redfern standing over her, telling her to write something nice.

We usually wrote each other long notes in our birthday cards. Last year Jocelyn and I had written our birthday notes in our secret code. I would've expected her to say something terrific in her card, something like "Sorry about Banana. Iced Tea won't let me call you. BFF."

I read what she actually wrote, examining it over and over for secret signs or messages. But then I had to face the fact that the card was empty, like Jocelyn herself. I knew we would never be friends again.

Mrs. Ramirez picked me up after school, and when I got in the car, there was a bouquet of thirteen yellow roses sitting on the passenger seat. "Happy birthday, Ah-bee-hail."

I put the roses on my lap, then held them up to my nose. Their scent was intoxicating, delicious. This was the first time anyone had ever given me flowers. I was somewhat embarrassed that they came from Mrs. Ramirez. I would've wished for them from a boy or my father at the least. But still, the flowers were perfect and sweet, and it was the first time that I felt glad for Mrs. Ramirez, so happy that someone was trying to do something special for me on my birthday. "These are really cool," I said. "Thanks."

"You put them in water right away. Otherwise they die." I nodded. I knew my mother kept a few vases under the sink. My father usually bought her flowers for her birthday and their anniversary, pink calla lilies, her favorite and, my father always used to say, just as beautiful as she was.

"You know tomorrow is Becky's birthday," I said. I'd been thinking about Becky all afternoon, all through advanced English and intro. to Western civ., thinking about how tomorrow she'd be eleven. And I wondered if she'd get any presents wherever she was.

"*Si.* Just like twins. I remember when she born."

I don't, though I've heard the story a million times. Becky was born six weeks early, her lungs so tiny and undeveloped that she had to spend a week on a breathing machine before my parents could bring her home. Becky and I should've had birthdays nearly two months apart, but some small act of fate had Becky born all those weeks early.

My mother always called us the September Sisters and told us that someday we would appreciate it, that it would be a nice time to share. She was always telling us that when we were older, we would love each other, we would be friends, we would be happy to have a sister. Usually, though, we fought over birthday cakes and birthday dinners and birthday parties, and every hour on the hour during my birthday Becky would hold a countdown to hers.

"I took care of you," Mrs. Ramirez said. "Every day for a week. And you cry and cry and cry. I thought you dying, you cry so loud."

I tried to remember even a moment of it, but I couldn't. My earliest memory is of the day my parents finally brought Becky home from the hospital. They'd let me sit on the couch and hold her, just for a minute, as they hovered over me and protected her head. She was my little doll, my amazing sister. As soon as she started to crawl, talk, walk, we fought constantly, but for a few months she was perfect.

When I got home, my mother was in the kitchen, cooking something at the stove. I hadn't really seen her since the day I'd stayed home sick the week before, except for one evening when she came downstairs to watch TV with my father and me. We watched an old movie together, something with Katharine Hepburn that my parents remembered having seen at some earlier point in their lives. When my parents discussed it, my mother smiled, and I thought her smile seemed genuine.

I was surprised, but then again I wasn't, to see her in the kitchen. I didn't really think she could ignore my birthday. I wondered if for her, the ache of missing Becky was subsiding. It was odd, but for me, the feeling was getting worse. I realized I was beginning to miss her, to think I really loved her, that in some odd way we had a special bond. When she was here, she drove me crazy on my birthday. I hated her on this day more than any other. But on the day of my thirteenth birthday something felt more missing than it had any other day since she'd been gone.

"Nice flowers," my mother said when I walked in.

"Mrs. Ramirez gave them to me."

"Oh, how sweet. She's always been such a darling." She reached under the sink and pulled out her favorite vase, a gift she'd gotten for her wedding. It's hand-painted up the side with these lovely purple windy lines. "Here. Trim the stems first."

I'd seen my mother do it a bunch of times, so I knew exactly how to cut the flowers and place them in the water. I suddenly felt like such a grown-up. Here I was with my very own flowers. "I should put them in my room, " I said.

"Or you can put them right here." She picked up the vase and put it in the middle of the kitchen table, like a centerpiece. "They brighten up the room."

"You're right. They do." She went back to the stove to check on the food. "What are you making?"

"Spaghetti and meatballs. Your favorite, sweetie." She smiled at me.

"Great." Actually, spaghetti and meatballs were Becky's favorite, the meal she always requested on her birthday, but I didn't want my mother to see how disappointed I was. For my birthday I usually asked for chili and cornbread, my mother's two original specialties. The truth is I don't even like meatballs all that much. They're okay. I don't hate them or anything, but my mother's are usually a little chewy and overspiced.

"Set the table, sweetie. Your father will be home soon, and I want to eat early tonight."

We hadn't eaten as a family since Becky disappeared. I set three places at the table instead of four, Becky's old spot so awkwardly empty.

"Can I go watch TV until dinner?" I was suddenly desperate to see something else, to be absorbed in someone else's life instead of my own. I didn't want to look at the oddly empty table. I didn't want to watch my mother cook Becky's meal.

She turned away from the stove to check the table. "Abby, set another plate."

"Why?" I asked. "Who's coming to dinner?" I imagined she might say Harry Baker, Mrs. Ramirez.

"Becky."

"Becky?" I didn't expect to hear her name, even though I was thinking about her, even though I wanted her empty space to be filled, wanted to hear her brag about her birthday the next day. I suddenly had visions of a life returned to normal, of the two of us pulling each other's hair and squabbling over an inner tube, of a family that ate dinner together, of a mother who spaced out only occasionally when she lounged around with a cigarette in her hand.

"She'll be home for her birthday. Becky wouldn't miss her birthday."

"You're right," I said quickly. "You're right." But I didn't really believe it. I set the fourth place because I was afraid if I didn't, my mother would make a silent retreat back into her own hazy world.

All through my birthday dinner my mother kept getting up to look outside, to peek through the front window. "I thought I heard something," she said.

Finally my father said, "Elaine, have a seat. Relax."

"I can't relax, Jim. Don't tell me to relax."

I chewed my meatballs, pretending they were the best birthday dinner ever. But I was afraid to say anything. I knew if someone moved the wrong way, said the wrong thing, my mother would storm upstairs, and my father would run after her. I preferred this strange dinner party of my mother's to being alone on my birthday.

"I remember when you were born, Ab, just like it was yesterday." He tried to change the subject.

I nodded. He says this every year. Then he recounts the

story of my mother going into labor, of how the first time he held me, he thought I was boy because the umbilical cord was still attached. He did the same thing to Becky on her birthday, only then he talked about her small, weak lungs, and she'd use this to her advantage. She'd crawl on his lap and hug him until he'd start to tear up, just thinking about how she been so blue, helplessly unable to breathe for the first seconds of her life.

By the end of dinner my mother was a wreck. She paced through the front hallway. While my father and I cleared the table and put the dishes in the sink, we could hear the clicking of her feet, back and forth and back and forth. It was all very odd, really—not that it wasn't odd anyway—but it was still my birthday. When I looked at this with my mother's logic, I wondered why she thought Becky would come home today, not tomorrow. I wondered if my mother might be confused, if somehow she'd collapsed the two of us into one person in her mind, one little girl. I wondered if I'd become invisible.

"Dessert," my father called to her. "Time for cake." He'd picked up cupcakes on the way home from work—chocolate with vanilla icing, my favorite. At least he'd remembered that.

My mother came back in. Her hair was messy, falling out of the neat, tight ponytail it had been in earlier. She looked oddly disheveled. "I don't understand it," she said to my father. "I just don't understand it."

He went to her and gave her a hug, and I could see he was solid but defeated. This was quite possibly the nicest exchange I'd ever seen my parents have. There was something so sweet, so desperate in their hug that I knew instantly how much they loved each other. "People don't just disappear," she said. "Little girls. Little girls don't just disappear."

My father stroked her hair back into her ponytail. "It's time for cake. Let's sing 'Happy Birthday.'" I knew my father was trying to do this all for me, and I felt ashamed that I would even want him to. I wasn't even sure if I should have a birthday anymore.

I heard the grandfather clock in the hall chime, so I knew it was six o'clock. If Becky were here, she'd be hopping around the kitchen saying, "Six hours until my birthday!" "Be nice, Becky. It's Abby's day," my mother would say, but she would smile, so I'd know she thought Becky was adorable, that she didn't really mean it. It was strange that I missed that, that it didn't quite feel like my birthday without it.

"I'm not really hungry," I said. "It's okay. We can have the cupcakes later."

My father shook his head and let go of my mother. "Ab, sit down. We'll have them."

I didn't want it to become an argument, so I did what he said. I wasn't sure what he whispered to my mother, but then she sat down too. He put a candle in my cupcake and carried it to the table singing "Happy Birthday" in that funny off-key way he has of singing things. He put it down in front of me. "Make a wish."

He looked me solidly in the eye when he said this, so I knew what he wanted me to wish for. I was surprised. I didn't think my father believed in wishes.

Chapter 7

BY THE END of September, work on Becky's case had slowed down considerably. My father complained that the police weren't doing enough, weren't looking hard enough for her. He told me that he blamed the lack of progress in Becky's case on the fact that we lived in such a small, clean suburban county. "The police aren't used to crime here," he said. "What do we have? A burglary every once in a while, some minor vandalism?" He waved his hand in the air, as if all that were nothing, that compared with Becky, it meant nothing.

But the police did finally manage to find the man in the blue van, something that my father did not exactly give them credit for. "How long does it take to find somebody?"

he said, and I think the fact that it took them that long was not a good sign.

His name was Oscar P. Derricks. The police found him after pulling him over in what Harry called a routine traffic stop. They found a Baggie of marijuana in the glove compartment and took him into the station, and someone there put two and two together. It was Kinney, not Harry, who called my father to tell him about it. This was when we also found out that Kinney had been put in charge of the case in order to avoid a "conflict of interest," something my father said was bullshit.

What I know about Oscar Derricks came from the little I overheard of my father on the phone and the very little my father told me. Oscar was twenty-four years old; he was a high school dropout; his permanent residence was listed as a subsidized apartment in Camden. Apparently he worked as a delivery driver for FTD, delivering flowers and such. Sometimes he'd make deliveries in Pinesboro, though not often, only when the regular guy was sick or flooded with calls. He hadn't made any deliveries in Pinesboro the week of Becky's disappearance.

When the police asked him what he had been doing on my street, sitting in his van, he denied ever being there at first. The police got a search warrant for his van, his apartment, his workplace, but the only thing they turned up was fourteen pounds of marijuana, which he admitted he'd been selling.

Oscar's story checked out when the police turned up one of Oscar's best customers, Shawn Olney.

"I can't believe there drugs in this neighborhood," Mrs. Ramirez clucked one day on the ride home from school. "Used to be safe for the children."

"Do you think he knows where Becky is?" I asked her.

She shook her head. "He sell the drug. Little Shawn. I remember him when he this high." She held up her hand to show the size of a toddler. "He always such nice boy. He shovel my driveway when it snow." I thought about Mrs. Olney attacking my father in the supermarket aisle, and I felt a cruel sense of satisfaction that Shawn had indeed been doing something wrong.

A few days after the police found Oscar, they charged him with drug-related crimes, but they were thoroughly convinced that he had nothing to do with Becky's disappearance. "If he didn't take her, then who did?" I asked my father.

He shrugged. "That's the same thing Kinney said to me

earlier." Only I guess what my father meant was that Kinney had said it in a much more accusatory way.

After Oscar was cleared, my father hired a lawyer and a private investigator. I heard about the private investigator through Mrs. Ramirez, because he was a friend of one of her sons-in-law. "He good man," she told me. "He find your *hermana* just like that." She lifted her fingers from the steering wheel to snap, and I felt the car jerk to the right a little bit. "You no worry now."

I found out about the lawyer only because he called one day right after I got home from school. When my mother didn't answer the phone in her bedroom, I picked up. The man on the other end asked for my father, and when I told him he wasn't home and asked if I could take a message, he informed me that he was my father's attorney, Raymond Garth, and that he would appreciate it if my father could please return his call.

It made me nervous that my father had a lawyer. I wondered if the police were planning on arresting my parents.

I thought about what would happen to me if they did, where I would live. Both sets of my grandparents are dead. My father has a sister in Ohio he doesn't talk to much, Aunt

Claire. I'd met her only once, and she seemed like the sort of cold woman who would sew a lot and ask children to mind their manners. I didn't think I'd have to live with her, but maybe I would. After all, she was my only blood relative.

I didn't think Mrs. Ramirez would take me in, as much as she'd been watching me lately. All her children were grown, and she was always talking about the trips she was going to take to see her grandchildren in Florida—someday, once she saved enough money.

It was just after my birthday that I saw my father hand Mrs. Ramirez an envelope. "Oh," she said. "Thank you, Mr. Reed. This going straight to my grandkid fund." I realized that my father was paying her to pick me up from school, to cart me around, that in all actuality she was nothing more than my babysitter. I didn't think my father had enough money to pay her to watch me full-time.

Suddenly I started to get angry with Becky. *You've ruined everything*, I told her. *You're ruining my life.* And I wondered if she could hear me, wherever she was.

The weather the last week in September was cool and beautiful, and I talked Mrs. Ramirez into going outside in the backyard instead of watching TV. She sat on the back patio, in my mother's smoking chair, while I ran behind the pool to the edge of the yard, where I could see Morrow's field. I told Mrs. Ramirez that I wanted to practice my cartwheels, but really I wanted to see what the police were doing in the field. It didn't seem like much; I saw an area that had been roped off with yellow tape, but I never saw a person out there doing something, looking for her. I wanted to go out there and start looking myself, but I couldn't get away from Mrs. Ramirez's sharp eyes. It was frustrating, standing there on the edge.

One afternoon Mrs. Ramirez seemed to be paying particular attention to me, and every time she looked up I remembered I was supposed to be doing cartwheels, so I must've ended up doing about twenty of them across the yard until I saw it. A little blue glint, it caught the edge of the afternoon sunlight, and I bent over and reached out for it. When I realized what it was, I gasped at a sight so unreal and unbelievable that it was almost like finding Becky herself: Becky's necklace, sunken in the dirt by a maple tree root, right by the edge of Morrow's field.

I was so excited to find the necklace that I picked it up and ran over to show it to Mrs. Ramirez right away. I didn't think that maybe I shouldn't touch it, because I had to; the necklace was something that was so real, such a part of Becky, that it wasn't something I could leave just lying there in the dirt.

A few years back, just before my grandmother got sick and died, she gave Becky and me these necklaces for our birthdays. Each necklace had a little sapphire (our birthstone) shaped like a heart on a thin gold chain. I didn't like to wear mine. I was afraid I'd lose it, and I'm not really a big fan of necklaces anyway. Usually I feel like they're choking me, and they make my neck itch. But Becky put hers on and decided she would never take it off. Becky loved jewelry, and this being her only authentic piece, she wore it and showed it off constantly.

Mrs. Ramirez called my father, who called Detective Kinney, and a few minutes after my father got home, Kinney arrived. My mother, hearing all the commotion, got out of bed and came downstairs. I held out the necklace and showed it to her, feeling this oddly enormous sense of pride that I'd done something useful, but as soon as she saw it, my mother started shaking violently, as if she were sobbing; only she wasn't crying. I knew that I was the one who'd made her shake, so I just stood there, all of a sudden sort of dumbstruck.

Kinney took the necklace from my hands and dropped it into a clear plastic bag. "You shouldn't have touched it." Kinney sighed. "You contaminated it."

This only made my mother start sobbing harder, and I felt so terrible that I wished I'd never been the one to find it in the first place. I think it suddenly occurred to my father that I had the same necklace because he said, "Where's yours, Ab?"

"She has one too?" Kinney sounded annoyed, and I hated the way he referred to me as "she," as if I weren't even in the room.

"It's in my room," I said.

"Let me see it," Kinney said, and I knew he didn't believe the necklace was really Becky's, that he couldn't imagine that I'd found something he'd missed. Something I hated more than anything about Kinney was the way he never believed me; he always suspected me of lying or doing something wrong just because I wasn't an adult. Kinney's way of looking at things was on the surface: I couldn't know anything because I was young; my mother must be guilty because she was sad. Sometimes I wonder, if Kinney had been a different person, someone who dug deeper, who believed there was more to every story, if we would've found her right away.

I kept my necklace in the little blue velvet box it had come in on top of my dresser, next to my bin of barrettes. It was there, right where I'd left it. Before I went back downstairs, I opened the box and ran my finger over the sapphire heart. My grandmother's heart. Becky's heart.

"Here." I handed the box to Kinney. "It's in here."

He opened it, glanced at it quickly, then shut it and thrust the box back at me.

"Then that's Becky's," my father said. "That's Becky's necklace." He said it again, as if he couldn't believe it was really true.

"Could she have lost it earlier in the summer?" Kinney asked.

"Did she have it on, Elaine? Had the girls been playing back there?" My mother was no longer shaking and stood perfectly still. She had this look on her face that reminded me of this sick bunny Becky and I had found in the pool once. It was almost drowned in there, half alive, its face glazed and afraid.

"Elaine, goddammit." My father shook her a little, but she didn't say anything.

I tried to think if Becky had been wearing her necklace in the pool the last night we were in there, and I couldn't remember. I can picture it on her, certainly, bobbing up across her chest in the black night water, but I wasn't sure if that image was that night or another one. I'd seen Becky swim with her necklace hundreds of times.

"She loved that necklace," my mother finally said. "She always wore it."

What my mother meant was, if Becky had lost her necklace when she was playing earlier in the summer, we would've heard about it. Becky would've noticed right away.

"Can we have it?" my father asked Kinney. "Can we have it back?"

Kinney shook his head. "I'm sorry, Mr. Reed. Evidence."

"No," my mother said. "She'll need it back. When she comes home, she'll want her necklace." Kinney looked uncomfortable, and he rubbed his top lip with his forefinger a few times. "You can't keep my daughter's necklace. It's not yours to keep."

"Elaine." My father put his hand on her shoulder. "Elaine, calm down."

It was one of those moments when I think the adults had forgotten I was there. They were so wrapped up in Becky's necklace that they didn't notice me. Kinney had put the bag with the necklace on my mother's sofa table, so it was sitting there, right in front of me. Just within my reach. I thought about taking it, putting it in the velvet box next to mine, so the two hearts were together, touching. It's not so much that I wanted the necklace. But I agreed with my mother; it wasn't the police's to have. Besides, I was the one who found it.

Before I could do anything, Kinney picked the bag up. I think he was afraid of my mother's picking it up and screaming bloody murder.

"You don't think she's coming home, do you?" My mother looked him straight in the eye when she said this, and he began tugging on his bottom lip a little.

"Mrs. Reed—"

My father cut him off. "Abigail, why don't see you Detective Kinney out? Your mother needs to lie down." He put his arms around her and murmured something in her ear.

She nodded. "Yes, Jim. I know."

I wondered what he had said to her, and I felt left out, as if some secret comfort had passed between them. My father looked at me and nodded toward the door. I expected Kinney to congratulate me, to thank me, to tell me that I'd done a good job, but all he said was: "No more snooping around, young lady. Why don't you try to let us do our job?" He sighed heavily, as if I had just made things so much harder for him, a sigh that I couldn't feel bad about because I believed they would've found the necklace weeks ago if they had really been doing their job.

I nodded because I realized Kinney wasn't ever going to listen to me, but I crossed my fingers behind my back. There was no way I was going to leave things up to the police.

After Kinney left, I took my necklace and went up to my room. I took it out of the box and put it around my neck. I admired the blue sapphire, the way it caught the afternoon light through the window. It really is a beautiful necklace, something Jocelyn envied on Becky all the time. That was part of the reason Becky wore it, I thought. I decided right then that I would wear my necklace all the time, the way Becky had.

Our grandma Jacobson gave us these necklaces right before she got sick. It's the last time I remember her perfectly whole and smiling. She was an amazing grandmother, one of those old people who act young and totally understand you. Not like Mrs. Ramirez.

The time she gave us these necklaces, Becky and I were

staying with her in Pittsburgh. Our parents had dropped us there before leaving on a vacation to Bermuda. It was the first and only time Becky and I stayed there without our parents. When we were younger, the four of us had gone to stay there every year for Thanksgiving. But my father and my grandmother hated each other; they bickered over everything. "Marge is the goddamned turkey," my father would say to my mother before we arrived.

One time when I asked my mother why my father hated her so much, she laughed and said, "Oh, don't be silly. Of course he doesn't hate her." But I always thought it had something to do with the fact that Grandma Jacobson teased my father for being so rigid, and he couldn't stand the fact that she didn't really like to listen to rules. They were like oil and vinegar, my father and my grandmother, which was something my grandmother told us more than a few times.

But Becky and I loved her, and we didn't get to see her that much since she lived about six hours away from us. She was the only grandparent we ever knew. My father's parents both died before he met my mother, and our grandfather Jacobson died right after Becky was born.

Grandma Jacobson had this funny red hair that she teased up in a poof on the top of her head. The hair was dyed;

underneath, it all was gray, which we saw a few months later after she got sick. We saw pictures of her when our mother was younger, and her hair was the same rich blond that my mother's is now. But unlike my mother, Grandma Jacobson was short and a little pudgy, round and soft and full of energy. She'd take trips with her friends all over the world and send us presents—little wooden dolls from Sweden, stones from Israel, the sapphire necklaces from Madagascar. Becky and I weren't even sure where Madagascar was. We pictured it as some exotic place where people ran around in jungles. My father had called her a crazy old bag for traveling there in the first place.

The night before we left, she pulled out the necklaces. "I want you to have these," she told us. "My heart. I'm giving you girls my heart."

She was always giving us presents and saying nice things like that, but that was the nicest, most adult present she ever gave us. We thanked her and jumped up and down and hugged her.

The next day, when my mother and father arrived to pick us up, Becky ran up to my parents to show them her necklace. "Really, Mom, you shouldn't have," my mom said. "They're too young for this."

"We're not too young," Becky and I chorused defiantly.

Grandma winked at us. "Oh, hush now, Elaine."

Becky and I were amused when our grandmother told our mother to hush. Usually it worked, and we got to witness what it might have been like for our mother as a little girl. That day was no exception. Our mother didn't say anything else about the necklaces until we were driving home in the car. "I wonder what she paid for those," she said to my father.

He shrugged. He was driving with one hand and had his other hand on my mother's knee. "She can afford it."

"That's not the point." My mother turned to face us in the backseat. "Now, girls, you take good care not to lose those necklaces."

"We won't," we chorused. When she turned back to face front, Becky and I rolled our eyes at each other.

A month later we found out our grandmother had cancer, and then the next time we saw her, that Thanksgiving, she was only ninety pounds and her hair was this crisp silvery gray. She couldn't walk anymore, and she had a nurse who came in and fed her and wheeled her around in her wheelchair. "You don't remember me this way," she said to Becky and me over and over again.

We nodded, and I squeezed her bony hand, but sometimes it is hard to remember her any other way. Whenever I wanted to remember her the way she wanted me to, I'd take my heart necklace out and hold it in my palm. Her heart, she'd said. It was bright blue and sparkling, just the way she'd been that summer after her trip to Madagascar.

My grandmother died in March of that year, and that was the first time I ever really saw my mother sad. Her sadness lingered on for months, until she started smoking again and crying sometimes in the bathroom.

One night right after Grandma died and my father was working late, my mother took Becky and me for pizza. The light in the restaurant caught Becky's necklace so it sparkled, catching my mother's eye.

She picked the heart up her in hand. "Sometimes I wonder if she's with us, watching over us." I wasn't exactly sure what she meant. But since then I sometimes wonder if my grandmother can see us. If she's floating up somewhere watching our every move. I wonder if she knew when I touched the sapphire heart; I wonder if she felt it, a short, soft thump in the chest.

Chapter 8

MAYBE IT WAS the necklace that set my mother off, that pushed her to believe that Becky wasn't coming home, but three days after I found the necklace, my mother decided to leave the house for the first time in two months and ended up crashing her car into a tree.

I was at school when it happened, and my father came to get me, pulling me out of last period. When I was called out of class to go down to the office, when I saw my father standing in there through the square windows, I thought they had found Becky. I felt something in my chest drop a little; then I felt the sharp, rapid pounding of my heart. Right after I had found the necklace, the police started digging up Morrow's field along the edge of our backyard, convinced they might find more clues, or worse, something my father didn't say out loud, her body.

"Ab." My father grabbed me in a hug, and I squirmed a little.

"What?" I asked. "Did they find her?"

He shook his head, and I exhaled. It was odd, but I felt a little relieved that Becky was still missing. Deep down I knew that any news about Becky wasn't going to be good news.

"Your mother had an accident."

The way he said it, I pictured my mother falling down the stairs, cutting her finger on a knife. "What happened?"

"Come on. Let's go."

I followed him to the car, suddenly nervous. My father had never come to pick me up from school before. And he wouldn't have come if she'd only had a little fall, a few stitches. "What happened?" I asked him again when we got into the car.

"She hit a tree." At first what he said didn't register. I pictured her running into a tree in our backyard, the thick maple whose low, leafy branch Becky liked to climb. I imagined my mother running around the yard, crazy, trying to see what was going on in the field and smack, right into the tree. "On Old Juniper Road. You know where it curves real hard."

I knew exactly where he was talking about. Old Juniper Road runs up along the outer edge of Pinesboro, winding from east to west above us. It was the road we sometimes took to the mall, only my mother hated driving on it because it was so winding. I wondered what my mother was doing out. As far as I knew, she hadn't gone anywhere since Becky disappeared. "Is she okay? Is she hurt?"

"I don't know." My father ran his hand over his thinning hair, in a sort of odd combing motion. "She's at Pinesboro Hospital. I got the call, and I stopped to get you on the way."

"She called you?"

He shook his head. "No, someone from the hospital."

"Oh." It was odd, but I didn't feel frightened. I felt numb in a way, used to the tragedy of what had become my everyday life. I wonder if that was how my mother felt those first weeks after Becky disappeared, if that was why she was able to stay in bed for so long.

In another way, I felt like an adult with my father for the first time. This was the only time in my life I'd felt somewhat like his equal. I was pleased that he'd picked me up from school to take me to the hospital with him rather than sent Mrs. Ramirez to fetch me and make me supper.

It turned out that my mother had only a mild concussion and some pretty bad bone bruises even though she hadn't been wearing her seat belt. The doctor, who seemed obnoxious and much younger than my father, told us it was amazing, that he'd seen accidents like this before where much worse had happened, even when people were wearing their seat belts. "She was just lucky, I guess," the doctor said.

"So she's okay then?" my father asked.

The doctor cleared his throat, looked quickly at me and then back at my father. "Physically she will be, yes."

It seemed like an odd answer to me right away. But as soon as the doctor said my mother wasn't wearing her seat belt, I realized that something just didn't add up. My mother is a staunch seat belt enforcer; she never starts the car until she hears a click from everyone. We were reading *Hamlet* in English class, and I immediately thought of a line from it that we'd discussed earlier in the week. Something was rotten in the state of Denmark.

"Can we see her?" my father asked.

The doctor nodded. "We'd like to keep her for a

few days for observation."

"A few days?" I couldn't tell if my father sounded relieved or upset. I figured he must be putting the pieces together. A winding road that my mother hated driving on. No seat belt. Observation. I wondered exactly what they would observe her for. But I thought this might have been my mother's idea of a suicide attempt. She loved drama, and she hated blood, so I didn't think she'd slit her wrists in the bathtub or anything like that.

My mother was resting in a hospital bed in a private room. When we walked in to see her, she had the TV on. She looked like she was watching it, because she was staring right at it, but when I looked at her closely, I saw her eyes were glazed over, that she was actually staring right through the TV, past it to somewhere else, somewhere invisible to us.

My father went to her and kissed her forehead. "Jesus, Elaine, you scared the life out of me." She stayed perfectly still, like a glass doll that might break if you shook it. And it looked like my father was tempted to shake her, to make her react to him in some way, because he stood back and stared at her for a minute, as if he weren't sure what he should do next.

I hung back by the doorway, not sure what to say or do, afraid to interrupt my father's moment. The doctor came up behind me and put his hand on my shoulder. I tried to shake him off subtly, and he took the hint and walked toward my father.

"Maybe you two should go," the doctor said.

My father shook his head. "I can't leave her. I have to stay here."

"She needs her rest. Really, it would be better."

"Elaine." My father shook her shoulder gently. "Do you want me to stay?"

She didn't answer him. I started to feel invisible again; only this time I wished I weren't there at all. I wished this had been something my father tried to shield me from, something he'd come home from and told me barely any of the details of. Just hearing that my mother had a mild concussion and would be home in a few days would've been fine. Suddenly I didn't want to be an adult at all.

My father and I left about fifteen minutes later. The doctor finally convinced my father that he should take me home, and as soon as he mentioned "your daughter," my father seemed to remember me, his duty to try to protect me from things, and he shuffled me out to the car.

"You can go back," I told him. "I can go over to Mrs. Ramirez's."

He shook his head. "I already called her. She's picking her grandson up at the airport tonight."

"Oh." I hadn't known her grandson was coming. It was strange that she hadn't mentioned it to me, when usually she'd talk and talk and talk about how wonderful her grandchildren were, how someday she would move to Florida to spoil them. So that was why my father had picked me up from school himself. He hadn't really had a choice other than leaving me there, stranded, or allowing me to walk home on my own. "I can stay by myself," I told him.

"No, Ab, there's no way."

"I'd be fine."

"It's not up for discussion."

When we got home, my father called Harry Baker to find out about my mother's accident report and the condition of the car. Apparently the car was totaled, a twisted wrap of metal.

My father got off the phone and sat at the kitchen table with his head in his hands. I felt bad for him. I wanted to comfort him, but I never said the right thing, so I just sat there with him, saying nothing.

After a few moments of sitting like that he looked up. "It's been hard for you, hasn't it, Ab?"

I shrugged, not willing to admit, even to myself, how lonely I was, how tired I was of being involved in a terrible, terrible mess. "I'm okay."

"You're a good kid," he said. "You know that. A real good kid."

It was quite possibly the nicest thing my father ever said to me, so I didn't want to tell him that I wasn't a kid anymore, that I wished I could be a kid more than anything.

Chapter 9

THE DAY AFTER my mother's accident was a Saturday, and when my father went back to the hospital to visit her, he dropped me off at Mrs. Ramirez's house on the way. Secretly I was relieved. I hated hospitals anyway. The way sickness smelled so clean, so much like the Lysol my mother used to use to clean the bathroom.

When I walked into Mrs. Ramirez's house, I saw her grandson, Thomas Greer, for the first time. He was sitting in Mrs. Ramirez's living room watching Saturday-morning cartoons, drinking orange juice from a juice box. "This my grandson." Mrs. Ramirez pointed to him. I could tell she was excited. She was hopping a little bit and smiling, so her chubby brown face looked as if it were about to burst. "He live here now."

I was surprised. I'd thought that he was only coming for a visit, not to stay. Then I instantly began to dread all the long afternoons I'd have to spend with him. At first glance he didn't look like the kind of boy I'd want to associate myself with.

He was tall, taller than I was anyway, with skin that looked even darker than Mrs. Ramirez's, and he had this big bushy mop of black hair that fell into his eyes. Mrs. Ramirez reached over and pushed the hair back behind his ears, and he cringed. He looked right at me, and I saw his eyes, huge deep brown eyes that stared at me like lost, open holes, so he suddenly reminded me of one of those skinny, needy kids you see on TV; you know, the ones you can help save with forty cents a day, the price of a cup of coffee. "You sit." Mrs. Ramirez pointed to a spot on the couch right next to him. "This Ah-bee-hail. My little neighbor girl I tell you about."

I felt myself blushing. I wondered exactly what Mrs. Ramirez had said about me, and I felt the way I did in school, out of place, ridiculous. "This Thomas, my grandson." Only when she said his name, it sounded like toe-moss. "You be friends." She pushed my shoulder down, practically forcing me to sit next to him. "You sit. I get you drink." She left the two of us sitting there and went into the kitchen.

It's funny that Mrs. Ramirez thought pushing me to sit on the couch next to him would make us become instant friends. Since Jocelyn had started ignoring me, I'd begun to give up on the idea of friendship, on the idea that there are other people in the world who will love you unconditionally, aside from your parents and your grandparents, who are required to love you that way. But I didn't want to be mean to Thomas, to snub him or anything like that. So I just sat there for a minute or so, trying to figure out how to achieve the balance between friendly and polite, between declining Mrs. Ramirez's offer of friendship and being mean. Finally I said, "So, Thomas, how come you came to live here?"

"You can call me Tommy," he said. "That's what everyone called me in Florida."

I nodded. "Well," I said, trying to think of something interesting to say, "you must like your grandmother." Even as I said it, I couldn't really picture anyone loving Mrs. Ramirez the way I had loved Grandma Jacobson.

"She's okay." He picked up the TV remote and turned up the volume, so it would've been impossible for us to talk to each other without yelling.

Mrs. Ramirez came back in with my juice, but then she left us to go clean upstairs. "You be friends," she said three times before leaving, "right, Thomas?" She pushed his hair back away from his face and tucked it behind his ears, and he pulled away again. She kissed the top of his head and went upstairs.

I tried to make eye contact with him, to show him I sympathized on some level. I hate it when adults manhandle me, like I'm their toy or something. But he wouldn't look at me. He stared straight ahead at the TV, occasionally sipping his juice.

We sat there in silence for the rest of the morning, until my father came to pick me up around noon.

Just after I got home from Mrs. Ramirez's house, the doorbell rang. My father was upstairs taking a shower. He hadn't said it, but my guess was he was trying to wash off the smell of the hospital. I was thinking about Tommy, wondering why exactly he'd come to live with Mrs. Ramirez. I couldn't imagine a time when my parents ever would've sent Becky or me to live with Grandma Jacobson permanently.

I didn't think my father heard the bell since he didn't come down, so I answered the door and saw Kinney and

Harry Baker standing there. Every time I saw a police officer on the porch, I felt my heart race. I felt the way I had when I'd seen my father at school the day before: suddenly excited, alarmed, wondering if my life would change into something even more terrible or something hopeful.

Kinney nodded at me in that uptight way he had of looking at everyone. Harry gave a funny little wave, and I had the sudden image of him in his catcher's mask reaching out for the ball.

"My dad's in the shower," I told them.

But I guess he had heard the doorbell after all, because before I knew it, he was downstairs, walking up behind me, clamping his hand on my shoulder. "Paul, Harry. Be right with you." Before then I didn't know that Kinney's first name was Paul. It felt odd to think of him as a real person, with a real first name. When I thought of him as Kinney, he seemed like this distant, unreal thing. I preferred him that way.

"Ab, why don't you go to your room?" He was back to being fatherly again, back to trying to shield me from the world. Only this I didn't want to be shielded from. I wanted to know every detail of what was going on in Becky's case.

I could tell my father was preoccupied, and I was

convinced he wouldn't notice if I pretended to walk up toward my room; but I actually sat at the top of the stairs, where I could hear most of what they were saying.

I think Kinney and Harry were doing what is always called "good cop bad cop" on TV. I'd seen something like that in a movie before, where Eddie Murphy is the good cop and the other guy looks like a real jerk. Harry was the good guy, trying to sympathize with my father and so on and so forth. And Kinney was asking all sorts of questions, trying to get my father to break down.

Basically, the police had looked at my mother's accident, her withdrawal, her mental state and combined them with the fact that they had no suspects, no witnesses, no proof, no signs of "forced entry." Then they had, as Kinney put it, put "two and two together."

"Jesus Christ, Harry," my father yelled, probably louder than he meant to because after that he lowered his voice, and I couldn't really make out what he was saying.

A few minutes later I heard Kinney saying something about my father's trying to convince my mother to tell him what she knew. Then he said something about getting her the help she needed.

I knew that my mother wasn't the one responsible for

Becky's disappearance. And it took every ounce of common sense I had to keep from running down there and screaming that at them. I wondered if my father believed them, or if, like me, he was furious that they were wasting their time, that they weren't out there trying to figure out what really happened to Becky.

They left a few minutes later, but before they did, I heard Harry say to my father, "We could use your help, Jim. Becky could." It made me feel so angry to hear him say that, so deeply betrayed.

I realized then that I was going to have to find the person who took Becky. This would be the only way to convince the police that it hadn't been my mother.

Chapter 10

THOUGH HE DIDN'T tell me about it, I suspected my father had the same thought I did after the police officers left on Saturday, because Monday morning before school I met his private investigator, Hal Brewerstein, for the first time. Hal was a burly man, even bigger than my father, with curly blond hair and a deep, raspy voice, a voice that I guessed had felt the effects of too many cigarettes, because he always reeked of cigarette smoke. He reminded me of a football player, and I couldn't imagine him creeping around, glancing into people's lives without their knowing he was there. But supposedly he was very good at his job.

My own idea of how I could find the kidnapper myself was still a little vague in my mind. I didn't know yet what

I was going to do exactly, just that I had to do something. I started to think that maybe the police were right, that it had to be someone close to us, maybe one of our neighbors who had taken her, but I wasn't exactly sure yet how I was going to figure out which one.

The day I met Hal was also Tommy's first at our school. Tommy is a year older than I am, and a grade ahead of me in school, and truthfully I hadn't really given him a second thought since Saturday morning, so it hadn't crossed my mind to look for him.

After I sat in what had become my usual seat at the outcast table at lunch, I saw him wandering through the cafeteria, holding on tightly to his tray, his bushy hair falling into his eyes. He shook his head a little in a motion meant to look cool, I thought, and to push the hair away from his eyes so he could see where he was going, but he just ended up looking silly, like a young tree wobbling in the wind, seconds away from falling over.

I waved to him and motioned to the seat next to me, which was empty. It was sad, but even the outcasts wanted to keep their distance from me now. He pretended not to see me at first, kept looking around, flipping his hair away from his face, until James Harper walked into him, catching Tommy a little off-balance and almost knocking him and the tray to the ground. "Watch where you're going, Brownie," James said. I felt bad for Tommy then, the only dark face in a sea of pale white. Right after that, he acted as if he had seen me waving for the first time, and he carried his tray over to sit with me.

It was the first time I'd really eaten lunch with anyone all year, if you could count Tommy as anyone. I'd gotten used to reading a book at lunch, so I wouldn't feel so awkward, so left out, eating in my own little world. That's how I'd gotten ahead in *Hamlet.*

After Tommy sat down, we didn't say anything to each other for a few minutes. He'd bought tomato soup in the lunch line, and I had my chicken nuggets. "The first day sucks," I said to him. "Actually, this whole school sucks."

"This whole town sucks," he said. I was surprised that he said anything, and it caught me off guard for moment.

I guessed he must have been missing Florida. I'd been to Florida only one time. A few years back the four of us went to Disney World. I just remembered the thick, humid air and the tall, thin palm trees. Tommy sort of reminded me of one of those palm trees in a way. "You don't like your classes so far?"

He shrugged and started slurping up his soup. That is one of my mother's pet peeves—soup noises—and I had the urge to knock the spoon right out of his hand the same way my mother would have if Becky or I had made that noise, but then I realized he wasn't doing it to be obnoxious. He just didn't know any better. "What are you reading?" He looked up from his soup and pointed to my book.

"*Hamlet*," I said.

"Oh, I read that last year."

"Oh." I found myself disappointed. Tommy had read *Hamlet* in eighth grade too. Mr. Fiedler had told us that we were special, that our advanced English class was way ahead. Usually, he said, you didn't get to read *Hamlet* until eleventh or twelfth grade.

"It was pretty cool." He said this with an air of superiority, as if to suddenly remind me that he was older and oh so much cooler than I was.

"Yeah, I guess." I chewed on one of my nuggets and watched as he finished off the soup by holding the bowl up to his mouth and drinking the remains.

"That's really disgusting," I said.

"What?"

"Never mind. It's on your chin." I handed him my napkin. He took it and wiped his face sheepishly. "So," I said, "were you popular at your old school?"

He shrugged. "Not really. I don't know." Tommy struck me as the type of boy who was not popular or even aware enough to want to be. That didn't mean he didn't want to be cool. He reminded me more of the tech kids who were cool in their own slick sort of way, not the same kind of cool as an athlete. That's why his *Hamlet* comment surprised me. I hadn't expected him to know anything about English. For some reason, I'd pictured him as the kind of boy who was obsessed with cars and finding new ways to use curse words.

"I used to be almost popular," I said. "See that table over there." I nodded toward the one Jocelyn and I had sat at all last year. "That's where I used to eat lunch with those girls up there and that one over there." I tried to nod my head toward Jocelyn without making it obvious that I was pointing her out. Jocelyn was laughing at something that Andrea said and shaking her long blond hair against her back. She was wearing hot pink lipstick, an amazing, enviable shade that I could see even from my seat a few tables back. They looked in our direction and started laughing again, and I quickly averted my eyes.

"She looks like a snob," Tommy said.

"She's not." My old instinct to defend her kicked in. "Well, I don't really know." I finished off my last nugget, while Tommy stared at me intensely, as if he were scrutinizing me, squinting his eyes a little, turning his head to the side. It made me feel uncomfortable, the same way I felt when older boys would stare at my chest, and I knew I was blushing.

"What's it like?" Tommy asked.

"What?" I pretended not to understand him, but of course I knew that Mrs. Ramirez had told him everything about me.

"You know."

I shook my head, but I suddenly felt myself blinking back tears. I bit my lip. The last thing I wanted to do was cry in front of him. "I have to go." I stood up and threw my book on my tray. "I don't want to be late for class."

Later that day, in English class, we talked about Hamlet's need for revenge. Mr. Fiedler asked us why we thought Hamlet went to the lengths he did to try to avenge his father's death.

We were quiet for a few minutes. I think none of us were sure what he wanted to hear. I thought about my mother's idea of my grandmother's spirit. I wondered, if she were to come to me and tell me where Becky was and how she'd gotten there, what I would do, how I would feel. Then I thought that Hamlet wasn't really trying to get revenge; he wanted justice, wanted things to be set right, and they weren't really the same things. I didn't want to say it out loud, though. I didn't talk much in school anymore; I didn't want to feel everyone's eyes on me, everyone's stares or giggles, so I kept the thought to myself.

I began to think about Becky and the lengths I could go to to find her. I thought about how Hamlet was going to put on a play to catch his father's murderer. What a joke! If only it were that simple. I tried to imagine us putting on a play, me and my father, Mrs. Ramirez, the detectives, my crazy mother as the star.

When Mrs. Ramirez picked Tommy and me up after school, we pretended that our lunch had never happened. "How you day?" Mrs. Ramirez asked. Neither one of us said anything. Mrs. Ramirez was used to my being quiet, but I'm not sure what she was used to with Tommy. "You meet all Ah-bee-hail's friends?" Nothing. "So quiet." She shook her head.

I was surprised to find both my parents at home when I got there. It was another moment that sent off a warning signal in my brain. Something about Becky. Only the reason they both were there was that my mother had been released from the hospital and my father had taken the afternoon off work to bring her home.

My mother looked surprisingly with it, seminormal even, except for the large bruise on the left arch of her forehead that was this purplish yellow color. "That looks painful," I said, and reached my hand up as if to touch it; only I was afraid to, so I left my hand suspended in midair.

"I'm okay," she said. "Come here." She held out her arms to hug me, and I went to her, relieved. I'd been needing comfort from my mother for weeks, been needing her in a way that I couldn't even begin to need my father or Becky or Jocelyn, for that matter. She kissed the top of my head and stroked my hair.

"Are you really okay?" I asked. I had this sudden surge of hope that the doctors had cured her. Three days in the hospital and she was a new, fabulous woman, the mother I'd known years ago.

"Sure I am, sweetie. I'm just a little depressed, that's all." I understood her depression to mean a sadness for Becky, an empty hole, and I understood it completely. But I was hopeful that she had come back a new person, that the old person, the woman who'd stayed mostly in her bedroom since Becky's disappearance, had been left at the hospital.

After dinner I sat up in my room staring at a blank piece of paper that was supposed to be an essay for Mr. Fiedler about Hamlet's revenge. But all I could think about was Becky. Finally I wrote at the top of the page: "Where is she? Who took her?" I tried to imagine Shawn Olney and his father as suspects, but they just didn't seem to fit. Then I thought about the man in my dream, the one who was vaguely familiar and yet a stranger to me. I wondered if he was someone else in the neighborhood, someone I didn't know as well.

As I sat there, I started to draw a map of my neighborhood, marking the houses of the people I knew and the people I didn't really know that well but whose names I knew. The neighborhood I live in is small enough so that I at least know who lives in every house.

After I finished my map, I sat there, looking at all the

houses, all the names; the possibilities of where to start, what to do next, rambled around in my brain, like prematurely exploded fireworks, popping so loudly that none of the colors even made any sense.

Chapter 11

A FEW DAYS after I had met Hal for the first time, he brought my father thick manila folders filled with all sorts of information about the people of Pinesboro, mostly my neighbors. Some of it didn't surprise me: Shawn Olney did drugs, and the hard-core stuff, not just marijuana. Mrs. Olney had been married before, and Mr. Olney was not Shawn's biological father. Mrs. Ramirez had signed up to become an Avon lady (but had never sold a drop of makeup). But other things I found shocking: Mr. Peterson was cheating on his wife, his lovely, perfect wife, with the beautiful red hair and lovely heels. Detective Kinney had been arrested as a teenager driving in a stolen car (a crime deleted from his record after he had performed 150 hours of community service).

Harry Baker's real first name was Edward.

I watched my father pore over the information with Hal and then throw up his hands in disgust. "It all means nothing," he said.

"Nothing means nothing," Hal told him.

But I agreed with my father; everything that Hal had brought him seemed useless.

Tommy and I began playing Uno after school and on Saturdays, when my father took my mother to her therapy sessions. Tommy had brought the game with him from Florida, but I already knew how to play. Becky and I had played it sometimes on snowy days and Saturdays when there was nothing else to do. It's a pretty simple game actually, where you match colors and numbers and so on, but we played it enough that we began to take it seriously, and we each developed our own strategy.

The odd thing about the game is that it doesn't really require you to talk. Once you have one card left, you have to say "uno," but other than that you don't have to say anything. Tommy and I didn't. We'd just sit there for a few hours, throwing cards into a pile, back and forth. Sometimes, if one of us spaced out or was too slow, the other one would say, "Your turn." Otherwise we were quiet.

It's not that we were hostile to each other. It was more that I found a sort of comfort in playing cards with him and not having to say anything at all. For a few hours I would concentrate on strategy, on winning a game. It was an odd sort of friendship—if you could even call it a friendship—very different from what I'd had with Jocelyn, where all we would do is talk. But there was something nice about it, I had to admit.

One Saturday, a few weeks after my mother had started seeing a therapist, Mrs. Ramirez came in and interrupted our game. Usually she left us alone. She'd stopped bugging us about being friends, but she'd get this sort of smug, satisfied look on her face when she'd walk by and see the two of us playing cards, so I knew she thought we were friends. When she came in, she told Tommy that she was on the phone with his mother, and his mother wanted to say hello to him before they hung up.

Tommy put his cards facedown on the table and started swinging his hair a little to move it out of his eyes. I'd noticed this was something Tommy did when he got nervous, and I wondered why talking to his mother would make him nervous. "I don't want to talk to her," he said. I was surprised by the forcefulness of his voice, the finality of his statement.

"She you mama. You talk."

He shook his head. "Just tell her I'm not here."

"I not going to lie to my *niña*." Mrs. Ramirez held her hand over her heart.

He shrugged. "Then don't lie. Tell her I don't want to talk to her." He looked at her so defiantly that for a moment I thought Mrs. Ramirez might slap him. But she was the one who retreated, looking wounded.

I can't imagine not wanting to talk to your mother. As crazy or as distant as my mother seems, I always want her to talk to me. I found it strange that Tommy pushed his mother away while I constantly wished for mine to come closer.

Tommy picked up his cards and started playing as if nothing had happened. I debated leaving it alone, but I was too curious. "Why won't you talk to your mother?" I asked him.

He looked directly at me, his brown eyes as wide and lost as I'd ever seen them. "I'll tell you someday," he said.

I nodded. I was okay with that answer. It was an indication that Tommy actually intended to be my friend.

Strangely enough, it was my mother who told me why Tommy hated his mother, not Tommy himself. My mother came to know all this from Mrs. Ramirez, who'd offered to drive my mother to the supermarket and such. We didn't get another second car after my mother's accident, and I'd just sort of assumed that my father was no longer going to let her drive. I was sure he was paying Mrs. Ramirez for these trips, as if she were babysitting my mother too, but I was also pretty sure my mother didn't suspect, because she seemed to think that Mrs. Ramirez enjoyed her company.

The whole thing came up when my mother started asking me about Tommy and how I liked him so far. "He's okay," I told her.

"That poor thing," my mother said. "That poor, poor thing."

"What do you mean?"

"Now don't you repeat this, Abby, you hear? What I tell you stays in this room."

I nodded. I always thought that was a funny thing to say, as if what she would tell me would literally hang above us in the kitchen for the rest of our lives or something. "He walked in on his mother having an affair." I tried to imagine Tommy entering a dark room and finding a younger, prettier version of Mrs. Ramirez in bed with a man who wasn't his father. "And then his father left. Just walked out of the house and hasn't come back yet."

It may have been an odd comparison, but I immediately thought of Becky. Tommy's father was a grown man, and he left on purpose, but it seemed to me that once a person was gone and you didn't know where, it didn't matter how he'd left or why. It was being left behind, not knowing, that was worse than anything. I began to see Tommy differently then, and not because he was the first person my age I knew to have witnessed something relating to sex, but because I began to understand him—his quiet stare, his lost eyes, his nervous hair flips. "I guess Tommy blames his mother for a lot," I said.

My mother laughed, a nervous, guilty sort of laugh, and I felt bad because I didn't want her to think that I blamed her for something. "Oh, I don't know," she said. "It takes two to tango, honey." She paused and played with her hair for a minute, tucking the wispy strands behind her delicate ears. "You know Tommy's father is black." She lowered her voice a little when she said this, as if this were something that should be kept more secret than anything else she'd told me.

I didn't see how his being black had to do with anything that had happened, but I don't know anyone else who is a racial mix. We don't talk about things like that in my family—race or ethnicity or even divorce. Where we live almost everyone is white with the exception of a few Hispanic and Chinese people, and the parents of everyone I knew in my junior high were still married. "His mother is Mexican," I pointed out, wondering what my mother thought the difference between black and Mexican was.

"I know," she said, "but still."

I nodded in agreement, so I pretended I understood what she was saying, but I didn't. Grandma Jacobson once made Becky and me promise that we wouldn't marry black men. "You marry for love," she told us, "as long as he's not black." When I asked her why it mattered, she said, "Oh, I wouldn't care, except for the children. I have nothing against black people, don't get me wrong, girls." I didn't understand what she meant then, and when she said it, I'd felt this vague sense of discomfort, though I didn't understand exactly why.

"Well, anyway." My mother undid her ponytail and tried to tuck those stray hairs in, but they just didn't fit, and she paused for a moment as if trying to decide whether or not to tell me the rest. "Apparently, Tommy was getting in a lot of fights at school. That's why Maria sent him here." I couldn't really imagine Tommy fighting. He seemed too quiet to be a fighter. I guess he just had all this pent-up anger that welled up inside him until he let it burst out. "I guess I shouldn't be telling you all this. Shit." It was the first time I heard my mother curse, and the harshness of it shocked me. "I need a cigarette."

She went out on the back patio, sat in her usual chair, and smoked her cigarette the way she'd been doing for the few months before Becky disappeared.

I felt slightly off-center, the way I had the day my father took me to the hospital. I felt as if my mother had forgotten whom she was talking to, that she too had mistaken me for an adult.

Chapter 12

AT THE BEGINNING of October I started having the dream every night. Sometimes the man seemed so vivid, so close, that I thought I would even be able to describe him to Kinney, to make Kinney believe that he was real, but every time I woke up, the image fell away, so I knew I'd have nothing more to tell him than what I already had.

But I had to talk to someone, so I told Tommy about the dream one afternoon at lunch. Though Tommy and I had been sitting together at lunch for weeks, we rarely talked, and when we did, it was briefly, about the food, our homework. It must have come as a surprise to Tommy, because it was somewhat a surprise to me when I blurted out, "Do you think dreams can be real?"

"What?" He flipped his hair back, and for a moment I could see his eyes, deep, round saucers, like the eyes of a deer I'd once seen startled in Morrow's field.

"I keep having a dream about that night." I saw him nod, so I knew he knew exactly which night I meant, as if he understood that there was no other night important enough to speak of. I told him about the man in my doorway, about the one time I could see his face.

"You should tell the police," he said.

I thought about the way Kinney looked at me when I told him about the man I thought I saw. "No. They don't listen to me. They're useless."

"My father is a cop," he said. It was the first time Tommy had mentioned his father to me, and I tried not to look alarmed, to give away what my mother had told me about him. I thought Tommy was going to be mad that I called the police useless, but what he said next surprised me. "Maybe I can help you."

For Halloween I dressed up as a loaf of Wonder bread. It was my mother's idea, and even though I thought it was a little strange, I went with it because she offered to make me the costume.

She'd been acting pretty normal since she'd come home from the hospital, but since she'd started going to therapy, she'd stopped talking about Becky altogether, and she didn't want anyone else to talk about her either. Once my father said something to my mother about a report from the private investigator, and she covered her ears and ran out of the room. I thought this was strange, but I found it better than the alternative. I was disappointed, though. I'd wanted to hear what the investigator had to say, but when I asked my father, he just said, "Not now, Ab." And he stormed out after her.

My mother made my costume out of a white trash bag and colored paper. She cut out the letters and the little circles and glued them on the front of the trash bag. Then she got me a white turtleneck, pants, and shoes to wear underneath, and some white face paint for my face. It was a pretty interesting-looking costume, I had to admit.

Tommy dressed up as a gladiator. Mrs. Ramirez made his costume out of cardboard and tinfoil. He had a sword and everything, though the tinfoil blade wasn't exactly straight. Mrs. Ramirez topped the costume off with a tinfoil crown that held Tommy's hair back away from his face, something like a headband. I didn't think that gladiators had actually worn crowns, but I didn't say anything to Tommy. I didn't want to make him feel bad.

Tommy and I went trick-or-treating together, while my father and Mrs. Ramirez agreed to follow along behind us and keep a respectable distance, so no one knew they were actually with us. I told my father we were old enough to go by ourselves, but he shook his head and said, "Absolutely not, Ab."

Mrs. Ramirez agreed. "Used to be safe neighborhood, but now with the drug and the"—she looked at my father and paused—"other bad stuff . . ."

Tommy didn't want to go trick-or-treating in the first place. He said that he was too old for it. Maybe he was right, but I'd never thought about it that way before, probably because I always went with Becky, so I'd never felt too old to go. Until this year Becky and I had gone with Jocelyn and some of the other kids in our neighborhood. We formed a big group, a pack, and several of the parents walked behind us, talking, while we skipped ahead. It was different, though, just me and Tommy, my father and Mrs. Ramirez. Quieter.

I convinced Tommy to go when I told him about my plan to scope out the neighbors. I told him we both could get a glimpse into everyone's house, to try to notice anyone who might be acting strange or seemed suspicious. "That's a good idea," Tommy said, a comment that made me feel a little excited.

Halloween night was unusually chilly, and we were expecting a frost. My father made me wear my coat over my costume, despite my protests. "No way. It'll ruin the whole effect."

"I don't care," he said. "I'm not going to have you catch your death out there."

I tried to recruit my mother to my side, since she'd so carefully made the costume, but she was upstairs resting, and when I called out for her into her dark bedroom, she didn't respond.

So I was Wonder bread with a coat on, which actually made me look more like a ghost nurse because all you could see were my white pants and shoes and my white painted face.

"Nice costume," Tommy said when we met him out by the curb.

I felt a little hurt, and I almost made fun of his sword or his crown, but he already looked so silly that I just didn't have it in me. "Whatever," I said.

Tommy and I talked my father and Mrs. Ramirez into

staying back in the street while we went up to the individual houses. We tried to attach ourselves to the ends of other big groups so we didn't look so silly: the ghost nurse Wonder bread in a coat and the lopsided gladiator.

We skipped right over the Olneys' house, and no one said a word about it, so I knew even Tommy knew about Mrs. Olney's contempt for my family. It was a shame, really, because Mrs. Olney always gave out the best candy, the full-size chocolate bars, not the teeny-tiny miniature ones that we got from most of the other neighbors. And as we started out and I saw other kids bouncing away from her door with their pumpkin candy holders looking extra full, I couldn't help feeling a little bit jealous.

So we ended up starting a little bit down the street, with the neighbors who didn't really know Tommy since he was so new, but all of them knew me, even with the white face paint on. It took us some extra time at every house as each neighbor got me an extra piece of a candy, a pat on the head, a "How's your poor mother doing, dear?" I found their condolences oddly insincere and too late. Where had all these people been since Becky had disappeared?

To be fair, I knew that some of them had joined my father in his initial search parties, but after that their interest had tapered off. My neighbors were too busy with their own lives, too busy being afraid of my family and what had happened to us, to offer any real help.

"I could just punch that woman," Tommy said after we'd gone to Mrs. Johnson's house and she'd pinched my cheeks, leaving a mark in the white makeup. "How do you take it?"

I was strangely pleased with Tommy's urge to protect me. It was not the same way I felt about my father's suffocating sense of protection. This was different. I thought about what my mother had said about Tommy's getting into fights in Florida, and I wondered if he really would punch someone for me.

As we went from house to house, I felt sort of lost without Becky. The year before, we'd both dressed up as bees, another set of costumes my mother fashioned out of trash bags and colored paper. That whole night we kept buzzing at each other and stealing each other's candy. It wasn't the same, trick-or-treating with Tommy, searching for suspects. Somehow none of it seemed fun anymore.

Mr. Barnesworth had lived in our neighborhood for years, and Becky and I had always found him exceptionally creepy.

He's probably only a little older than my father, but he lives all by himself and never mows his lawn or anything, so the grass out front gets all ragged and weedy, and his house is what my father calls an eyesore. When we rang his doorbell, he didn't answer. You could tell he was home because some of the lights were on inside. I wondered what he was doing in there, all by himself, and I wondered if he didn't answer the door for anyone or just for us.

To me, this made him seem suspicious, as if he were avoiding us for a particular reason. I wondered if he could be hiding Becky in his house. Maybe he'd locked her in the basement. Maybe she could hear us on the porch, hear my father's booming voice and Mrs. Ramirez's chuckle from the street. But I knew I had no real reason to suspect any of this, so after we had rung the doorbell three times, we gave up.

When I got home, after I had separated my candy into piles on the living room floor and allowed my father to inspect it, piece by piece, for evidence of poison, I went up to my room, chewed on a peanut butter cup, and thought about Mr. Barnesworth. I wondered how I could find out more about him.

The knock at my door caused me to jump, and I was surprised when it was followed by my mother sticking her head into the room. “How was it?” she asked. She sat on my bed, right next to me, and smoothed out the front of my costume with her hands. “It got crushed.”

“Dad made me wear a coat.”

“Oh, he did, did he?” She sounded more amused than annoyed. “Here.” She handed me a jar of her cold cream. “I brought you this. For your face.”

“Thanks.” Last year our faces had been painted black and yellow, and Becky and I had taken turns sitting on the toilet seat in her bathroom while she’d cotton balled the goopy stuff onto our faces. I guessed this year, as with everything else, I was on my own.

“Did you get a lot of candy?”

I shrugged. “I guess so.”

“Good.” She kissed me on the top of the head. “Don’t eat too much tonight. You’ll get sick again.”

I nodded, but I didn’t remind her that it was Becky who always ate too much candy and got sick, that Becky was the one who’d thrown up in bed last year and cried out in the night for her.

The next day Tommy pleaded with me to call Harry Baker and tell him about Mr. Barnesworth. “I thought *you* were going to help me," I spat at him; he turned away quickly as if he'd been slapped. I felt a little bit bad for snapping at him, but I didn't apologize.

I called Harry Baker at home the next morning because I wondered if maybe, unlike Kinney, Harry, a friend of my father's, might actually listen to what I was saying. I got up early, before anyone else was awake, and I got his home number from the little address book my mother kept in the kitchen drawer. He answered the phone, sounding sleepy and slightly annoyed, but as soon as I said who I was, he cleared his throat, which I took as a cue for me to continue. "I have someone I think you should look into." I told him all about Mr. Barnesworth's strange behavior.

His silence on the other end was deafening. He cleared his throat again. "Abigail, you have to let the police do their job."

"You don't understand," I said. "You don't know what to look for." I heard a muffled noise, and I thought he might be laughing at me, and I felt my cheeks turning bright red. "It couldn't hurt to check," I said, trying to sound more nonchalant, as if I had other things on my mind, but of course I didn't.

I worried all day that Harry would give me up to my father, that when I got home from school, my father would be there waiting for me, ready to yell and scream and ground me. I hadn't been grounded since Becky's disappearance. I wondered if my father would suspect that it wouldn't have the same effect on me that it used to. Unless I was sent next door to Mrs. Ramirez's, I spent all my time at home anyway. But if my father knew about my call to Harry, he didn't mention it, so I figured he didn't know. It isn't like my father to keep quiet about something like that.

I had a hard time keeping quiet myself, waiting for Harry to call me back. Over the next few days I let my imagination run away with me. I imagined all the clues the police might find if they actually looked in the right places, that they might even find Becky herself, and she would come home, and everything would be back the way it was.

I waited until the end of the week, and when Harry still didn't call me back, I tried calling him. I dialed his home again, but I got his answering machine. So then I called the station. Somehow I got transferred to Kinney, who picked up his line with a short clipped "Yes?"

"Mr. Baker."

"No, Abigail, it's Detective Kinney."

"I need to talk to Harry Baker," I said.

"He's not in today." The realization startled me: that Harry Baker continued to have a life, that he did not spend every waking moment working, looking for my sister.

"Did he tell you about our conversation?"

"Hmm?" It was clear Kinney didn't have a clue what I was talking about.

I took a deep breath before I repeated my spiel about my suspect, because I already knew before I started talking that Kinney was going to yell at me.

Kinney was silent for a moment. Then he said, "Abigail, we've already looked into everyone in your neighborhood." He sighed. "I thought I told you, you need to let us do our job."

I hung up on him. I closed my eyes and felt tears welling up against my eyelids, and I blinked, trying to hold them back.

Chapter 13

IN ENGLISH CLASS we finished *Hamlet*, and we moved on to *To Kill a Mockingbird*. It was a little disappointing, after Shakespeare, to be reading a book that the rest of the eighth graders were reading too. But Mr. Fiedler said it was a classic book nonetheless.

The English class I was in was strange, because the advanced classes in our school didn't have to follow the same curriculum as the regular classes. Mr. Fiedler could decide whatever he wanted us to read, whenever he wanted us to read it, as long as the books were on the district approved list. He told us that he didn't normally have his advanced class read that book second, that normally he continued on with something else by Shakespeare, but he'd geared up for a change. I thought that maybe after listening to what we had to say about *Hamlet,* he decided we were idiots after all, so he sent us back a bit to something more our speed. Or maybe he just really liked *To Kill a Mockingbird* and decided we shouldn't miss out just because we were supposedly super-smart in English.

And so, as I started reading the book, Mr. Barnesworth became my Boo Radley. I imagined him pale and ghostlike, a criminal, inside his house waiting to be discovered. Since I'd read only the first few chapters of the book when I got this idea in my head, I didn't know about the ending of the book yet. I didn't realize that Boo Radley turned out to be a nice guy who saves the day. No, at first I thought this novel was fate, a sign that Tommy and I should cut school one day and break into Mr. Barnesworth's house.

I'd convinced myself that Becky was in his basement, that Mr. Barnesworth kept a stash of little children in there, and that when Tommy and I broke in and rescued them, we would become heroes of our school.

"Why do you think he has your sister?" Tommy asked.

"I don't know." Why anyone would've taken Becky was beyond me in the first place, but Mr. Barnesworth gave me the creeps, so who knew exactly why he would do anything?

"If you don't want to go with me, I'll go myself." He sighed. I knew that would get him. I'd learned to tap into Tommy's instinct to protect. I felt almost ashamed of myself for using him this way, but honestly I was afraid to go to Mr. Barnesworth's on my own

"Fine," Tommy said. "But if we get caught, I'm telling everyone it was your idea, that I only went along to make sure you were safe."

"Whatever." But the way he said it made me blush, and I had to look away so he wouldn't notice.

We waited until the next Tuesday to cut school. Tuesday mornings Mrs. Ramirez volunteered at the library, so we knew she wouldn't be at home, and we knew she wouldn't have a chance to see us walking around when we were supposed to be at school.

Tommy and I both went to homeroom, so we could be counted on the attendance. Otherwise the office would call home to ask our parents why we weren't there. We knew there would eventually be a problem if our morning teachers counted us as absent and compared that with the list of homeroom absences, but I was hoping no one would notice. Teachers didn't always do these time-consuming comparisons; most of them just didn't care enough. I knew the only teacher who would notice if I was missing was Mr. Fiedler, and that class was last period, so I'd be back for that.

After homeroom Tommy and I met by the front doors. As everyone else shuffled on to first period, we opened the doors and ran away through the side parking lot of the school. We avoided the front lot because we knew that's where the monitors usually stood, waiting to catch cutters like us. I'd never cut school before, but I could see the monitors out the window of my first-period algebra classroom, stopping the occasional student trying to get away with skipping. Luckily we didn't get caught, and before we knew it, we were walking down the treelined street toward our neighborhood.

I had this sudden eerie sense of déjà vu. I hadn't walked through these streets since last spring, when I'd walked them with Becky and Jocelyn. Walking them with Tommy, I had this overwhelming feeling, this sense of lightness. "We used to walk home from school this way," I told him.

"I walked home in Florida," he said, "except when it got too hot or it rained. Then I took the bus."

I'd never ridden on a school bus, except for the occasional field trip. Our neighborhood is too close to the elementary school, junior high, and high school for the district to provide us bus service, so I always walked or got a ride. "A bus would be cool," I said.

He shrugged. "It was okay." The way he said it, I could tell he was thinking of something unpleasant that had happened to him on one of those bus rides. I wondered if he'd gotten in a fight or if someone had tried to beat him up. I didn't want to ask him, though. I didn't want him to get mad and change his mind about going to Mr. Barnesworth's.

The dumb thing about our plan was that we planned our escape from school perfectly, but we did no planning on how we were going to get into Mr. Barnesworth's house. I didn't really start thinking about that until we actually got to our neighborhood and began cutting the back way across the development behind us, so we would avoid being seen. Even though Mrs. Ramirez was at the library, we were afraid one of our other neighbors would see us and dutifully call my father. I tried not to think about what would happen if he found out about this.

I asked Tommy how we should get into the house.

"I don't know," he said. "I thought you had a plan."

"I did," I lied. "I do. I just wanted your opinion."

"Well." He sounded a little nervous. "Maybe we should

ring the doorbell first. I don't know, pretend we're selling something for school."

It was a good idea, and it seemed much less scary than breaking in. But I wondered if it would work. On Halloween, Mr. Barnesworth hadn't even opened the door. Besides, I assumed he wouldn't even be home, that he must have a job. That's why I'd convinced Tommy that the only way to do this was if we went during the school day.

It was odd the way I'd pictured myself inside Mr. Barnesworth's house all week, finding Becky, seeing her standing there. I imagined the way it would feel to see her again, what I would say to her. I thought I would hug her, that I would hold her body close to mine and tell her that everything would be okay now that we were there. Tommy and I would be instant heroes. But I hadn't imagined how we would get in there until right then.

We crept along the back of his property a little first, trying to peer into these two small windows that went into his basement. We have similar windows to the basement in my house, and I knew from playing in my backyard that we wouldn't be able to see anything. "This is a waste of time," I told Tommy. "Let's just try to go in the front."

Before we went to the front yard, up the walkway to the

door, we hid behind this large oak tree and kept a lookout at the street. The street looked virtually empty; all my neighbors were at work or at school. "Let's go," I said. Tommy looked at me, his eyes wide and more lost than I'd ever seen them, and I could tell that he was afraid. This made me nervous, and I felt this little runner of sweat begin to trickle down the back of my neck.

When we got up to the door, I told Tommy to ring the bell. He argued with me. "Why don't you do it?" he said. "This was all your idea anyway."

I gave him a look. "I'm watching out for the neighbors who know me."

"The street's empty."

"You never know. Someone could decide to walk his dog or something." But the truth was I was nearly paralyzed by fear, almost too afraid to move my finger to the doorbell.

"Fine." He put his finger on the bell. I could feel my heart thumping in my chest so loudly that I thought I might give myself away.

When we heard the lock begin to turn, the creak of the door beginning to open, we both jumped. I hadn't expected him to open it, hadn't expected to come face-to-face with the man I'd convinced myself was a crazy kidnapper. I was suddenly afraid for me and Tommy, for my parents, for Mrs. Ramirez. What would they do if we disappeared too?

When the door opened, Tommy and I took a step back, almost in sync with each other. But standing there, in the foyer of the house with an identical layout to mine, was a short middle-aged woman with brown highlighted hair. The highlighted part was right down the center, and it reminded me of a skunk stripe. "Can I help you?" she said.

I suddenly wished that Tommy and I had come up with a plan B, the way they always do in movies. We hadn't expected this strange woman to answer the door. I wasn't sure what we were supposed to do, and I felt oddly frozen, paralyzed.

"We're selling raffle tickets," Tommy said, before I could even think to say anything. "For school."

"Oh," she said. "Shouldn't you be in school now?"

"We have off today," Tommy lied.

"Parent-teacher conferences," I said. I was surprised by the squeaky sound of my own voice.

"Would you like to buy a raffle ticket?" I wasn't sure where Tommy was planning on going with this, since obviously we didn't actually have tickets to sell. And I began to wonder how any of this was going to get us into the house. It also dawned on me that this woman made Mr. Barnesworth seem more normal. Whoever she was, old skunk hair didn't seem like the type to hide children in the basement.

"Hmm, I don't think so. Not this time," she said. She began to shut the door.

"Wait." I was desperate, not actually sure what I was going to say until it popped out of my mouth. "What about Mr. Barnesworth? Would he like some tickets?"

"Oh, no. I don't know," she said. "He's very ill. I don't think so."

Tommy looked at me. "He's ill?" I said.

She looked us over, up and down, as if sizing us up. "Do you two know him well?"

"Yes," Tommy lied. I almost reached over and pinched him. What a stupid thing to say! I was beginning to worry he was getting us into more trouble than we were already in. Whoever this woman was, there was a good chance she'd know that Mr. Barnesworth didn't even know who we were.

"Well, nice to meet you then. I'm Sara Alban, his nurse." She looked at us, expecting our names, but we pretended not to understand and just smiled at her. I felt myself sweating, even underneath my too-tight bra, making it more uncomfortable than it already was before. I thought about how sick my grandmother had been when she needed a nurse to come to the house, and I felt suddenly guilty for thinking of Mr. Barnesworth as my sister's kidnapper.

Tommy must've had a similar thought, because he said, "Sorry to bother you." He grabbed my hand and started to pull me away from the house. We walked quickly down the street, and as soon as we thought she couldn't see us anymore from the doorway, we cut behind Mr. Barnesworth's next-door neighbor's evergreen tree. Tommy's hand was sweaty, but it felt nice to hold on to.

By the time we got to the tree, I was out of breath and shaky, and I felt like I was about to cry. "I don't think he's it," Tommy said. I nodded. "Come on. Keep walking." He was shaking his hair out of his eyes, but his voice sounded even, in control. He still didn't let go of my hand, and I didn't want him to.

We walked behind the properties, down the treelined divider between our development and the one behind it. As we walked, I felt my heart slowing down. I began to be able to breathe again. "This was stupid," I said, "wasn't it?"

"No," Tommy said. "No, it was fine. Now you know."

"I guess so." I felt like an idiot, though, suspecting Mr. Barnesworth, calling Harry Baker early in the morning. Then I began to feel deflated. I felt like we would never find Becky, that she wasn't trapped somewhere in our neighbor's basement, that she could be anywhere in the entire world by now.

"Hey," Tommy said. He let go of my hand and pointed up to the street in front of us. "Isn't that your mother?"

I looked to where he was pointing, unable to register what he'd said to me. I'd worried about seeing Mrs. Ramirez, Mrs. Johnson, but not my mother. I didn't believe that she ever left the house when I was in school. I imagined her solidly fixed to it, as if she were somehow attached to the foundation, like another wall.

Sitting in a strange red car at the stop sign that divided our development from the main road was a woman who looked eerily like my mother and a man I'd never seen before. Before I could get a good look, they pulled out onto the main road. "I don't know," I said. "I can't tell."

"Well, it probably wasn't her anyway." But he sounded the way I felt, unsure. I began to get an uneasy feeling in the pit of my stomach, and I was afraid I was going to be sick right there in front of Tommy.

൭

We were back at school for lunch, and if anyone had noticed we were gone in the morning, no one said anything to me. For the rest of the day I thought about my mother and the man in the red car. There was a chance that it hadn't been my mother, that I was worrying for nothing, but it had looked so much like her, her blond hair pulled back the way she always did, in a ponytail. I wondered what she'd been doing, who'd she'd been with. I felt afraid for her, worried about her being in the wrong place.

When Mrs. Ramirez picked us up from school, Tommy and I didn't say anything to each other in the car. It was as if the morning had never happened, as if Tommy and I had never held hands and run, sweating, through the trees. It was as if we'd discovered a whole new world together in the morning, but by the afternoon that world had vanished, become something hazy that I couldn't be sure had ever quite existed in the first place.

"Did you see my mother today?" I asked Mrs. Ramirez. Tommy was sitting up front, and I was in back. He turned around and gave me a look that seemed to say, *What the heck are you doing?*

"No, Ah-bee-hail. Not today. Tomorrow we have big shopping trip!"

"Oh, right," I lied. "I thought today was Wednesday." I thought that I could safely ask Mrs. Ramirez about my mother's whereabouts without her suspecting a thing. My mother, on the other hand, was a completely different story.

By the time I got home, I'd convinced myself that my mother would be gone, that the man in the red car had driven her somewhere far away. So I was almost surprised when I found her sitting out back, in her chair, smoking a cigarette, just like any other day.

I let myself out onto the patio and sat in the chair next to her. She had her eyes closed, but I knew she was awake because she moved the cigarette to and from her mouth. "Hey," I said, "I'm home."

"Hmm." She reached out blindly for my hand, and I gave it to her. "How was your day, honey?"

"It was good," I lied.

"Good."

I sat there holding her hand for a few minutes, trying to figure out how to grill her without getting her to suspect anything. "So," I said, "what did you do today?" It wasn't an unusual question. It was something I might have asked her every other day and not even thought twice about her answer, but I held my breath, waiting to hear what she had to say.

"Oh, nothing much." She opened her eyes, sat up, and smashed her cigarette in the ashtray. "It's getting too cold to stay out here. Don't sit out too long." She stood up and kissed the top of my head.

It wasn't an unusual way for her to respond, but if there was anything I'd learned, it was to suspect everyone and everything.

Chapter 14

THE LAST TIME I remember my family's being completely whole and ridiculously normal was June, nearly two months before Becky disappeared. My father took a Thursday off work, and the four of us went to the beach in Ventnor. On the way there in the car, my father had one hand on my mother's thigh and the other on the steering wheel. We drove with the windows down, and it was this perfect blue-sky June day, so the breeze that came into the car was just right and not too hot, even though it was already summer.

My mother was wearing a wide-brimmed straw hat and her black bathing suit with her white linen cover-up. Becky and I had on our brand-new pink bathing suits (hers was a bikini; mine was a one-piece). My father wore his navy swim trunks and his Pitt T-shirt. In the trunk of our car, my mother had packed towels and a coolerful of peanut butter and jelly sandwiches and root beers.

When we got there, Becky and I collected seashells by the edge of the ocean, and our parents watched us from their towels. I remember looking up once and seeing them sitting there, my father's hand on my mother's thigh, as if it were permanently attached there. She leaned in close to him, so I could tell she liked it. Even though they were looking at us, it was clear they were thinking about each other.

We picked up pearly shells, black-blistered shells, and little chipped ridged shells that looked like potato chips and collected them in an old bucket. "She sells seashells by the seashore," we sang over and over, taunting each other into saying it faster and faster.

Later my father went into the ocean with us and taught us how to bodysurf so we could catch the front hooks of the waves and ride them all the way back to shore. Becky ended up swallowing a whole lot of salt water, and she came up sputtering. My father swam to her and picked her up so he was holding on to her while he was treading water. "You're okay, Beck," he said. "You're all right."

"Baby," I whispered to her, so she could hear me but my father couldn't.

"Shut up." She jumped off my father and tried to catch another wave, just to prove she could do it. And she could. When she stood up at the edge of the water, her blond hair tangled and in her face, she gave my father the thumbs-up sign.

"Way to go, Beck," he said, shooting the thumbs-up right back to her.

"I'm getting out," I told him. "I'm starting to feel pruny." But really, I'd decided if Becky could steal my father, I'd have a go at my mother.

She was reading a book on her towel, a romance; she loves romance novels. When I sat down next to her, she said, "Sweetie, you're dripping all over me. Take a fresh towel." But she didn't even look up from her book; she just kept on reading.

"Dad taught us how to bodysurf," I told her. "Becky swallowed a lot of water."

"Uh-huh. Good, hon."

Before we left, we changed into dry clothes in one of the public changing rooms by the beach. I watched my mother dress with fascination, in complete awe of the womanliness of her body, the sharp curves of her hips and the plumpness of her breasts. I wondered how long it would take for me to be like her, to *be* her.

It was Hal who eventually told us who the man in the red car was, not my mother. "Do you know who this is?" my father asked me, showing me the picture of them that Hal had brought over earlier in the day.

"No." I shook my head. Even though I'd thought I'd seen her the day I'd cut school, it was still a shock to see the picture. In the picture I could see her face. Her eyes were wide and bright, and she looked like she was laughing. I hadn't seen her laugh since before Becky disappeared, and the sight of it was so strange and moving that I almost wanted to cry.

My father leaned down to inspect the picture, as if some minute detail he might have missed the first time through would tell him everything. You'd think after what my mother had told me about Tommy, I would've immediately suspected her of having an affair, that this was some man she was cheating on my father with. But I didn't. The thought didn't even cross my mind. I didn't think my mother was capable; she couldn't have it in her. I'm not sure what my father suspected, but he was visibly shaken.

It may seem strange that my father started to come apart over a picture of my mother in a car just because we didn't recognize whom she was with. We both knew she didn't have a car, and before Becky disappeared, no one would've cared or noticed what she did during the day. But we both also knew my mother was different now; everything was different now.

"Why don't you just ask her?" I said. "There's probably a simple explanation." I was hoping if he found out, he would tell me too. But I knew he wouldn't ask her. My parents hardly talked to each other at all anymore; since my mother had stopped wanting to talk about Becky, it was almost as if they didn't have anything to say to each other.

It took Hal only a few days to find out who he was. His name was Garret Walker, and my father had no idea how my mother knew him.

When my father asked me if I'd ever heard of him, I repeated the name a few times before telling him it was unfamiliar. It's a strange name, a uniquely snobbish-sounding name. I'd never known a Garret before. "Garret," I said to my father. "Garret. Garret."

"I know," he said. It was weird the way we understood each other, the way this odd connection passed between us.

The night my father confronted my mother about the whole thing, he sent me over to spend the evening with Mrs. Ramirez and Tommy, so I missed what actually happened between them.

Instead of playing cards, Tommy and I did our homework at Mrs. Ramirez's kitchen table. I kept thinking about what was going on over at my house. My father hadn't told me specifically that he was confronting my mother about Garret, but he'd said as much when he told me they had a few things to discuss in private.

As I sat there at Mrs. Ramirez's kitchen table, I began to wonder about the nature of love—how it could be lost and found and twisted into horrible and ugly things. I wondered if my parents still had a piece of their love for each other, something large enough to hold on to, or if it, like everything else, had vanished.

"His name is Garret Walker," I said to Tommy.

"Who?"

"The man we saw with my mother."

"You know him?"

I shook my head. "My father's investigator has pictures."

Tommy looked up so suddenly, I could tell he was startled. I knew he was thinking if the investigator had pictures of my mother, he might also have pictures of us on Mr. Barnesworth's doorstep, but my father hadn't mentioned it, so I knew he didn't know. I wondered if Hal had taken the pictures on a different day entirely, if there was the possibility that my mother and Garret had been spending a lot of time together. "I don't want to go back to Florida," he said.

"Don't worry," I told him. "He doesn't know." Tommy flipped his hair, so I could tell the whole idea of my father knowing we'd cut school together made him nervous. "Why don't you want to go back?" I had this peculiar notion that it had something to do with me, even though I already secretly knew about Tommy's hatred of his mother.

"I just don't want to," he said.

We sat there quietly for a few minutes, and Tommy looked like he was deeply involved in a math problem. I couldn't tell if he was just pretending to do the work the way I was. "My mother was laughing," I finally said, because I just couldn't stop thinking about it, couldn't stop replaying her face over and over again in my head. "She looked so happy in the picture." I was sure Tommy knew about my mother's depression, her breakdown after Becky's disappearance. I was sure Mrs. Ramirez had told him everything, so I knew I didn't need to rehash it, that he would understand exactly what I meant.

"Is your father mad?"

Tommy's question sounded innocent, but I thought about everything my mother had told me about him, and I felt myself blushing. "No," I said. "It's not like that. She's not cheating on him or anything."

"My mother cheated on my father with a man named Irwin," he said. "Can you imagine that, Irwin?"

I tried to pretend I was surprised about his mother cheating on his father, but I'm a terrible liar, so I don't think I was very convincing. Tommy didn't seem to care, though, what I knew or didn't know about him. So finally I decided it was a safer subject if I just stuck to talking about my own mother. "She's not cheating."

"I mean, really," he said. "Irwin."

"What's your father's name?"

"Thomas," he said.

"Thomas. So you're Thomas junior."

"He always called me Little Tommy, LT for short."

"LT." The name seemed to give him a whole new character, a different personality. I could picture LT, the tough guy from Florida who picked fights to defend himself. But that wasn't Tommy, the boy who flipped his hair when he was nervous and held my hand as we ran from Mr. Barnesworth's.

"He was the only one who called me that."

"What happened to him?" I asked, although I already knew. It seemed like the right question to ask.

"He's going to come get me soon, and I'm going to go live with him." Even though I didn't think this was true, it made me a little nervous. I didn't want Tommy to leave. I wasn't sure what I would do without him. Maybe he was reading my mind, because he said, "Maybe you could come with us."

"Maybe." I doubted that my parents would let me leave, but it seemed like a nice dream, so I let Tommy hang on to it.

As my father and I walked home from Mrs. Ramirez's, I asked him to tell me what had gone on with him and my mother. "None of your beeswax, Ab." He tugged on my hat a little to pull it down over my ears. It was cold, and our breath looked smoky in the air.

"Did she tell you about Garret?"

"It's getting cold. It's almost winter."

I wanted to scream at him not to change the subject, but I knew it was no use. "Are you getting a divorce?" I whispered this, so when he didn't answer right away, I couldn't be sure if he heard me or not.

"Jesus, Ab. Of course not. Why would you think that?" He stopped walking and turned to look at me. "Your mother and I love each other very much, no matter what. You know that?" He shook my shoulders a little bit until I nodded.

I didn't understand their love anymore, not the way I'd thought I understood it the day on the beach. In fact I wasn't sure I understood love at all.

Garret Walker. All I knew about him was that he drove a red car, and he could make my mother laugh. I hated him.

I sat up in bed after my parents had gone to sleep and doodled his name over and over again on a piece of paper. I wrote his name in curvy letters and sharp-edged brisk letters, until it became just letters on a page, nothing more than that.

I had my own theory about Garret. I decided that Garret was my mother's private investigator. During the day, when

I was at school, she went with him, scouring Pinesboro for traces of Becky, for clues that the police might have missed. When Garret found Becky, we all would be sorry for doubting him and, more important, for doubting her.

This theory didn't explain why he made my mother laugh, but maybe she wasn't laughing at all. Maybe I was wrong about that. Maybe the camera had caught her at a funny moment, where she'd contorted her face in agony or grief, in knowing that another day had passed without finding Becky.

But the thought of who Garret was gnawed at my insides, and I knew I needed to know the truth. I decided that if my father wasn't going to tell me anything more about Garret, then I was going to have to find out myself. Though I felt a little embarrassed about my failure with Mr. Barnesworth, Tommy and I had managed to cut school successfully without getting caught, a thought that made me feel more than just a little exhilarated.

Chapter 15

BY THE END of November the ground had begun to freeze. We had an early winter, with our first official snowfall a whole week before Thanksgiving; it was large enough to get us a day off school.

I stayed in bed until ten, and then I sat by the front window and watched the snow. I saw Mrs. Peterson outside shoveling her driveway in her black high-heeled boots. I envied her pink-patterned scarf, which seemed to be wrapped in perfect order around her neck, unlike the scarves I wore, which hung funny and smacked me in the face. I wondered what the woman Mr. Peterson was cheating on her with looked like, and for some reason I instantly thought of my mother and Garret.

When Tommy rang the doorbell right after lunch, I still had Garret in my head. I couldn't shake the feeling that I had to keep him away from my mother, that if only she stopped spending time with him, everything would be okay. I decided that if I could talk to Garret, somehow I could fix things. I'd gotten out the phone book and begun searching to see if he was listed. He was.

I answered the door to let Tommy in, and before he could say anything, I said, "Come on in. I'm going to call Garret Walker."

"What?" His breath came out frosty on my front porch. "Are you nuts?" Maybe I imagined it, but I thought his eyes lit up just a little bit when I said it, as if he didn't think I was nuts at all but had just added an element of excitement to an otherwise dull day.

I led Tommy into the kitchen and picked up the phone and started to dial. "What are you going to say?" Tommy asked.

I hung up the phone quickly, realizing he was right. What was I going to say? It was just like the way I'd planned our escape from school but hadn't really thought about how we'd get into Mr. Barnesworth's house. "What do you think I should say?"

He shrugged. "You could pretend to be your mother."

I didn't know if I could pull my mother's voice off, so much scratchier than my own, but I wasn't sure yet how well Garret and my mother knew each other, so I thought maybe I could make it work. "That's not bad," I told him. I figured I had nothing to lose. Even if my father found out about this, I had a feeling he wouldn't be too angry with me, and if my mother found out, well, I didn't think things could be much worse between us.

I picked up a napkin from the table and put it over the receiver, thinking that this would help disguise my voice or at least make it sound more muffled. I'm not sure if Garret even knew about me, so he probably would have no reason to suspect I wasn't my mother.

As I started to dial, I realized that Garret might not even be home, that he could have a job like my father and be at work despite the snow, so it almost surprised me when he picked up on the second ring. "Hello," he said. His voice sounded a little high for a man's, not at all what I expected, and though I'd seen the pictures Hal had taken, I suddenly envisioned Garret as a small and very thin rat. When I didn't answer, he said it again. "Hello. Hello. Is anybody there?"

I cleared my throat and tried to speak softly and do

my best to imitate my mother. "Hello," I said. "Yes, this is Elaine. Elaine Reed."

"Oh, hi there." His voice softened, and my stomach sank, because I could hear that he was fond of my mother, just from his tone. "How are you?"

"Fine," I said. I tried to choose my words carefully, to sound mature, the way I'd overheard my mother on the phone in the past. "I'm doing well, thank you." Tommy nodded at me, so I knew he thought I sounded authentic. "I'm calling to tell you that I can't see you anymore. I need to spend more time with my husband."

There was silence for a minute, and I felt my heart beating rapidly in my chest, a drum so loud that I was sure Garret could hear it even through the phone. Finally Garret spoke. "Elaine," he said. "Elaine." I had this feeling he was about to profess his love for me, no, my mother, so I hung up the phone as fast as I could.

"Well, what did he say?" Tommy said.

I shook my head. "Nothing." It was his pause, the way he said my mother's name as if it were something close to him, something that belonged to him, that really got to me, and I wasn't sure how to explain this to Tommy.

But I hoped that maybe my phone call had been enough.

If Garret stayed away from my mother, maybe she would stay away from him too, and that would be the end of it.

Just after the first snowfall Harry Baker paid us a personal visit to tell us that the police were calling off their search of Morrow's field until spring. It was the first time I'd seen him since my early-morning phone call, and when I saw him walk in the front door, I felt ill. Maybe it was a feeling of helplessness, but suddenly my stomach felt as if it were about to capsize, to refuse to keep down the dinner I'd just eaten. I thought I would be able to see it in his face, the way he pitied me, but I couldn't. He was just the same old Harry.

My father didn't take the news well. "Jesus, Harry," he said, "you can't call it off."

"Not calling off," Harry said, "just postponing until spring."

"Until spring?" My father sounded incredulous. Spring seemed so far away, such a long time to go without any answers.

"The ground is frozen," Harry said.

"Well, you don't even know that she's there." It sounded silly the way he said it, as if Becky were alive and simply hiding in the field.

"You're right," Harry said. "So we're following up on any other leads."

"You have other leads?"

"Not right now, no."

My mother came downstairs in the middle of the conversation. She hadn't gotten dressed, and she was wearing a pair of ratty green sweatpants and one of my father's old holey undershirts. Her hair was messy and matted in a funny way in the back, and she wasn't wearing any makeup. "Harry," she said. Her voice sounded scratchier than normal, thickened and dulled by sleep.

"We're doing everything we can." I watched him pity my mother, watched his eyebrows twist this funny way so he looked sad and distraught. But it wasn't a genuine sadness, like my mother's; it was a tired sadness, and I wondered if I was imagining the sense of relief in his voice. I wanted to punch him. I wanted to tell him that he hadn't tried hard enough, that he'd wasted half the fall suspecting my mother.

For Thanksgiving, Mrs. Ramirez cooked a turkey and invited my family over to eat with her and Tommy. My father seemed relieved by the invitation, as if he were afraid to ask my mother to cook for us, afraid to expect it from her, even. The year before, Thanksgiving dinner without Grandma Jacobson had felt strange enough, but this year, without Becky, would've been even more bizarre. That's why I was glad Mrs. Ramirez invited us. It seemed to break tradition, in a way, to create this whole new holiday.

Mrs. Ramirez cooked enough for an army: a huge turkey, which my father carved, mashed potatoes, stuffing, salad, bread, and three kinds of pies. I hadn't expected her to be so good at cooking such American foods. I'd thought she would be good at making tacos or nachos, so when I saw her feast at dinner, I felt ashamed. In truth she is an excellent cook. The food we had at her house was probably the best Thanksgiving dinner I ever had.

Tommy's mother called in the middle of dinner, and we all got quiet as Mrs. Ramirez took the phone into the kitchen to talk to her. I watched my mother smile at Tommy. She gave him her fake, flashy smile, the one she gave to lost dogs and poor people. I was ashamed of her, and I wanted Tommy to look away.

We ate in silence for a few minutes until Mrs. Ramirez came back into the dining room. "Toe-moss," she said, and she handed him the phone. She sounded stern, insistent. I was surprised to see Tommy get out of his chair and walk into the kitchen. I wondered when he'd started talking to his mother again. I felt surprisingly alarmed. I liked it better when he hated her. I wondered, if he started talking to her on a regular basis, whether he'd eventually move back to Florida, leaving me here all by myself.

Right before dessert my mother got a headache, something she'd been having a lot lately and something that the doctor said could be a residual effect of the concussion. My father ushered her out but ordered me to stay behind for pie. It felt a little strange to be there without my family, what was left of it.

After Mrs. Ramirez watched me dutifully eat a piece each of pumpkin and apple pie, she let Tommy and me go into the living room to play cards while she cleaned up from dinner.

"What did you talk to your mother about?" I asked him as I dealt the first hand.

"I don't know." He shrugged. "The snow."

His answer surprised me at first, but then I remembered that there's no snow in Florida. I thought it must be strange to live in a place where it didn't snow in the winter, and in my mind Florida turned into this surreal place, with orange and purple sunsets and soft breezes. "That the first time you've seen snow?"

"Yeah. I guess so. Except my mom said once when I was a baby, we came here for Christmas and it snowed then, but I don't remember it."

I nodded. I wanted to ask him if he was going back to Florida, but I didn't have the guts. I was afraid if he said he was, I would start to crumble like my mother.

"She asked me what I was thankful for."

That was something we used to do at Thanksgiving at Grandma Jacobson's every year. We'd go around the table one by one and say one thing we gave thanks for. My parents usually said each other, and Becky and I would say something silly like a television show we enjoyed watching or a present Grandma Jacobson had given us earlier in the day. My grandmother would always say she was thankful for her girls, and she'd smile at my mother and Becky and me. I guess this left my father out, but it didn't seem strange at the time. I don't think he would've wanted her to include him anyway.

"What did you say?"

"I told her I was thankful for snow," he said. "It was all I could think of."

"I know what you mean. We used to do that at dinner, and it's hard to come up with something."

"I'm thankful for these cards," he said, and held up his hand.

"You have a good hand?"

"Maybe yes, maybe no."

I smiled. "I'm thankful for this game," I said. Though I meant it to be a joke, it was serious in a way. This game passed the time. Spending afternoons with Tommy kept me away from my parents, took me out of this whole messed-up life of mine for a few hours.

He paused for a moment and looked at his cards. I thought he was planning his next move, planning on stealing the game from me or something. But then he looked up at me and shook the hair away from his eyes, so I could see that he was serious, his deep brown eyes open wide, as if poised and waiting for rejection. "I'm thankful for you," he said.

I felt my heart flutter a little, the way it used to around James Harper. I couldn't help smiling. "Me too," I said. We looked at each other for a moment, and just like the day a few weeks earlier when we held hands behind the evergreen tree, I felt this intense connection to him.

Then, without even moving his eyes, he threw down another card. "Uno," he said.

I wondered if he'd said he was thankful for me to butter me up, just so he could win the game, but I didn't think so. I wanted to believe that he was beginning to need me, just the way I needed him.

Chapter 16

IT SNOWED SIX more times between Thanksgiving and Christmas, and by Christmas break we had ended up using a total of five snow days, which was almost our district's whole allotment for the entire school year.

After the day when Harry told us about the police not searching the field anymore till spring, the snow began to depress me. If Becky's body really was buried in Morrow's field the way the police thought, I knew the ground there must be terribly cold, and I wondered if she could feel it, if she knew cold the way neither one of us had known it before. This made me so sad; I couldn't bear to watch the snow fall anymore, and I ended up spending most of the days off up in my room, reading the second half of *To Kill a Mockingbird*.

Despite my own miserable failure with Mr. Barnesworth, I began to like the book as I read more. In particular, I was affected by Tom Robinson, the black man who gets convicted for a crime he didn't commit just because he was black. As I read, I thought about Tommy and how my mother had commented on his race and how James Harper had called him Brownie on his first day of school. It made me sad for him.

One snowy day, as I was reading and I'd just gotten to the part where Tom gets convicted, I told my mother about what was going on in the book. We were lying in the living room together. She was reading a book that her doctor had suggested during therapy, something about grieving, when she looked up and asked me how my book was.

"It's good," I said. "It really is." And I meant it. I really felt for Scout, for the way the adults didn't understand her. "It's kind of like a mystery," I told her. And then I told her all about the whole case, about how Mayella Ewell was raped and everyone thought Tom did it just because he was black. "Even though Scout's father proved at the trial that it would've been impossible for Tom to be the rapist, the jury still just convicted him," I told her.

"Well, that's terrible," my mother said. "That's just a shame."

I was surprised by her response. I'd pictured my mother as one of those members of the jury who might deliberate and say, *Well, jeez, the evidence does make it look like he's innocent, but still, look at him, he's b-l-a-c-k.* "I thought you didn't like black people," I said.

"Abby, what are you talking about? Why would you say that?"

"Well, the way you talked about Tommy's father, I thought—"

"What a terrible thing to say. Do you really hate me that much?"

I didn't hate her at all, but I was trying to understand her, and I realized I had failed horribly, that I'd suddenly turned our quiet relationship into something ugly. "I'm sorry," I said. "I didn't mean it like that."

"You think you're so smart," she said. "Reading all your books the way you always do for that darn English class, but you don't know anything, Abigail Reed." She slammed her own book shut and stormed out of the room.

I felt particularly bad because I knew this wasn't her crazy, irrational anger; this was my mother, and she was actually, truly angry with me for the first time since Becky had disappeared.

About an hour later Tommy rang the doorbell; he was dressed in a snowsuit that made him look like an Eskimo. "Maybe we could go sledding," he said. His hair was underneath a big black hat, and for the first time I could see every inch of his face perfectly. He looked different this way, cuter.

"I'll ask," I said. "You can come in if you want." This was only the second time Tommy had ever been inside our house, and I felt a little nervous, leading him in to sit on the couch.

My mother was lying in bed. I saw her eyes were open, so I knew she was awake. She was staring out the window. "Who was at the door?" she asked before I could say anything.

"Tommy. He wants me to go sledding with him. Can I go?" I was expecting her to say no, expecting her to tell me I was grounded or she didn't want me leaving the house. That's what my father would've said if he had been here. I was sure of it.

"Just don't sled in the street," she said.

"I can go?"

"As long as you're with Tommy," she said.

It was odd the way she said it, as if she thought Tommy could protect me from something. She would've never let me go sledding by myself, not this year anyway. I suddenly realized the way boys were looked at differently from girls. I could have been insulted, except I wasn't. I was excited about sledding, about leaving the house. "Thanks," I said, though I wasn't sure this was the right thing to say.

"Abby." She stopped me as I turned to leave. I thought she was changing her mind. "Turn off the lights on your way out." I turned them off, and because I was thinking about sledding, I didn't think about what it meant for my mother to be back in bed in the middle of the day in darkness.

Becky and I loved to go sledding when it snowed. The Petersons have this oddly shaped, winding hill in their side yard that's perfect for riding down on the orange, saucer-shaped sleds our mother had bought us a few years earlier. Mr. and Mrs. Peterson told Becky and me we could use the hill to sled whenever we wanted to, and we had come to think of it as our own, an extension of our property in the winter.

Sledding was one time when we never fought (we had identical sleds) and when we laughed a lot, giddy to be home from school and so freezing cold that we were out of our minds. We'd stay out in the snow so long that our faces would start to hurt, to feel like they were cracking, as we'd yell things to each other going down the hill. It was as if the snow had numbed our jealousy of each other, given us a break from being sisters, from having to share so much that we didn't want to share.

"You ever been sledding?" I asked Tommy as I pulled the two orange sleds from our garage. I hesitated for a moment as I took them out of the storage area, feeling somewhat uneasy giving away Becky's sled to Tommy. I told myself she wouldn't mind, that she would want him to use it, but I knew that wasn't true. Becky didn't like anyone touching her things.

"No."

"It's not hard," I told him. I handed over Becky's sled. "Here, take this. I'll show you."

I led Tommy to the top of the Petersons' hill, plopped my sled down, and sat on it. I moved back and forth, pushing the sled into the snow to start marking out my path; then I crossed my legs and put my hands onto the snowy ground. Tommy mimicked me, in this funny way. He looked uncomfortable touching the snow.

"Now you have to push off with your hands, " I said. "The first time going down is sort of slow, but once you make a path, it'll be better." He nodded. "Okay," I said. "On your mark, get set, go."

I pushed as hard as I could, and then I was going down the hill. The whole experience was magnificently freeing. Though I'd been down this hill this same way so many times in my life, it felt unbelievably new. I felt something on the way down that I hadn't felt in so long, this tiny surge of joy.

When I got to the bottom, I stood up and looked for Tommy. He'd fallen off the sled halfway down the hill and was trying to stand up and regain his balance but kept slipping. "There you go," I yelled. "You almost have it." Then I watched his face as he finally made it, as he went down the hill. He looked fearless; it was a look I'd never seen from him before, something genuine and perfect.

"Good job," I said when he reached the bottom, and I lifted up my hand to give him a high five. As he reached up to high-five me, he lost his footing, and he started to slip. He grabbed onto my hand, as a reflex, I guess, so I went down with him.

I started laughing, and then Tommy started laughing

too, and we both ended up on our backs in the snow. I rolled onto my side to look at him, and I was still laughing, but he'd stopped.

"Abigail," he said. It was the first time anyone had ever used my full name so sweetly. I liked the way it sounded when he said it, even though usually I preferred Abby.

He put his hand on my shoulder and leaned his face close to mine, and that was when I realized he was going to kiss me. Even though I was freezing, lying in the snow, I felt my cheeks getting hot, and I could feel my heart pounding underneath all my layers. I'd thought about my first kiss so many times, imagined what it would be like with James, how his lips would feel. Jocelyn and I had spent some afternoons last year practicing kissing our hands, just in case. I remembered Jocelyn saying, over and over again, that the worst thing you could be labeled at our school was a bad kisser.

But when Tommy went to kiss me, I wasn't thinking about any of that or about being cold or the fact that we were lying in the snow. I was just thinking about how much I wanted him to, how I wanted to know what his lips tasted like.

I leaned toward him and tilted my head a little, and

then I felt his lips on mine. His lips were much softer than I would've imagined and a little salty-tasting. When he kissed me, I felt this weird sort of electricity, this tingling sensation in my legs.

The kiss was short, and when he pulled back, I could see his breath, like frosting, lighting up the air. "Abigail," he said. I smiled at him and watched my own breath like little puffs of smoke from my mother's cigarettes. "Abigail." And this time I instantly noticed the way his voice curled on the second syllable, as if he'd suddenly seen a ghost.

"What? What is it?"

"Are you sure they don't mind us sledding here?"

I shook my head, feeling giddy from the kiss. "Nope, not at all. Besides, they're at work."

"But what about her?" He pointed to the window. I turned but saw only the curtain being drawn across the window. "The girl," he said. "What about the girl?"

Chapter 17

THERE WAS A moment after Tommy kissed me when I felt warmth, when I was alive, and then Tommy's words sank in. The Petersons didn't have a little girl.

Tommy slipped and fell as I grabbed his hand and started running toward the Petersons' door, and he called after me, "Abby, wait." But the cold had made my ears numb, and as I ran, I let myself tune him out, the frosty air like cold, cold water rushing through my eardrums. Before Tommy could get up, I was ringing the doorbell, two, three, four times, then banging on the door, as hard as I could, so hard in fact that when Mr. Peterson opened the door, I almost fell.

"Abigail Reed, is that you? What is it, are you hurt?"

I was out of breath and shaking, but I managed to

say, "Where is she?" By then Tommy had reached me, and I pointed to him and said, "He saw her, a girl, in your window."

"I'm sorry?"

"Where is she?" By this point I was crying, and the tears running down my cheeks felt so warm that I felt as if I were melting. I wiped them away because they stung and because I was embarrassed.

"Why don't you let me walk you home?" he said, and he stepped outside even though he didn't have his coat on and put his arm around my shoulder.

Tommy reached for my hand and pulled me hard. "It's okay, sir," he said. "I'll take her home. Abigail," he said in a whisper, "I don't think it was her."

I calmed down by the time Tommy and I were sitting in Mrs. Ramirez's living room, drinking the hot chocolate she made. "Ooh, you two catch you death out there." She shook her head.

"Grandma, please." It surprised me that Tommy's annoyed look was enough to get her to leave the room, but it was.

"I'm sorry," I said. "Who was she?"

"I don't know. But she had very dark hair, much darker than . . ." I don't think he could bring himself to say Becky's name.

My mind wandered quickly to all sorts of places—there were hair dyes, plastic surgeons, there were people who could make you look completely different—but then I thought about how foolish I'd felt after meeting Mr. Barnesworth's nurse. "It's no use," I told Tommy. "What can I do?"

"No." He shook his head. "We are not giving up." When I heard him say the word "we," I felt my heart beat a little faster, the way it had when he kissed me on the hill.

Tommy and I kissed one more time before Christmas break. It was funny, the way nothing changed between us, and yet everything changed. Neither one of us said it, but I could tell that he assumed that if Mrs. Ramirez or our parents were to find out about the shift in our relationship, we would somehow be torn apart.

I knew, despite my mother's anger when I'd implied that she didn't like people of other races, that if she found out that Tommy and I had kissed, she'd be furious. My father would become even more overprotective. Mrs. Ramirez would be ashamed that her amazing grandson liked the daughter of the crazy neighbors. Maybe Mrs. Ramirez would send Tommy back to Florida; maybe my father would find another "babysitter" for me. This was why we pretended that nothing had changed.

The second time we kissed was the day I took Tommy to Morrow's field after school. It had started snowing again earlier in the day, and by the time Mrs. Ramirez picked us up from school, there was a nice white coating on the ground.

"Maybe you have off again tomorrow," Mrs. Ramirez said to us in the car. Tommy turned and caught my eye and smiled. I felt my face beginning to turn hot, thinking about the last day off, the afternoon on the snowy hill. "Roads little bit slippery." She hit the brakes as if to make a point, and I felt us slide. I put my hand on the door and held on tightly.

When I got home, my mother was up in her room. She was lying in bed with the TV on, and she hadn't gotten dressed. She'd been in her room again since the snow day the week before, when I'd unintentionally insulted her. I tried to tell myself that this retreat wasn't my fault, that it had more to do with Christmas coming up and the fact that

Becky wasn't here, but it was hard. I started to blame myself for her behavior, and I started to despise myself just a little bit. I filled up with such self-pity that I felt like a plump helium balloon that, if let go for a second, would rise so high into the sky it would disappear.

"It's snowing again," I told her.

She nodded. " I know."

"We could take a walk in the snow if you want." This was something she used to love to do when it was snowing just a little bit. The three of us—me, her, and Becky—would take a short walk outside and point out shapes of snowflakes. The flakes would hit our faces and melt, and my mother would hold on to our hands and laugh.

"I don't think so." She pulled herself deeper under the covers, retreating farther and farther away from me. "Why don't you take a walk with Tommy?"

I tried not to react when she said it. I tried to shrug and pretend like it didn't matter to me if I walked with him. But I felt my heart start to pound at the thought of being alone with him again.

"Show me this field," Tommy said, after we'd walked once down our street. "I want to see it."

"I don't know." The truth was I was afraid of Morrow's field. I worried that Becky really could be there somewhere: her body, or her spirit, whatever it was. I was nervous that if I went back there, she'd begin to haunt me more than she did already.

In years past Becky and I and a lot of the kids in our neighborhood played in Morrow's field when it snowed. It is the perfect flat place to build snowmen and make snow angels on the ground. The field is surrounded on all sides by trees, so it is like this secret, hidden world. We thought of it as this semimagical place where we were far away from everything, yet oddly close too. On one side it has a tiny, slanted hill where, after a few successive snowfalls, the snow begins to build up in drifts. That was where we'd make snowballs and throw them at one another.

Last year we'd had only one big snowfall, but it was big enough to get two days off from school. Becky and I had gone back there to build a snowman, but we ended up having a snowball fight. She threw the first one at me, and I guess she was trying to be funny because she started laughing and laughing. "Shut up," I told her. She threw another one at me, and this one hit me square in the middle of my thigh. "Stop it." She laughed even harder, so I started making snowballs too and throwing them at her. I was throwing them hard, harder than I even realized I could, and one hit her on the cheek.

"Ouch." She lifted a mittened hand to touch her face. "That stings, Abby. I'm telling Mom." She ran toward the house.

"No, wait." I ran after her. "Becky, come on. We were just having fun."

Becky had a red welt on her cheek that turned into a purple bruise and lingered there for days. "What were you thinking, Abigail?" my mother said to me as she put her hand to Becky's cheek. "Why would you do this to her?"

"She started it," I said, and I stuck my tongue out at her when I knew my mother couldn't see me.

"Honestly, Abigail. You're older. Act your age." She kissed Becky's cheek, right on the sore spot, right where I hit it. I remember thinking that I wished I'd knocked her eye out, that I wished I'd really hurt her, made her pay for everything she did to me.

The field was quiet when I went there with Tommy. I think everyone had been forbidden to play there, snow or no snow.

People were suddenly afraid of the field, the same way they were now afraid of my family, as if it too held this strange, mystical power to transform them into something ugly.

The field looked different from how I remembered it, I guessed because the police had been digging there. I think they'd tried to put the dirt back, to make it look as if nothing had ever happened there, but the snow had this weird brownish tint to it, as if it had mingled too closely with the disturbed earth.

As soon as we stepped behind the first row of trees that divided the field from my backyard, Tommy grabbed for my hand. I couldn't feel warmth from him through the thickness of my mittens and his gloves, but his grip was firm, reassuring.

I heard the snow and the earth crunch beneath our feet, and I cringed, thinking of Becky, thinking of the cold sting of a snowball against her cheek and how that had made her run away from me.

We walked across the field until we were standing in the center. Tommy looked around. "It's not as big as I thought it would be."

"It's big," I said, thinking about how the police had spent all fall looking for Becky and had turned up nothing.

"It's big enough so you could get lost here."

"I don't know," Tommy said. He faced me and put his arms around me. I could almost feel him there, through the thickness of our parkas. Our faces were close, but not touching, until he bumped his nose against mine in a way that was sweet and sincere.

"So this is it," I said. I was talking about the field, but when it came out, it sounded like I was talking about so many other things.

That's when he leaned in to kiss me for the second time. The kiss was longer this time. His lips lingered there for a minute, and when he pulled back, he kept his face close, so I could feel his warm breath tickling my nose.

For a second I thought about what Becky would think if she could see me. I knew she'd be insanely jealous, and she would be the one to tell my parents everything. But then I wondered if she were watching me from somewhere else, someplace near my grandma Jacobson, and if there, wherever she was, she could be happy for me, because there wouldn't be any more jealousy. I wondered if she and Grandma Jacobson would clap their hands and hug each other and say something like "Good for her. She deserves to be happy."

I'm not sure I was happy, standing there so close to

Tommy. But I was feeling something, and for the first time in the longest time it wasn't hurt, and I wasn't afraid, and I didn't hate myself.

"We should go back," Tommy said. "It's getting dark. They'll worry." He pulled away from me and started walking. I followed behind him, looking around the field for a moment, trying to listen for my sister's voice.

Chapter 18

I THOUGHT ABOUT the girl Tommy had seen in the Petersons' window, and some nights, I dreamed about her, a raven-haired Becky, handcuffed to a post on a wall, held captive by a madman who cheated on his wife. "Why can't you save me?" she asked, only when I heard the words, they came out in my voice, sounding small and empty, as if I'd gotten lost in an echo chamber.

Though he didn't mention it for nearly two weeks, Tommy hadn't forgotten about her either. In the days before he left with Mrs. Ramirez to go to Florida for Christmas, he devised a plan to find out about her. "We'll break in," he told me on the last day of school before the vacation. I nearly choked on my sandwich when he said it. "I've been watching," he said. "They leave for work around six-thirty." Tommy must've noticed my shocked expression, because he said, "I can see their front door from my bedroom window."

"How will we get in?" I asked him, and I can't tell you how the question rolled off my tongue as if it were the most perfectly normal thing in the world.

"We will," he said. "I know how."

The next morning Tommy watched my father leave for work, then watched Mr. and Mrs. Peterson kiss good-bye in the driveway. I watched them kiss too from my front window, having already put on my boots and winter coat and lied to my mother about going over to Mrs. Ramirez's house. I caught myself admiring the way Mrs. Peterson had curled her hair, the way it fell in soft red loops out from her hat and onto her shoulders, and when I saw Mr. Peterson's hand on her back, I felt a chill, remembering his hand on my shoulder and the file Hal Brewerstein had created about his affair. It surprised me the way their kiss disguised everything else, and it scared me too, the way something could look so beautiful but could secretly be hideous.

Five minutes after they left, I met Tommy in the street

with our sleds, just as we had planned, and then we ran across to the Petersons' hill, which was still covered in snow, so if anyone should see us, it would look like we planned on sledding.

"Come on," Tommy said, once we were away from the street. "Follow me." He led me to the laundry-room window, the same tiny laundry-room window that sat on the side of my house and Mrs. Ramirez's house.

"Through here?" I said. "We won't fit."

"We will."

I wasn't surprised when Tommy pushed on the window and it opened immediately. Before Becky disappeared, I was sure, my mother had never locked our tiny laundry room window either. "What were you going to do if the window was locked?" I asked him. But he didn't answer.

Tommy gave me a boost, and before I knew it, I was inside the Petersons' laundry room. Officially a criminal, I tried not to think about what would happen to my mother's mood if Tommy and I were arrested for breaking and entering or about the smirk on Kinney's face as he booked me into jail. As I grabbed Tommy's hand and helped pull him into the house, I pushed the thought out of my mind.

With Tommy's hair under his winter hat, I could see

every bit of his face, his eyes, and he was illuminated. He suddenly seemed to have an easy confidence, a solid gaze, that made me feel both at ease and unnerved. Tommy was enjoying this.

We made our way out of the laundry room and into the Petersons' house, which was identical to both our houses, yet decorated with expensive-looking white leather furniture that I guessed people weren't actually allowed to sit on. My mother despises furniture like that. Everything seemed to be in order, seemed to be terrifically adult and glamorous, the way I always imagined the inside of their house to be.

We went up to the master bedroom, to the window where Tommy had seen the girl, but there was no sign of her. The Petersons' bed was perfectly made up with a red velour comforter and mounds of pillows. I thought about Mr. Peterson's affair, and I had to look away because I wondered if he had brought her here, his mistress. "There's nothing here," I said to Tommy, and I turned around to face him.

"There's this." In his hand was a doll, her blond hair pulled back into a perfect ponytail and tied up neatly with a red ribbon.

A few hours later I watched Tommy pack for his trip. It was the first time I'd ever been in his bedroom, and it felt strange, me sitting on his bed in Mrs. Ramirez's house.

He had Becky's bedroom, but it was eerie to me how different it looked, how boyish. In Tommy's opposite but identical room, Mrs. Ramirez had hung up pennants from various sports teams, ones from Florida and ones from some of the East Coast teams near us. And his walls were painted this deep royal blue.

I hadn't been inside Becky's bedroom since before she disappeared. I was afraid to go in there at first, afraid I would destroy evidence or touch something I wasn't supposed to. But then it became something like a shrine, a secret place that I'd lost access to. Everyone in my family left it alone; we pretended that that room wasn't even there. It seemed almost sacrilegious to go in there, to touch Becky's things.

"Are you going to tell your father about the girl?" he asked as he folded some clothes into a suitcase.

"I don't know." It seemed a little silly when I rolled it around in my brain.

Tommy nodded. His hair was back in front of his eyes again, and it hid his expression, so I couldn't tell what he was really thinking.

"Are you excited to go back to Florida?" I said. I tried to sound cheery when I said it, but really I was annoyed that he was leaving, even though I knew it was out of his control.

He shrugged and went to his closet to pull out some shirts. "I don't know. I guess so."

"It's probably warm there, nice."

"I kind of like the snow." He turned and looked at me and smiled, so I knew it wasn't the snow he was talking about, but the two times we'd kissed, standing in it. I had to look away because I didn't want him to see me blushing.

"Will you get to see your father?" I asked, just to change the subject. Talking about us made me nervous, made it seem like there was something real there, like Tommy and I were boyfriend and girlfriend.

"I don't know. Probably not."

I could tell this made him sad; there was a sense of remorse in his voice that he was usually able to hide. I wondered if Irwin would be there, if Tommy would have to bear Christmas with Irwin and his mother. I didn't want to ask him, though. I didn't feel right talking about Irwin unless he was the one to bring it up. Instead I said, "Becky loved Christmas."

He didn't say anything, which was okay, because there

wasn't anything I wanted him to say. I thought about how Becky got so excited every Christmas morning, how she'd stay up half the night before, singing Christmas carols, usually until my father told her to go to bed or Santa would skip our house. She seemed too old to believe in Santa still, and maybe deep down she didn't, but on the surface she pretended to believe.

I'd discovered that Santa wasn't real when I was six and I'd found all my Christmas presents in my mother's closet two weeks before. Even though I taunted Becky with this memory, she refused to listen. When I tried to tell her over and over again, she'd put her hands over her ears and start singing.

I thought Christmas was just okay. My mother is Jewish, and my father is Episcopalian, so until Grandma Jacobson died, we celebrated both Hanukkah and Christmas. I've always preferred Hanukkah to Christmas, maybe because it is a little unusual, something that sets me apart from most of the other kids in Pinesboro, who on the whole are purely Christian. But I also love the meaning behind it, the miracle of the oil, the eight nights of celebrating. I missed that we didn't celebrate it anymore.

Eventually Mrs. Ramirez came up to tell me my father

was downstairs waiting for me. "You be good girl for your parents when we gone." She patted my shoulder in this funny way. I could tell she was trying to be nice, but it felt more like a slap.

I hardly heard her. I was thinking about how much I would miss Tommy, how depressed I was that he was leaving, but it would've been too weird to tell him any of this, especially in front of Mrs. Ramirez. The only thing I could bring myself to tell him was to have a good trip.

"Merry Christmas," he said as I walked toward his bedroom door.

"Yeah," I said without looking behind me. "You too."

If he stayed in Florida, if I never saw him again, I wanted to remember his face the way it looked in the Petersons' laundry room, not the way it looked as he stood in his bedroom, when I knew he looked sad.

When we got home, I told my father about the girl in the window, but I only told him how Tommy saw her when we were sledding, not about our trip into their house or the doll. For some reason, maybe because he could detect the urgency in my voice, my father didn't get angry with me, but he immediately called Harry Baker and left him a message.

Then he ran to the front window to watch the Petersons' house, sitting there so still for two hours that I thought he might've fallen asleep.

"Dad," I said, my voice sounding tiny in the dark front room of our house.

"Ab." He sounded tired.

"Are you all right?"

I listened and listened, but there was no answer.

Chapter 19

THERE WAS THIS Christmas song that Becky liked to sing: "I'll Be Home for Christmas." My parents had an old Elvis Presley record where he sings that song. Becky would put it on my father's record player from college and sing along with him in the living room. She'd use her hairbrush as a microphone and stand on her "stage" in front of the fireplace.

My mother played that Elvis Presley record over and over, starting two days before Christmas. Every time it got to the end of Becky's favorite song, she'd go in and move the needle, replaying the song two, sometimes three times. It was strange, really, to hear Elvis singing about being home for Christmas if only in his dreams. I knew my mother noticed it too, that she was thinking that Becky might come home, that she would be here somehow, in some way.

My mother loved to hear Becky sing. "You have a voice like an angel, sweetie," she'd say. Becky did have a beautiful voice, even though I never admitted it to her when she was here. It may have been what I was most jealous of.

I never understood the concept of pitch; I couldn't get myself to sing on key even when I tried really hard. Mrs. Richards, our elementary school music teacher, told me that she thought I might be tone-deaf. When we practiced for choir, she used to look right at me and lift her palm in the air a little bit, as if she believed the force of her hand hitting the air could bring me to the right pitch. But she loved Becky. In fact she'd told my mother a few times that she thought we should get Becky voice lessons, that she believed Becky really had something special.

I wondered if Mrs. Richards missed the sound of Becky's voice in her choir, if Becky's absence was noticeable there.

We didn't even have a tree until Christmas Eve, when my father dragged in a scrawny leftover one that he'd found in the picked-over tree lot. My mother and I watched him drag it in the front door, neither one of us moving to help him.

"Can't have Christmas without a tree, ladies." He was out of breath, and his cheeks were bright red.

"Oh, I don't know, Jim." My mother had her hands on her hips.

He dropped the tree in the entryway and shut the door behind him. "Elaine, it's Christmas." He looked at me. "Help me get this in the living room, Ab."

We put it in the corner by the fireplace, in the same spot where we put the tree every year, but this tree was smaller than usual, and it looked so sad, forlornly misshapen and out of place. "Bring down the ornaments," my father said to my mother. She looked paralyzed, and I expected her to ignore my father, but she didn't. She went upstairs and came back with the box of ornaments a few minutes later.

In the box of ornaments Becky was everywhere. As I pulled them out of the box, one by one, I saw the ornaments she'd glued together in school; the ones that were her favorites, the blue with silver painted stars; the ones she liked to place near the top of the tree but couldn't reach, the little red shiny balls that she'd hand to my father, giving him explicit instructions about which branch to place each one on.

"Just put them up, Ab. Don't think about them." It sounded so harsh, but I didn't think he meant it that way.

I think he just wanted the tree to be there and decorated, that he wanted the world, our house to have some sense of normalcy.

"You don't have to do this for me," I said.

"I'm not." But I wondered, If he wasn't doing this for me, then who was he doing it for?

The record moved to Becky's song, and my mother reached over and turned it up. Maybe she was trying to drown out me and my father hastily decorating the tree; maybe she thought that if she turned it up loud enough, she'd be able to remember the sound of Becky's voice, the clear crystal pitch that could sing out above the record. I can still remember it. If I close my eyes, I can hear it.

On Christmas morning my mother refused to get out of bed, but my father came and woke me up and told me to have a look at the presents Santa had left for me under the tree.

"Please," I groaned. "I haven't believed in Santa for like seven years."

"Well, luckily," my father said, "he still believes in you." He sounded almost cheerful, and I wondered what exactly had put him in such a good mood. Maybe he still believed in holidays, in peace and happiness and miracles and all that stuff. Maybe for one day he made himself believe.

There were more presents under the tree than I'd expected. I picked up the first one I saw and started to unwrap it. "Hey." My father pulled it from my hands and put it back down. "That's not for you."

In years past my parents had divided the tree down the middle, with my presents being on the far side near the fireplace and Becky's on the side by the window. I'd inadvertently reached for a present on her side. It was strange, but in the past few months I'd forgotten about the lines we'd used for dividing things.

You might think it was odd that my father put presents for Becky under the tree, but I didn't, not really. In fact I felt guilty about starting to unwrap her present. After Christmas, I knew, my father would save these presents for her. When she came back, we wanted her to feel as if she hadn't missed a thing.

Sometimes at night, when I couldn't fall asleep, I'd think about what I'd tell her when she came back. What I planned on saying: *The only thing you've missed is missing you.* I thought this over and over again. What made that true were things like this, her Christmas presents, neatly wrapped and waiting for her.

When I moved to my side of the tree, I saw that there were just two presents there. I'm ashamed to say it, but I felt jealous of Becky, even without her being here. There were five presents on her side and only two on mine. Even vanished, she was a stronger force than I was, something to be reckoned with.

"It doesn't look like much," my father said. "But usually your mother is in charge of these things."

"No," I lied. "It looks like a lot. It does. Thank you." I felt genuinely grateful that my father loved me enough to go out and buy the presents on his own, even if he'd bought Becky more.

I opened the bigger, heavier present first, which turned out to be a boxed set of Shakespeare's plays. "This is great," I said. "Thanks." I really meant it. I was surprised that my father had thought to get this for me and excited that I could occupy the rest of my break reading.

"I knew you had your nose in *Hamlet* all fall."

I nodded. "Yeah. Thanks."

The second, smaller present was a thirty-dollar gift certificate to the Pinesboro mall. I thought about what I would buy with the money, and I realized it was the first time in a long time that I'd thought about clothes or buying something or shopping. Those things seemed like part of a different life now, almost like something I'd done in a dream, somewhere very far away from here.

I stood up and hugged my father. "Thank you," I said.

"Merry Christmas, Ab." He held on to me a minute longer than he usually would in a hug, and then he patted me on the head before letting me go. "Do you want to know what I got her?"

For some reason, I thought he was talking about my mother at first. He'd often share his ideas for presents for her with me or Becky or ask our advice if he wanted to buy her a girl thing like jewelry. Becky was better at helping him than I was. But then I saw he was staring at Becky's presents, so I knew he was talking about her. "Sure," I said. "Tell me."

"There's something here for each month, " he said, and pointed to each present. "August, September, October, November, December. There's something that she missed in each one, something I've been saving for her."

I'd had no idea that my father was saving things for Becky. I'm not sure why this surprised me exactly, but it didn't seem like something I would expect from my father. Becky's disappearance had changed him. "That's nice," I told him. "She would've liked that." After I said it, I realized that I'd used a verb tense that made it sound like she was never coming back.

I think my father noticed too, because he looked away from me and didn't say anything else about his presents. I wanted to know what he'd saved for her each month, but I knew he wasn't going to tell me after what I'd said. He sat down on the couch and just stared at the tree, as if he were expecting something beautiful to jump out of it.

"It's quiet," I finally said, just to say something, to break the awful, piercing silence.

"Turn on a record or something."

"That's okay." I didn't want to hear Christmas songs again, didn't want to imagine Becky singing, Becky jumping up and down in front the tree. "I think I'll go upstairs and read."

"Okay," he said, but I knew he hadn't really heard what I'd said.

"Merry Christmas," I said before I took my presents and went upstairs.

"Yeah." He nodded. "Merry Christmas." But his voice sounded flat.

Harry Baker rang the doorbell around noon. It was the first time he'd come by since the day in November when he told us they were postponing the search. As I looked out my bedroom window and saw him standing by the front porch, I felt a surge of hope. It was Christmas. There were miracles on this day. It's the day Jesus Christ was born, and that had to mean something.

I guess my mother thought the same thing I did, because by the time Harry was in the entryway saying hello to my father, we both were racing down the stairs. "Elaine." He nodded at my mother and sort of half nodded at me without really looking at me.

"What?" she said before she even made it down the steps. "What is it, Harry?"

Harry shook his head, so we all knew instantly that they hadn't found her, that he hadn't come with any news. He was here only because it was Christmas, and he used to be one of my father's friends, and now he felt sorry for us.

I knew it was impossible, but it seemed like my mother was shrinking right before my eyes. I watched her crumpling, smaller and smaller, but then I realized she was just slouching to the floor, where she held on to my father's leg.

"It's Christmas," she said.

"I know, Elaine." My father reached down to pat her shoulder and help her stand up. He hugged her. "Why don't we get you back into bed?"

"That's a good idea," she said. "Yes, that's what I should do." Her voice sounded frantic, a little bit crazy, and I started to get frightened for her all over again.

"Ab, show Harry into the living room. I'll be right down."

I felt silly leading Harry to our couch, because he'd been in our house a dozen times in the past few months; he knew where it was. Luckily my father returned quickly. I didn't want to look at Harry. I despised him for the way he failed to understand me, us, our family. I believed he was the one who could've stopped the others, who could've told them that it was not my mother they were looking for but someone or something else.

"Harry," my father said when he came back downstairs. "Harry Baker."

"I didn't mean to upset her." Harry's voice was quiet, almost timid sounding, not like the Harry I remembered on the baseball field.

"Ab, why don't you go back to your room?"

"It's okay," Harry said, "I'll only be a minute. I just have something I wanted to give you." He fished around in the inside pocket of his coat for a minute. There was this uncomfortable silence in the room, as Harry searched his pockets and my father and I stared at him. I felt this intense tension between my father and Harry, and it was strange, because I could picture the two of them laughing in Harry's backyard, as they held on to their cans of Budweiser and their barbecued hamburgers.

Harry lifted Becky's necklace out of his pocket and let it dangle over his hand so we both could see it. "Here," he said, and he handed the necklace to my father.

My father rubbed his temple and then reached over for the necklace. "Jesus. I thought you needed this as evidence."

Harry shook his head. "We checked it over for everything. Prints, fiber, what have you. But nothing turned up. It was just sitting in a box. I thought you'd like to have it. Detective Kinney wanted to keep it just in case, but I said just in case what, you know?" Harry laughed a little; I was surprised by how nervous he sounded. I wondered if he'd taken the necklace and brought it over here without Kinney's permission. I began to see this as Harry's peace offering, as a gesture that he wanted to go back to being friends with my father.

My father clapped Harry on the shoulder the way he used to when Harry left a picnic at our house and they were saying good night. "Thank you," he said.

We all were silent for a moment, as if we were mesmerized by the necklace hanging from my father's hand, the tiny sapphire heart sparkling like a little star on a crisp, cloudless winter night. I don't know what my father and Harry were thinking about, but I was thinking about the look on my grandmother's face when she gave us those necklaces, a round, glowing smile, her full wrinkly face lit up and pink. It was a look I hadn't remembered in a long time, something that had been covered up by the hollow eyes and sharp bony lines left on her by the cancer. "I should go," Harry said. "I don't want to interrupt your Christmas."

My father and I walked behind him toward the door. "Merry Christmas," my father said as Harry began to walk away. Harry turned around and nodded to us, as if to say, "The same to you." I saw his face then, and it was oddly contorted with something. I didn't know Harry well enough to say for sure, but I guessed it was guilt or sadness or his failure to really do his job.

This was the last time I ever saw Harry Baker. Two weeks after Christmas he left the police force, and he packed up and moved to Arizona.

Chapter 20

WHEN TOMMY CAME back from Florida, he had this really, really short hair, a buzz cut. He looked so foreign to me that I knew instantly something would be different between us, that Tommy's haircut symbolized a change for him, even if I was the only one to recognize it.

His mother and Mrs. Ramirez had bought him a skateboard for Christmas, and the first time I saw him after he got back, he was skateboarding down our street. "Is that Tommy?" my mother said as she peered out our front window. "Come look at his hair, Abby."

It was him all right, gliding down the street as if he didn't have a care in the world. I wondered why he hadn't come over to show me the skateboard, why he was flying down the street on his own. "I don't know," I said. "I kind of liked it the other way."

"He looks so much more grown up this way."

I shrugged. "I guess so." I was trying to act nonchalant, trying to pretend that Tommy's hairstyle had absolutely nothing to with me, but inside, I felt sort of stung, deceived almost, which was stupid. Tommy had a right to cut his hair and to skateboard and not tell me about any of it.

"I don't know," my mother said. "He's sort of cute this way."

Her comment made my cheeks turn red, and I wondered if she suspected how I felt about him. "He's all right," I said. "Nothing special." And then I felt disloyal to Tommy. I knew I would have been hurt if he'd said the same thing about me.

"So why'd you cut your hair?" I said when I saw him at lunch the first day back in school.

"My mother did it. She said it was too long." He sounded surprisingly pleased, though, not the way I was used to him talking about his mother. "Do you like it?"

I nodded. "Sure. It's nice."

"I don't know. I'm not used to it yet. It surprises me every time I see it."

I thought that was a strange thing for Tommy to say. I didn't think boys noticed their appearance the way girls did, but what Tommy said represented how I felt every time I saw myself in the mirror, every time I noticed my breasts and this serious, complicated look on my face that made me look foreign to myself.

Mrs. Ramirez had packed Tommy this huge container of enchiladas for lunch, and he scooped half of them out of the Tupperware container and onto my school lunch plate, which contained some scary-looking mashed potatoes. "Here," he said. "I can't eat all this."

"Thanks." I took a bite. "They're delicious." They were really good actually, even cold. It'd been a long time since I'd eaten a home-cooked meal.

"My grandmother makes the best enchiladas." There was this awkward silence where we both just sat there and chewed. "How was your Christmas?" Tommy asked.

"Okay," I lied. "Yours?"

"Pretty good. I got a skateboard."

"I know. I saw you."

"You did?"

It was strange the way I could see his eyes all the time, and they were so expressive that I could understand everything that he was feeling in each instant that he was feeling it. That's why I missed the hair, the anonymity it gave him. I could tell when I said I saw him on the skateboard that he was embarrassed, as if he'd been caught doing something he shouldn't have. "It's okay," I said. "I've been really busy."

"You have?"

"Well, you know." It was pretty obvious I was lying, but I didn't feel like explaining my way out of it at that point. "I got a set of Shakespeare's plays for Christmas."

"That's cool."

I smiled. I liked that Tommy thought that genuinely was cool. Jocelyn would've laughed at it, the way she did whenever I read or talked about books. "Seriously, Abby," she'd say, "why do you think God invented TV?"

"It's not a skateboard," I said.

"Still." He paused. "Did you tell your father?"

I nodded. "He called the police, but they weren't interested, so he has his investigator looking into it." I tried to sound nonchalant, even though I felt a surge of nerves just thinking about Tommy's hand on my back as he pushed me through the laundry room window.

"Oh, that's good, I guess."

We finished the enchiladas, and then we just sort of sat there. I wondered if Tommy would want to kiss me anymore or if those two moments had been something purely disposable to him, like his hair.

Right after we went back to school after Christmas break, the weather turned exceptionally warm, and the world around us began to thaw out and melt. The sun was shining, and the temperatures were in the fifties. Our backyard filled up with these big muddy puddles, and the street in front of our house was wet and glistening in the sun.

If it hadn't been for the warm spell, the police probably never would've discovered the body of a little girl in a riverbank in Philadelphia, about twenty-five miles from our house. If the weather had stayed cold, snowy, by spring she might've been too far gone for anyone to find her. The weather was so strange, it was as if someone had known she was there, someone had wanted the police to find her. I took it all as a sign.

No one in my family had talked about bodies before. We hadn't talked about Becky's being dead; we pretended not to consider the possibility. We talked about when she was coming home and what we would say to her. My father still had the Christmas tree up, with her presents underneath it. We weren't in denial; we were just hopeful, unable to imagine the permanence of Becky's absence.

It was Detective Kinney who came to tell us about the body. He came in person, instead of calling. When I saw him walking in through our front door, I knew that there was significant news. It was the same way I felt when I saw Harry Baker on Christmas morning, only, because it was Kinney, I knew he'd have something important to say.

When Kinney showed up, the three of us had just sat down to eat dinner. It was one of the rare occasions when we did this, when my mother felt well enough to get out of bed, when my father actually remembered to pick up a pizza on the way home.

We all jumped a little when we heard the doorbell ring. My parents exchanged a brief glance, a moment, before my father stood up. None of us would admit it, but I think we all were waiting for the doorbell; every day, every moment we sat in our house, we were waiting for something to happen.

I recognized Kinney's voice immediately. "Jim," I heard him say, "I hope I'm not interrupting."

"No, not at all," my father said. "Come in."

By this time my mother and I both had made our way

into the hallway. I tried to catch Kinney's eye, but he still wouldn't look at me. "Maybe it would be better if we just spoke outside for a minute," Kinney said to my father. My father let himself out onto the porch and shut the door behind him.

"I'm going out there," my mother said, but she didn't move. She stood frozen next to me in the hallway. I think she was afraid the same way I was. We both knew if Kinney wanted to talk to my father outside in private, he couldn't have come here with good news.

"It's probably nothing," I said to my mother, but I don't think either one of us believed it.

"The pizza's getting cold," she said, but we didn't go back to the table. We just stood in the hallway. It was probably only a few minutes—it couldn't have been more than ten—but it felt like ages, as if time had stopped and trapped us there.

When my father came back in, his face was completely white, paler than I'd ever seen him, eerily ghostlike. "Jim, what is it?" My mother finally moved and walked to him.

"Let's sit down, girls," he said. "Sit down."

We went back to the kitchen table, but none of us touched the pizza. "Jim, you're scaring me." My mother ran her fingers loosely through her hair, something I'd seen her do a million times, something seemingly careless, but I noticed then how tense it made her look.

"Okay," my father said. He took a deep breath and looked at me. I could tell he was debating whether or not to send me to my room.

"I want to know," I told him, and I guess the way I said it convinced him to let me stay, because he nodded.

"They found a body in Fairmount Park. A little girl. About her weight and height and age." I knew he couldn't bring himself to say Becky's name, to say her name in the same breath as "body." She wasn't a body; she was a person, my sister, his daughter. "They haven't identified it yet, but Kinney wanted to tell us. They thought it might be her."

"No," my mother said. She shook her head violently, back and forth and back and forth. I watched her hair whip into her face. "It's not her. It can't be her. How did she get to Fairmount Park?"

"Elaine." My father stood up and wrapped his arms around her from behind. I couldn't tell if he was trying to restrain her or hug her.

I thought about the body and what it might look like and how Becky could have been dead and rotting beneath the snow and we didn't even know it. I wondered if the ice had preserved her body, the cold. But if they couldn't identify the body, I didn't think it had. I thought of this movie I saw once where these kids find a dead body and the eye sockets have rotted out and there are maggots crawling in and out of them. The smell of the pizza suddenly invaded my nose, overtook my senses, until it overwhelmed me so completely that I thought I was going to be sick.

I stood up and ran to the powder room. I bent over the toilet coughing and gagging, and I felt my insides coil up and back, but I didn't throw up; I just gagged a few times. I sat down on the floor and leaned my cheek against the lid of the toilet. The plastic was so cool that it felt nice, and I couldn't bring myself to stand up and go back into the kitchen.

"Ab." My father knocked on the door. "You okay?"

"Yeah," I lied. "I'll be out in a minute." The last thing I wanted was my father coming in here, trying to talk to me or make me feel better. I didn't want him to see me like this. I wanted him to think I was old enough to know the truth; if he didn't, I'd never learn anything.

I stood up and opened the door, and my father was still standing there. "They don't know if it's her," he said.

"I know."

"It could be anyone."

"I think I'll go to bed," I said. "I'm tired."

He nodded. "Sleep well." It seemed like such a funny thing to say, after the news he'd just delivered. I wasn't sure how I would ever sleep well again.

I felt like a terrible person, but as I lay there awake in bed, I almost felt hopeful. If that really was Becky, we would know what happened to her. The police would find her killer and bring him or her to justice. We could have a funeral, and people would send condolences, and we would find a way to piece life back together into something whole, even if it was different from before.

It began to dawn on me that dead was better than missing, vanished, disappeared. At least dead was final. I started thinking that if only we could have a funeral, everything would be okay.

The only funeral I'd ever been to was Grandma Jacobson's. We'd gone to Pittsburgh for it, so we could bury her in a plot right next to Grandpa Jacobson. She died in the spring, so it was this beautiful, warm March day. For some reason I'd expected it to be just the four of us, but my grandmother had had a lot of friends. There must've been a hundred people there as we buried her, and afterward they came back to Grandma Jacobson's house, where my mother catered a lunch.

I remember hearing a lot of stories that I never knew about my grandmother. People were laughing and recounting wonderful memories, trips they'd taken with her, and times they'd spent with her. Becky and I sat on the couch in my grandmother's living room and listened to all these little old people tell us how wonderful she was. Her house didn't smell like her anymore—like cinnamon and sickness. It smelled clean, like Lysol, and something altogether new that I didn't recognize.

It was strange, but I hadn't been as sad as I'd expected to be. We'd known for a few months she was dying, and that whole time I felt the sadness like a weight in my chest, pulling something out of me that I didn't even know I had. But after she died, I felt better. My mother had said to me and Becky that we should be happy that she wasn't suffering anymore. That now she could be free of the cancer, that she could find Grandpa Jacobson again, and the two of them could be happy. I didn't necessarily believe any of that, but still, I'd felt this startling sense of relief that came completely to the surface at the funeral when I watched them lower her casket into ground.

My mother cried, and so did Becky. Becky clung to my mother's dress. I'm not sure if she was old enough even to understand what was going on, but I think the mere fact that my mother was crying frightened her. This was the first time we'd ever seen my mother cry.

I didn't cry, though. I held on to my father's hand, and I kept thinking, *This is it. This is it!* When her coffin was in the ground and people threw handfuls of dirt over the top, I knew she was gone. She was completely gone. It's not that I didn't miss her, that I didn't long for her after that, but at that moment I had this feeling of completeness, finality, the end of something. My grandmother was gone.

I thought that if we could have a funeral for Becky, then at least we would know where she was. We would be sad, and life would never be the same, but we could move on. At least I could feel something again; at least I could sleep at night; at least we could go visit her grave and talk to her. At least it would start to be over.

We didn't hear anything from Kinney for three days, and each day ticked by like an interminable moment. It felt like time had stopped, that it was holding us there, cruelly, while we waited. Most of those three days are a blur, and I can only truly remember this dull feeling of hope mixed with dread. It was the strangest thing I've ever felt, and it made my heart beat constantly faster and faster, my breath shorten, as if I'd been running. I'd have to stop to catch my breath, even if I'd just been sitting down.

Tommy knew about the body, though he didn't say anything about it. I could see it in his oddly exposed eyes, some sort of new pity for me, the way he stared at me just a little too long as I ate my lunch, as if he wanted to say something but couldn't.

"What?" I asked him, almost egging him on, almost wanting to pick a fight with him. But he looked away.

The body was a little girl a whole year younger than Becky. Her name was Anabella Girardi. Another missing girl, someone from the city.

Kinney didn't even come in person to tell us the news. "Don't be sorry," I heard my father say into the phone. "It's not her," he mouthed to my mother and me.

"Oh, I knew it," my mother said. "She's still alive." She smiled at me and rubbed my shoulder. I wasn't sure if I believed she was still alive or not. But I didn't feel relieved like my parents, didn't feel the slightest bit of hope.

I saw her school picture on the news, and there she was, in a pose similar to Becky's, with similar blond hair and a cute, toothy smile—frozen forever at nine.

We watched them interview the mother on the news as she stood outside their broken-down row house in West Philadelphia and cried. She was a small, skinny woman, with greasy, stringy hair, and she was missing a few teeth. "She was my baby," she said, sobbing. "My baby."

"Oh," my mother said, and she covered her mouth with her hand. "Oh."

It was a place you'd expect a girl to go missing from. Nothing like Pinesboro. Nothing like my perfect neighborhood, with its sprawling green yards and picket fences.

A few weeks later the police caught her killer, her own father, who'd been recently estranged from the family. Case closed. End of story.

Some nights I'd dream about Anabella Girardi. I'd see her swimming in the river, then sinking, slowly. I'd try to reach out for her, and when I did, her face transformed, a little like melting plastic, until it was Becky I was looking at, Becky drowning.

Chapter 21

THE NEWS OF the body not belonging to Becky catapulted my mother out of bed and back into the real world. She began walking over to the school to walk me home, and she did something that she hadn't really done since Becky had disappeared: She started cooking dinner.

I enjoyed those walks home with my mother. If she had dared pick me up from school the year before, I would've ignored her or pretended not to see her, and I would've kept right on walking with Jocelyn until she called out my name so embarrassingly loudly that I was forced to stop.

But I was so desperate for my mother to recognize me, to remember me, that I was glad when she came to walk me home. I was surprised she kept coming, even when it got cold again. She'd bundle herself all up and be waiting for me out in front of the school steps with a scarf wrapped around most of her face and her baby blue hat covering her ears.

"You don't have to come when it's this cold," I told her.

"I don't mind," she said. "I kind of like it. It's refreshing."

Mostly we walked home in silence. I'd watch our feet and try to match my mother's steps, her strides, so we were walking in tandem. Sometimes she asked me about my day, and I'd always tell her it was fine, even if it wasn't. I walked home delicately, on thin ice. I knew it was only a matter of time before she'd break.

At home I watched my mother begin to act like my father's wife again. It was little things that I noticed: She'd straighten his tie before we left in the morning; she'd take his jacket and get him a beer when he walked in; she'd smile at him across the table. I began to love my mother all over again for these simple things she did for my father, the ways she had started to reinvent us as a family.

One afternoon near the end of January Tommy walked home with us. Mrs. Ramirez had some kind of appointment and wasn't able to pick him up, and apparently she'd asked my mother to make sure he got home all right.

It was a little strange walking with both of them. I didn't want to walk too close to Tommy for fear my mother would notice I felt something for him, but I didn't want to walk too close to my mother either. I didn't want Tommy to think I had thrown him away now that my mother was acting normal again.

I ended up walking a little behind the two of them as my mother asked Tommy a million questions. She was putting on a show for him, I knew, because she talked more to him than she ever did to me.

"Well, we just love your new haircut, don't we, Abby?"

"Yeah," I said, but she wasn't really paying attention to me anyway.

She touched the top of his head with her hand. "Oh, it's so stubbly. You must be freezing. Didn't your grandmother give you a hat?"

"Naw. I'm not cold," Tommy said.

I rolled my eyes, even though neither one of them could see me. I was sure Tommy was freezing and that he'd stuffed the green and white Eagles hat that Mrs. Ramirez had bought him for Christmas into his backpack.

"Oh," my mother said, "boys will be boys, I guess. Girls

like their hats. We accessorize, right, Ab?" She laughed.

I could tell Tommy was uncomfortable because he moved his head like he used to when he flipped his hair. It looked funny now, more like a nervous twitch, since the hair was gone.

I felt slightly jealous. It was a strange feeling, something that had become unfamiliar to me these past few months. I knew it was silly, that my mother was just pretending with Tommy, not offering any of the real affection that I so desperately wanted from her, but still, I couldn't help myself.

"Did you have a nice trip to Florida?"

"Yeah, it was okay," Tommy said.

"Just okay? Oh, my, what I wouldn't do for sunshine like that." She laughed again, and Tommy did his nervous head shake.

"Remember when we went to Disney?" I said.

"Oh, Abby, that was ages ago. Another lifetime." This time the laugh caught in her throat, and it sounded more like a cough. I knew instantly that I'd said the wrong thing, that my mother was suddenly picturing Becky waving as she flew by on the Dumbo ride. She loved that stupid ride. I had to go on it with her five times, just flying sort of aimlessly in a circle, in this big plastic elephant. Personally, I'd thought it was ridiculous.

No one said anything for a few minutes until we crossed the street to enter our development. Finally my mother said, "You're a nice boy, Tommy, aren't you?" He shrugged. "Your grandmother tells me how sweet you are. That's good. You know, I was so glad when I had girls. I couldn't imagine raising a boy. They're so . . . I don't know, harsh, I guess."

Tommy didn't say anything, but I didn't know what he could say in response to that. She was starting to make me nervous; she sounded a little crazy. I wanted to shake her, to ask her to act like a normal person and not embarrass me in front of Tommy. But I kept my mouth shut.

"Tommy sounds so much like a kid," she said. "You should go by Thomas, with this new haircut and everything."

"He likes to be called LT," I said. Tommy turned around and glared at me. I'm not sure what made me say it, but as soon as it popped out of my mouth, I knew I'd revealed something sacred, something that would make Tommy hate me, and I was instantly sorry.

"LT. Oh, no," my mother said. "I don't think so. It doesn't suit you at all."

"Whatever," Tommy said. "I don't care."

"Thomas," my mother said. "We'll call you Thomas from now on, won't we, Ab?"

"Sure, I guess so." I was reluctant to disagree with my mother, afraid of what that might do to her, even though I knew I was probably hurting Tommy's feelings.

Tommy turned around and gave me this look I'd never quite seen from him before, something that said he despised me, that whatever he might have felt for me, it was gone.

For nearly three months I let myself believe that my phone call to Garret had worked, that his relationship with my mother, whatever it was, was over. But this little illusion came crashing down one night in February when I heard my parents fighting about him.

They thought I was in my room doing my homework, and I was, but my father's booming voice startled me, and I went to the top of the stairs to hear what they were saying.

"It's not like that," my mother said. "We just talk."

"You can talk to me."

"Jim, don't."

"For Christ's sake, Elaine, why don't you just talk to me?"

"It's not the same thing, Jim. Garret understands me."

"Goddammit, so do I."

When I heard Garret's name, I felt sick; I had this instant unsettling feeling in the pit of my stomach, like this was about to be the end of something else, the creation of an even larger gap in my family. Then I felt angry with myself because I'd allowed myself to be fooled by my mother's acting normal.

"Well, you don't give me a chance," my father said. "You cringe when I touch you. Jesus."

"Hush. Keep your voice down."

"I'm trying to understand. God knows I am, Elaine, but you're making me look like a goddamn fool."

"No. Nobody thinks that. I don't think that."

"Jesus, I miss her too. Don't you think I'm hurting?"

"It's not the same for you," my mother said. "Everything cuts me." It sounded so strange, but when my mother said that, I knew it was perfectly accurate.

"I don't want you to see him anymore," my father said.

"We just have coffee. And we talk. That's it, Jim. Nothing else."

"You see him more than you see me." I was surprised by the whininess of my father's tone. It didn't suit him, and I wondered if I sounded that awfully desperate when I whined to get my way.

"That's not true."

"Rosalie told me. Every day he comes here to pick you up." I felt sorry for my mother that Mrs. Ramirez had ratted her out, and also slightly annoyed. I hated it when Becky told on me.

"So what? So it helps me get through the day."

"Well, it stops today," my father said. "You're not seeing him anymore."

"Jim—"

"No, I mean it. Talk to me, or talk when you see that damn therapist I'm paying a hundred dollars an hour. That's what he's there for."

I wondered exactly who Garret was and how he and my mother had met. I'd always imagined an affair to be something sexual, something awfully torrid and steamy. It was how I pictured Mr. Peterson's affair. The thought of it was just enough to make me blush when I'd seen him getting his mail the other day. He'd been wearing a black suit, much like one my father would wear, but on him it looked distinguished, handsome even, and I caught myself wondering what exactly he might be doing when he cheated on Mrs. Peterson.

If my mother was telling the truth, her relationship with

Garret had nothing to do with sex, but I still felt this gnawing in my gut that she was doing something wrong, that she was cheating on my father in another, altogether different way. Wasn't my father the one who was supposed to make her laugh, make her feel better?

My parents had always told us that a marriage was a partnership, something with two equal halves, where you shared everything—responsibilities, joys, sadnesses. If that was the case, then I didn't think my mother was still considering my father her partner.

I wondered if Garret and my mother had kissed. In my gut I believed they had. I couldn't imagine sharing all that talking, all that understanding, and being able to resist the feeling of warmth that would inevitably follow. When Tommy and I shared two brief moments of complete understanding, they both resulted in small instants of passion. I suspected it was the same for my mother.

The next day my mother wasn't waiting for me outside school, and I had to ride home with Tommy and Mrs. Ramirez. "You mother not feeling so hot," Mrs. Ramirez said. "Get in. I watch you today."

"You shouldn't have told on her," I whispered.

Mrs. Ramirez cocked her head and gave me this funny, twisted look. I couldn't tell if she'd heard me at first, but then she said, "Ah-bee-hail, you too young to understand."

I hate when adults tell me I'm too young to understand something, because I always feel like it's their excuse to keep from explaining themselves. I knew in my heart that what Mrs. Ramirez had done was wrong.

Once we got back to Mrs. Ramirez's house, I tried to get Tommy to play Uno with me. Since the walk home with my mother two weeks earlier, we'd barely spoken at lunch, and this was the first day we'd been required to spend after school together in a while. I was hoping Tommy wouldn't hold a grudge.

"I don't know," he said. "I'm kind of sick of that game."

"Yeah, I guess you're right." The game had begun to get old, but it was the habit of it, the ritual that I liked. I enjoyed having something that felt like mine and Tommy's, something that belonged to us.

"Anyway, I have a lot of homework."

I thought that he was just saying that to avoid me, and I felt disappointed. "Don't be mad at me," I said. I didn't think I could take it if he hated me.

He shook his head. "I'm not."

"Are you sure?"

He nodded, but I could tell something was different. We had lost our closeness, an understanding of each other. I knew that the day I'd betrayed Tommy's confidence in front of my mother was not something he would easily forget.

"Your grandmother told on my mother, about her seeing Garret every day," I said.

"I know. I was here when she told your father." I felt a little angry that he hadn't told me about it before I brought it up. "She made me promise not to tell you."

"I understand," I said, but I didn't, not really.

I started to see the way loyalty worked, and it was odd the way you could feel a certain sense of loyalty to some people that interfered with your loyalty to others. It was the way I'd felt when Tommy walked home with me and my mother, that I needed to be on her side, even though a part of me had wanted to be on his. I guessed that Tommy felt the same about his grandmother. She'd saved him in a certain way, taken him out of Florida when his life had been bad, and I supposed he felt he owed her something for that.

"Are they having an affair?" Tommy asked.

"No, I don't think so. She told my father they just drink coffee and talk."

"Yeah, right."

"No." I felt slightly insulted, for my mother's sake. "No. I think that's all."

"Whatever," Tommy said.

"Do you think that's the same, though?" I asked him. "Is it cheating if you only talk?"

"I don't know," Tommy said. "I'm not sure."

"Hey, you two." Mrs. Ramirez walked into the living room and interrupted us. "I got to watch *Oprah* today. She having on a psychic." She sat down next to us and flipped on the TV.

"Can I go outside and ride my skateboard?" Tommy asked, and I knew he really was trying to avoid me. I felt slightly hurt that he would abandon me here with Mrs. Ramirez, Oprah, and the psychic.

"Too cold," she said. "You freeze to death."

"It's not that cold. Come on, just twenty minutes."

"Okey-dokey. But you wear you hat and gloves." Tommy jumped up to go bundle himself and left me sitting there on the couch with Mrs. Ramirez.

I was suddenly back where I'd started six months ago,

watching stupid TV with her while the whole world moved in circles around me.

It turned out that Garret was this guy my mother met through her therapist. His daughter had been killed six years earlier, shot through the head as she crossed the street in downtown Philadelphia with her mother. In the wrong place at the wrong time. She was only seven at the time, which meant that she'd be my age, that if she were alive, we would be in the same grade. Her name was Tiffany, Tiffany Walker.

Most of what we learned about Garret came from Hal Brewerstein, who presented my father with a file on Garret that seemed ten times thicker than all the others. I watched my father sort through the file at the kitchen table and then throw it all down.

"Maybe it's not my place," Hal said, "but I don't think this is what you're looking for."

My father appeared so angry that at first I thought he might punch Hal, but he surprised me by saying nothing. Finally he said, "Keep looking."

After my father had forbidden my mother to see Garret, I think she did start to die a little. She became instantly deflated, an odd ghost of her former, recovered self. I took my father's takeout dinners up to her room on trays. My father asked me to, afraid, I guess, to face her. I think he felt bad for their argument, only he was too stubborn to admit it. He spent several evenings eating dinner with me at the kitchen table, staring out the window, as if he were watching something amazing outside, something invisible to me.

My mother spent most of the week after their fight lying in bed, sprawled out and limp, her eyes round and empty. It reminded me of when I saw my grandma Jacobson in bed just before she died, her body stolen, devoured by cancer. Only physically there was nothing wrong with my mother.

When I brought her the trays, she didn't eat, didn't even acknowledge my presence. I was hurt by the blank stares or the shaking of her head when I tried to put the food in front of her, even though I knew it wasn't personal, that she'd distanced herself from everything, not just me.

So after a few nights I was surprised when she reached out for me, when she held out her hand for me to grab onto. I squeezed it, and she squeezed back. Her hand was surprisingly cold and dry; her fingers felt bony as they curled around mine.

"It's going to be okay," I said to her, though I knew

nothing would be okay. I wanted to reassure her, wanted to help her the way that Garret did. I thought if only I could talk to her, if only I could understand her, then she wouldn't need him. I guess that's exactly what my father thought, exactly why he was so destroyed by her relationship with Garret.

"Abigail. Abigail," she said. "Come lie with me."

So I did. I put her tray down on the floor and got into bed with her. I snuggled up next to her body, the way I used to when I was younger and I'd had a bad dream and I'd fled to her room so she would hold me against her and I would feel in her warmth this instantaneous sensation that everything would be fine. My father would get angry when I'd wake him up; he'd say, "Jesus, Ab, it's the middle of the night. Go back to sleep." But my mother would open up the covers on her side of the bed and let me in, and she'd let me sleep there all night if I wanted to.

For some reason I got up the courage to ask her about Garret. "Why do you need him?" I whispered. I thought if I could understand, I could help.

"Who?" she said, and then it was as if it had suddenly occurred to her who I meant. "Oh, Abby." She leaned over and kissed my head.

It surprised me when she started talking, when she told me the details, the things you can't get from a detective's file. Tiffany Walker had pale green eyes and long brown hair that she wore in two braids down her back, Indian style. After she died, Garret pulled his Volvo into the garage one evening, shut the door, locked himself in the car, and turned it on. Apparently his wife found him after he'd passed out, but he hadn't been there long enough to die. After that, Garret starting going to therapy with Dr. Shreiker, the same guy my mother saw, and by the time she walked in, six years later, he was still learning how to deal with his pain without wanting to die.

My mother met Garret in Dr. Shreiker's waiting room one afternoon when the doctor was running behind. My mother said the doctor came out into the waiting room to apologize to both of them and told them to chat, that he thought they'd have a lot in common. This seems like it'd be against some kind of code of ethics or something, but I don't know.

"And we just became friends," my mother said. "He understands me."

It was so different from the way my mother had met my father, something I'd always turned into a fairy tale in my mind. One winter day when they both were in college, my mother had gone ice-skating with her friends. I imagined it must've been beautiful then, snowy and magical outside. My father had a job working for the rink, driving the Zamboni machine. Every so often he'd clear the ice, yell for everyone to get off, and then drive around on the machine.

But people didn't want to stop skating, and as the day progressed, they started to get a little drunk and angry, and every time my father came on to clear the ice, people would throw snowballs at him.

My mother felt so bad that she left her friends, and she stood by the little hut where the machine was parked. "People are terrible," she said to my father as he got off the machine and wiped the snow from his face.

"Nah, just drunk," my father said. "They don't know the difference."

"Well, I think it's awful, just awful."

My mother started to walk away, but my father called out after her, "Hey, I get off in an hour. How about some hot chocolate?"

My mother smiled at him, and my father said he always remembered that smile, just the right amount of teeth, just the right amount of arch. When she smiled at him, he felt like all the snow was gone, and he was warm; the world was perfect.

But after my mother told me the story about Garret, I felt sick, and I didn't think I had it in me to try to help her. I wanted so much for her to make my world okay, for her to fix everything that went wrong, that when I cuddled up against her I felt tears running down my cheeks. I tried to stop them, but I couldn't, and before I knew it, I was leaning my face on her ratty sweatshirt and I was crying, and she was stroking my hair back softly, just the way she would have after a nightmare. "I need you," I whispered, and then I instantly felt guilty even though it was true. I didn't want to pressure her, but I wanted her to be there for me, to help me out of this the way a mother is supposed to help you out of things.

She didn't say anything, but she continued to stroke my hair back until I stopped crying. Then I was so tired, so unbelievably drained, that I couldn't move, couldn't lift my head. I fell asleep there, just like that, with my head on my mother's sweatshirt.

When I woke up the next morning, the bed was empty; my mother was gone.

Chapter 22

THERE WERE ODD similarities between my mother's disappearance and Becky's. I realized her absence when I woke up and went downstairs. My father had already contacted the police. I felt this sudden, nagging pit in the bottom of my stomach, this sensation of losing something so large, I'd yet to realize its importance.

The morning after my mother left, I walked downstairs and saw Kinney sitting at the kitchen table with my father. My father was crying. It was the first and only time I've ever seen my father cry. He didn't cry once the whole time after Becky disappeared, or at least not in front of me. This time I was instantly afraid; I knew something was terribly, terribly wrong.

"What happened?" I said. My voice shook, and I thought I was going to cry again, though not a relieved sort of crying the way I'd done the night before in my mother's arms, but a reckless, uncontrollable shaking sob, something that would completely take the life right out of me.

"Did your mother tell you she was going somewhere?" Kinney asked.

I shook my head. "She's gone," I said. But it wasn't a question; it was something that I automatically knew from watching my father cry, from listening to Kinney as he sat at our kitchen table.

There wasn't much Kinney or anyone else for that matter could do about my mother leaving. She was an adult, and there was no sign of foul play, no sign that she'd gone unwillingly. "People leave," Kinney told my father. "Happens all the time."

"But she's not well," my father said. "She shouldn't be alone."

Kinney looked sort of disgusted with my father, as if he thought we'd already wasted too much of his time. "Look," Kinney said, "I'm sorry. But this isn't police business."

Of course that wasn't true. Everything was police

business. My mother's disappearance aroused new suspicion that she had done something to Becky. Somehow her disappearance ended up on the news, only the newscaster made her sound like a common criminal, like someone who'd jumped bail. It didn't seem fair that every day husbands and wives parted, wives left their husbands and vice versa; mothers and fathers disappeared into the dark, silent night. But when my mother left, it became the whole town's business, the whole world's, really. When my mother left, it seemed like a crime.

I'd begun to blend in again at school, begun to feel a certain anonymity, but as soon as she left, that all disappeared. I heard the whispers again, felt the sting of being an outcast, as if there were something exceptionally ugly and wrong about me all over again.

You would've thought I would be angry with my mother, but part of me felt I could understand her, the need to get away, out of our house, away from everything Becky.

After my mother left, Tommy started being nice to me again. I guess he decided to forgive me for betraying his confidence to my mother, or maybe he felt sorry for me, felt we now had this new connection: His father had left him; my mother had left me. We were these two lost and abandoned creatures, unable to understand how we'd become so unloved.

"Hey," he said to me at lunch on the Monday after my mother vanished, "it'll be okay."

"No, it won't," I said.

"Where do you think she is?"

I shrugged. I'd already convinced myself that my mother was dead. I was sure she'd left my father and me to die, that she didn't want to die in front of us, didn't want us to see her suffer. She didn't want one of us to find her in the garage with the car turned on, barely breathing.

My other thought was that she was with Garret. I tried to convince myself this couldn't possibly be true. Strangely, I took more comfort in thinking of her dead than I did thinking of her with Garret. It didn't seem fair that my mother could leave my father for another man, not after Becky had left all of us, not after my father had been consumed by sadness.

"We can play cards after school if you want."

"Whatever."

He reached for my hand under the lunch table and squeezed it once, quickly. I couldn't look at him because I was too embarrassed, too ashamed. I didn't want to like him anymore, didn't ever want to fall in love or out of it. My father's love for my mother had become so ugly that it'd pushed her to leave us just so she could be free of it.

After school Tommy let me ride his skateboard for the first time. He taught me how to push off with my left leg, then jump on the board as if I were sailing on a boat down our sidewalk. I was sure my mother wouldn't have approved of my being on the skateboard. She would have said that skateboards were boys' toys and that even if Tommy looked cute riding one, I didn't. She would also have commented about how dangerous they were, how you could just slip right off the sidewalk and get hit by a car or something like that. But she wasn't there—

It was still cold outside, though it hadn't snowed in a while, so the ground was frozen but not white. I wasn't dressed warmly enough for being outside, and my ears turned red and numb almost instantly.

"Ah-bee-hail." Mrs. Ramirez came running out of the house after a few minutes with a worn black knit hat. "You freeze to death out here." She firmly pushed the hat over my head; it was too big for me, and I could tell it covered too much of my head and made me look ridiculous. But I really was cold, so I didn't complain. "Now you kids be careful out here."

"We will." Tommy sounded annoyed. Suddenly I felt a little jealous of him for Mrs. Ramirez's pestering, her concern. It's strange how I'd hated it when my parents had hovered; it had become annoying and seemed so trivial. But it was worse when they didn't do it, when it felt as if no one cared what I did or if got hurt or if I wore a hat when it was cold outside.

When she went inside, Tommy turned to me and said, "Jeez, she drives me crazy sometimes."

I nodded. "At least she cares about you. She really does."

"Too much, I think. Here." He took the board back from me. "I'll show you how to ride up the driveway and spin around."

It sounded dangerous to me, and I almost protested, but then I changed my mind. I didn't want Tommy to think I was a chicken, and I definitely didn't want him to get mad at me again. Then I'd be inside, sitting on the couch with Mrs. Ramirez, suffering through some talk show.

I watched Tommy speed up the driveway, then circle and flip the board up to fly down. "Look." He laughed and held his hands out as if he were surfing. "No hands." He skidded to a stop in front of me. "Here, you try it."

"I don't know if I can," I said.

"Sure. It's easy. It's all about balance." I took the board from him and stood on it like he'd shown me; then I started pushing off with my leg to get momentum. For a moment I felt wonderfully free, and I gave myself up to the cold afternoon, to the sensation of flying. I don't know if I was going too fast when I tried to turn or what, but all I know is that one moment I was floating on Tommy's skateboard and the next I was sliding down the driveway headfirst.

I didn't feel any pain; there was nothing but this numbness, this dull sensation that I'd fallen. I watched the skateboard roll the rest of the way down the driveway empty, until it ran almost right into Tommy, who was already on his way up to see if I was okay.

"Are you hurt?" he said. "Are you all right?"

I felt dazed, and I shook my head a little, and I felt this incredible warmth around my eyes, something so warm that it felt nice against my freezing face. I reached up to touch it, and when I withdrew my hand, I saw it was spotted with red, with my own blood. "I'm bleeding," I said.

He nodded, so I knew it must look bad; he must have

already seen it. Oddly I didn't feel panic at all, but I gave in to the warming sensation of my blood, a feeling of surrender. I'd fallen and hurt myself, and I was this broken thing in Mrs. Ramirez's driveway, and I felt like that was exactly where I belonged.

"Grandma," Tommy called. "Grandma." He sounded panicky, and his eyes were wide, round brown saucers.

"You have nice eyes," I told him, and I reached up for his face, but I felt my hand groping sort of blindly in the wrong direction.

Tommy ran up to her front door and banged on it a few times. "Abby's hurt," he said. "Abby fell."

Mrs. Ramirez walked outside, and when she saw me lying there in the driveway, she said, "Oh, *Dios mío*! Get in the car. Thomas, get her in the car."

Tommy pulled me up by my elbow, and I instantly felt dizzy. "I feel like an idiot," I told him, and I was smiling when I said it, but I didn't know why.

"Hurry up!" Mrs. Ramirez shouted.

She was already in the driver's seat, and Tommy laid me down in the back and sat next to me. For some reason I noticed that I wasn't wearing my seat belt, and I told Tommy, but he didn't do anything. Or maybe I didn't tell him; maybe I just thought I did. But all the way to the hospital all I could think about was how unsafe this was, how we could all die as Mrs. Ramirez sped down winding Tourret Road to take me to the ER.

Because I was bleeding when Mrs. Ramirez and Tommy brought me in, they took me back right away in the emergency room, something that I guess is pretty unheard of. But it turned out that my injuries looked a lot worse than they really were.

It looked like I had blood pouring from my eye, but really I'd only cut my face, just above the eye. As the blood ran down, it hid the cut, leaving Tommy and Mrs. Ramirez to think I'd been blinded. The cut needed two stitches, and the doctors thought I might have a mild concussion. I also had some pretty severe scrapes on my knees, which the nurse cleaned with antiseptic and bandaged up. The doctor said I would need to wear an eye patch bandage for three days, just to make sure the cut healed properly. But the doctors could see no damage to my eye itself.

By the time my father got there, I had been stitched and bandaged and was wearing my eye patch, which felt uncomfortable and itchy against my face. "Ab." He ran into the room, out of breath, just as I was about to be sent back out into the waiting room to Tommy and Mrs. Ramirez. "What happened? Are you okay?" He shook my shoulders a little bit and then hugged me close to him. "God, I was so worried. I thought . . ."

"I'm fine," I said. "It's nothing."

"Nothing." He reached up and touched the eye patch, traced its edge with his fingers. It was such a warm gesture coming from my father that it surprised me. "Everything's falling apart," he said. Even though he was touching my eye patch, I didn't think he was talking about me. I thought he was talking about my mother, about how if she had been here this probably wouldn't have happened.

"I'm okay," I said. "It's just a cut. I got two stitches."

"Thank God." He grabbed my hand and tugged on it. "Thank God you're okay."

"It's nothing." But suddenly I could feel pain. I don't know if the anesthetic was wearing off or what, but my eye started throbbing and my head started throbbing, and I was intensely aware of the raw, scraped skin on my knees. It hit me that I was in the hospital, that I'd been hurt, and I wanted to cry. "I wish she were here," I said. I realized instantly how unclear that was, that my father couldn't tell if I meant Becky or my mother.

I was thinking about my mother, about how I wanted her to hug me and tell me everything would be fine. But then I thought about Becky, how if she were here, she'd be fake sobbing in the waiting room, saying, "I don't want Abby to die. Don't let her die, Dad." Always the drama queen. She would've been the one getting all the attention, even as I sat in here and got stitched up, but I think I would've liked it all the same, just to see her cry over me, to see anyone cry over me.

"Let's get you home," my father said.

We walked out into the waiting room, and the first thing I noticed was Tommy, his face white, his lips trembling, his eyes so wide open still, it was as if they'd been frozen there. Mrs. Ramirez stood up and patted my father's shoulder. "Doctor say everything be A-OK, Mr. Reed. Just wear the patch for three day."

He nodded. I couldn't tell if my father wanted to thank her for bringing me here or scream at her for letting me get hurt in the first place, but he didn't do either one. He just reached up in this awkward, shaky way and grabbed onto her hand on his shoulder.

I wanted to say something to Tommy, to reassure him

that this wasn't his fault, that I would be fine. *No permanent damage*, I thought about saying to him. *Nothing doing.* That was something my grandma Jacobson used to say all the time, *nothing doing*, as if it were this hip sort of phrase that she'd caught on to. It used to make Becky and me laugh.

But all I could bring myself to say to him in front of my father and Mrs. Ramirez was, "They stuck a foot-long needle in my forehead to numb it." It was obviously the wrong thing to say, and I can't be held completely responsible for its stupidity because I wasn't exactly myself. But Tommy started to turn this weird shade of green, and he started coughing, until I thought he was going to throw up. So I told him that it didn't hurt, that everything was numb, numb, numb.

He stopped coughing and looked at me. "I know," he said. And I believed him. I knew he did know, that he understood my numbness, maybe even felt it the way I did.

Chapter 23

THE ONLY THING worse than going to school after both Becky and my mother had disappeared, with my mother and father suspects of terrible things, was going there under those same conditions wearing an eye patch.

I must admit, even I thought I looked freakish. The patch was large and white, and it covered most of my left cheek as well as my eye. I pleaded with my father to let me stay home from school, but he wouldn't let me. "The doctor said you would be just fine to go to school."

"But it hurts," I whined.

"Then I'll get you a Tylenol."

"I don't want a Tylenol. I want to stay home."

"Ab, stop whining."

"I'm not whining," I said, but I knew he was right, I was.

The strange thing was that people I thought had forgotten all about me came up to ask me what happened, if I was okay. When they talked to me, their eyes got shifty; they couldn't look directly at me, and when I told them that I fell off a skateboard, they sort of nodded and walked away. I suppose I should've come up with a better story, something grandly daring that would've made me sound terrific. Falling off a skateboard was kind of lame; it's not like you were that high up or anything.

At first I didn't know what people were whispering about me; apparently they thought falling off a skateboard was lame too, so lame that someone invented a story that was circulating around the school first as a rumor, then as "the truth." I didn't know about it until Jocelyn said something to me the second morning in homeroom.

"What happened to you?" she asked.

I was surprised that she had actually talked to me, that she wasn't ignoring me the way she had been for months. Lately she wouldn't even turn her head to the side I sat on, out of fear, I guess, that I might look at her and start up a conversation. So it took me a minute to answer her.

"I fell off a skateboard," I said.

"Really, Abby? Is that all?" I nodded. She stared at me, scrutinizing my face. I wondered if she was trying to remember her best friend, who was still inside me somewhere, underneath the eye patch and all. "Are you sure?"

"Yeah. I was there." I didn't mean to say it as rudely as I did, but I was already annoyed with her, and I didn't really understand what she was getting at.

"Your father, he didn't . . . do anything to you?"

"My father? He wasn't even there when it happened."

"Abby."

"What?" I had this sinking feeling in the pit of my stomach, an inkling of what people had been whispering about me, that they'd somehow implicated my father in some terrible wrongdoing.

"Well, never mind then," she said. "Just forget it." She turned back to face front and fluffed her bangs a little bit and pretended that she'd never said a word to me in the first place.

I was already miserable, down a mother and temporarily down an eye, and the accusatory sound of her voice made me so mad that I suddenly realized I no longer wanted her friendship even if she had offered it.

I tapped her on the shoulder, a touch that made her jump, but she turned and faced me. "I can't believe I ever thought you were my best friend," I said.

She looked around, a little embarrassed, maybe because once I got angry my voice got louder. "Abby, don't," she said.

"Don't worry," I told her. "You're not even worth it." And then I was the one to turn away from her, to stop looking in her direction.

At lunch I asked Tommy if he'd heard what people were saying about me.

"I don't know," he said. "It's nothing. It's stupid really."

"Just spit it out," I told him. My patch was beginning to itch, and the stitched cut underneath it felt moist. I had the urge to rip it off, but I knew I couldn't, so I sat there, twisting my hands, trying to keep them from doing something desperate.

He looked down at his food. "People think your father tried to kill you." I started laughing. I knew it wasn't funny, but there was nothing else for me to do but laugh. "What?" Tommy said. "What's so funny?"

My laughing fit stopped as abruptly as it began, and

I suddenly felt myself sweating. "Where did you hear that?"

"Just some guys talking in my math class, that's all. I don't know if everyone thinks that."

"They do," I said, thinking about Jocelyn. "Of course they do. Why would anyone think my father would try to kill me?" It sounded so ridiculous, even as I said it. It sounded like some terrible, terrible TV movie.

"Well," Tommy said. He still couldn't look at me. He was shoveling his sandwich into his mouth. "I don't know."

"You do," I said. "You're not telling me everything." He shook his head. "Tommy, come on. I thought I could trust you."

"Fine," he said. "But you won't like it."

"Do you think I like this?" I knew Tommy thought I was talking about the eye patch, but really I meant everything else.

"They're saying that your father killed your sister and your mother, and then he went after you; only he screwed it up and only took out your eye instead."

I put my hand up to touch the patch, to feel my eye moving underneath it. "Well, that's stupid," I said. "That's so ridiculous." He nodded. "My eye is fine. I just fell off a stupid skateboard." I realized I was yelling, and I felt sort of bad because it wasn't his fault; I shouldn't have been yelling at him for dumb things that other people were saying.

"I know. I was there."

"I didn't mean to yell at you. I'm sorry."

We sat there in silence, finishing our lunches. I thought about how strange it was that Jocelyn, who'd known my family and me for years, would believe such a rumor. Suddenly I hated her and all the other kids at my school so much. I wanted all of them to feel pain the way I had over the last few months, and not the falling-off-the-skateboard-stitches kind of pain but the pain of losing people, the pain of being so completely misunderstood.

"When I was in Florida," Tommy said, "people used to call me these awful names."

"Why?"

"I don't know," he said. "Just because they could, I guess."

I thought of that first day at lunch, when it was so obvious to me that Tommy's skin was so much darker than everyone else's at my school, and I wondered if it had been the same for him in Florida. "People are dumb," I said.

"I used to get in fights over it. I'd get so angry."

I nodded and pretended to look surprised (though it was

hard with only one visible eye). "How did you stop?" I began to wonder why things were different here, why he didn't beat up the obnoxious boys who probably laughed at him in his gym class.

"It's not worth it," Tommy said. "I don't care what they think. What does it matter anyway?" But he sounded hurt; his voice trembled a little bit.

"You're right," I told him. "None of the people here are worth anything. They don't know anything."

"I used to dream about running away," Tommy said. "I'd think about getting on one of those fishing boats that docked in the harbor and stowing away in the bottom and just becoming a fisherman for the rest of my life or something."

I tried to imagine Tommy as a fisherman, out on the sea all day, and he didn't seem like he had it in him. "I couldn't run from this," I said. "Everything would still be so messed up, even if I could leave."

"I know. I couldn't really run either. Who can ever really run from anything?"

Chapter 24

TWO WEEKS AFTER she disappeared, my mother reappeared just as suddenly. She was sitting at the kitchen table one evening, smoking a cigarette, when my father and I walked in. He'd just picked me up at Mrs. Ramirez's, and the two of us had gone to McDonald's before going home. She was sitting there in the dark, at the kitchen table, the only light coming from the glow of her cigarette, barely noticeable at first.

I smelled her there before I saw her, the woodsy intoxicating scent of her cigarettes, something I was used to smelling out on the back patio in the spring, but not in the house. "It's Mom," I said to him as soon as we came in the front door. "She's here."

My father flipped on the lights and started walking toward the smell. I followed behind him, not sure yet if I was angry or would be happy to see her. "Elaine," he said, when we both saw her sitting there, cigarette in hand. He sounded surprised, even though I'd already told him it was her. I'm not sure he let himself believe it until he actually saw her sitting there.

She nodded at him and then looked straight at me. "Abby," she said, "don't hate me." Her voice sounded shaky, unfamiliar almost, and I didn't know if I should go to her, so I didn't; I hung back with my father. "I need a goddamn ashtray."

She stood up and started rummaging around in the cupboards until she came back with an old clay bowl I'd made for her in elementary school. I don't think it was supposed to be an ashtray, but it was kind of lopsided, so it didn't quite work as a bowl either. "I know I shouldn't be smoking in here," she said, and she laughed a little as if this were something funny to her, something my father and I didn't get. "I didn't want you to worry."

"Jesus, Elaine." My father reached out for her shoulder, but she jerked away so quickly that it made me sad for him. "I didn't know what to think."

"Well, I'm not dead," she said, "if that's what you thought."

I don't know if my father thought that or not, but I felt my face turning red. I didn't want her to know that I'd thought that, that I'd expected Kinney to tell us they'd found her body. The fact that I'd believed she was selfish enough to kill herself made me feel slightly ashamed.

"Maybe you should go upstairs," my father said to me.

"Jim, calm down. I'm not going to do anything crazy. Here." She patted the chair next to her. "Have a seat, sweetie." I looked to my father first, because for some reason I felt I needed his permission to listen to her. I waited for him to nod at me before I sat down. "What did you do to your face?" She put her hand on my stitched-up cut, but I pulled away. "I'm sorry. I didn't mean to hurt you."

She hadn't hurt me. It didn't hurt anymore, even though it looked ugly still. I just felt uncomfortable when she touched my face, and I pulled away from her the same way she'd just pulled away from my father. "It's nothing," I said. I didn't want to tell her about Tommy's skateboard because I thought she'd be instantly mad at me, she'd crush me with a *Didn't I raise you better than that?* And then I was afraid I might yell back, *Well, where the hell were you anyway?*

"Jim, you sit down too. I want to talk to both of you." My father did as she asked. I realized this was the first time I'd ever seen my mother in charge, completely in control of the situation, my first indication that something drastic had changed in her since she'd left.

"Elaine," my father said, "I could take you upstairs, put you to bed. We all could talk tomorrow."

"Do I look like I need to go to bed?" she snapped. "I'm sorry. I didn't mean to yell." She ground the cigarette out in the bowl. Then she said, "Do you mind if I smoke?" My father shook his head, and she pulled another cigarette out of the pack and lit it. "I want to try to cut down," she said, "quit altogether,"

"That's good," my father said. He smiled at her. It was an awful awkward moment between the two of them, where I felt like they both understood something that I never would.

"Anyway," she said, "I can't stay long." My stomach sank when she said that. She hadn't come back for good; she'd returned for only this fleeting moment of explanation, and then she'd leave again, flee from our lives. I wondered if things would've been different for us if Becky had returned for just this short amount of time, just to explain to us what had happened to her and why.

I was surprised that my father didn't say anything, didn't try to stop her when she said she couldn't stay long, but I guess he was afraid of sending her away again without an explanation.

"It's no secret that I've been a mess," she said. "This house." She chuckled a little and tapped the cigarette in my bowl. I watched the ashes fall in there, and I tried to concentrate on them instead of her so I wouldn't start crying. "I had to get out of here. It was suffocating me."

"Elaine—"

"Don't interrupt me," she said. "I'm not finished, Jim." She turned to look at me. "Abby, you know I love you, and I'm not leaving you. We'll still see each other."

I felt a small bubble of relief that she hadn't forgotten me after all, but I felt sorry for my father. She hadn't said she still loved him. When she singled me out, I realized that this really was the end of our family. Suddenly I didn't even care that she was alive, that she sounded saner than she had in weeks.

"I've gotten an apartment down on Hardy."

"An apartment?" He sounded as if he couldn't understand the words. "On Hardy?" Hardy is this street that runs between Pinesboro and Break Point, a town just on the edge of New Jersey. I knew exactly the apartments she was talking about. There is this large, tall building there that is older than most of the surrounding buildings and almost something of an eyesore. I couldn't imagine my mother living there, a place where I imagined poor people and college students lived.

"It's nothing terrific," my mother said. "But it's something different. A place to start over. When Garret's daughter died, he said the only way he could get past it was to get away."

"So that's what this is about, Garret?"

"No," my mother said. "It's about me." She sounded angrier than I'd heard her in a long time. She stood up and looked out the back window. "I can see her everywhere here, Jim."

I thought of that expression, you know, "You can run, but you can't hide." I couldn't imagine my mother forgetting about Becky, even in an apartment on Hardy, even away from my father and me. I wanted to tell my mother that, but I was a little afraid of her anger.

"I'll want you to visit me, Ab, after I get settled."

"What about Dad?" I said, and then instantly, I wished

I hadn't. I was aware that the pain between them was private, something that was almost none of my business.

But she pretended I hadn't even asked the question. "There's this great little diner right down the street. I can take you there for breakfast on the weekend." I didn't want her to take me to a diner for breakfast; I wanted her to stay here and be my mother. It wasn't much to ask of her, I didn't think.

"Elaine," my father said, "don't you think you're overreacting?"

She shook her head. "Oh, Jim," she said. She walked over to him and touched his face. "You're trying so hard, aren't you?"

My father turned his head away; maybe because he didn't want her touching him anymore. I didn't understand how the ways they'd always touched each other could've vanished so quickly in these last few months, how Becky's disappearance could've stolen them, the way it had stolen everything else familiar to me.

My mother stayed for less than an hour. Then she claimed she had to go home. It hurt me to hear her say that, to realize that our house wasn't what she thought of as home. I know it hurt my father too, because he couldn't look at her when she was leaving.

I still don't know exactly what she did for most of those two weeks she was missing. Hal Brewerstein traced her credit card and told my father that she had ended up in Pittsburgh. And she told me, just after she had moved into her apartment, that it was Garret who had driven her there and that she had gone to Pittsburgh to see Grandma Jacobson's grave. My mother said that at the grave she'd felt Grandma's presence; she believed her mother had actually spoken to her. "It was the strangest thing," she says whenever she tells the story. "It was like I heard the sound of her voice coming off the wind. You know how distinct her voice was, Abby, so crackly and sharp, and she was telling me to save myself. Then I knew what I had to do."

After that, I guess, she came back and got the apartment, and that's when she started to realize that we must be worried about her. She claimed it really hadn't occurred to her to call, that we would miss her, not the whole way to Pittsburgh, not the whole time there. "I must've been in some sort of daze," she said; "otherwise I would've realized." I believed her; I knew that she could've been so out of it that she would've forgotten us completely.

I am not sure what her relationship with Garret was then, and secretly I envisioned the two of them rolling around in bed together in one of those roadside turnpike motels. But I don't know if that was true or not, or if Garret was only a friend to her, someone to listen to her, to understand her the way she felt my father and I couldn't. All I knew was that Garret and his wife had split up a few years after their daughter's death. Garret was unattached, even if my mother wasn't. I thought that must mean something.

Chapter 25

THE FIRST TIME I went to visit my mother in her apartment, I was surprised by how barren it was. I'd known going in that it would be nothing special, but there was something about it that was almost prisonlike, something I might expect to be military housing. The walls were this rough brown brick that was impossible to hang things on; the carpets were thin and speckled green. The floors creaked when you walked on them. "The kitchen isn't so bad, don't you think, Ab?"

I nodded because I didn't want to disappoint her, but the kitchen was as terrible as the rest of the apartment. It was very dark—no windows or anything, just the great big glaring fluorescent light hanging from the ceiling and this awful brown and white linoleum. It wasn't even big enough to fit a table. My mother had set up a card table in the living room near the kitchen, and I guessed that was where she ate.

Going to visit my mother in her apartment became a part of my routine, something I did every Saturday. My father would drop me off in the street below and then watch me walk up from the car. It was the most freedom he'd given me in a long time, since before Becky disappeared, but I guess it was just too awkward for him to walk up and see my mother.

There wasn't much for me to do in her apartment, and the days dragged on. She had only a small TV in the corner of the living room, propped up on a cardboard box. She'd tell me I could turn it on, watch whatever I wanted, but it was too hard to see. It made any show oddly miniaturized, like a poor imitation of the show, not the real show itself.

My mother started smoking constantly, inside the apartment and everything, and she seemed very shaky, maybe nervous to see me. She sat there at the card table with the cigarette hanging between her two trembling fingers, saying, "I'm going to quit, sweetie, in just a few days."

"Okay," I said, though I knew she wouldn't. Truthfully I didn't care. I found the smell of her cigarettes warming, familiar. It reminded me of a summer night in the pool with Becky.

My father sent my mother a check each month to cover the rent on her apartment and her food. Maybe he was so used to taking care of my mother that he didn't quite know how to stop, or maybe he let himself believe that he wasn't the one she was leaving; it was the situation. Or maybe he was just afraid that if he didn't take care of her, then someone else would.

My father may have supplied the money, but Garret was the one who took my mother places—drove her to the supermarket and such. It didn't seem fair that she spent so much time with him, but I knew that life was far from fair.

My mother and I never went to that diner she'd talked about. In fact when I went to visit her, we barely left the apartment. We'd sit there and play a game of cards or watch the small TV or read or something. We hardly talked.

There was so much I wanted to say to her, rational arguments in my head for why she should come back home. At first I decided not to say any of it, afraid if she got angry, she would leave again or, worse, do something terrible to herself. But after a few Saturdays with her in the apartment, I couldn't take it anymore. "Why don't you come home?" I said. "Dad really misses you."

"Oh, Abby." She sighed. "It's not that simple."

"I'll help you with everything," I told her. "We're doing a cooking unit in home ec now."

"That's nice, sweetie." She lit a cigarette and looked off into the distance, so I knew the conversation was over, that she'd stopped listening.

The next weekend I met Garret for the first time. He isn't as tall as I expected him to be, not nearly as tall as my father. In fact he probably isn't much taller than Tommy or my mother even. And his height gives him this strange air of childishness. I wondered if that was part of what my mother liked about him. He's completely the opposite of my father.

When I walked into her apartment, he was already sitting there. I knew him instantly from the picture, and I felt myself cringe. "It's so nice to finally meet you, Abby," Garret said right away. "I've heard so much about you."

I remembered his voice from the phone call, and I felt a little sick, wondering if he knew I was the one who had called him, if it was something he and my mother had laughed about. I wondered what exactly he'd heard about me. *Yes,* I wanted to say, *I'm the daughter who didn't disappear. I'm the one who's left, the one she abandoned.* I was annoyed with my mother for intentionally bringing us together, and I wondered if this was her way of showing me that she was never coming home.

If I'd known that Garret would be there, I wouldn't have come to see her at all. I would've told my father I had too much homework to do or that I wasn't feeling well.

"I should make some tea," my mother said. "Wouldn't it be nice if we all had some tea together. Abby?"

"Sure," I said. "Whatever."

"I hear that you like to read," Garret said, as we both sat down at the card table while my mother clanked around in the kitchen, trying to figure out tea.

"I guess so." I was unwilling to offer him anything, not even the smallest part of me. I already felt disloyal to my father simply by talking to Garret.

"Anything in particular?"

"Not really." I shrugged.

"What about that book you were reading before," my mother called from the kitchen. "The one with the bird in the title. You loved that, didn't you, sweetie?"

"*To Kill a Mockingbird.*" I almost laughed, thinking about my mother's reaction the day I'd been reading it and her falsely cheery tone now.

"Good old Atticus Finch," Garret said.

"Garret's quite a reader," my mother yelled from the kitchen.

I wasn't impressed by Garret's knowledge. It occurred to me that Garret and I probably had more in common than my father and I did, but this made me feel even more awful, so I just sort of shrugged and looked away from him.

"You read that in school?" Garret asked.

I nodded, and I remembered that Garret's daughter would've been my age had she lived. I felt this tiny bit of sympathy for him, this sadness that she hadn't gotten to do something as simple as reading a book.

"She's in a special advanced class." My mother carried the tea in paper cups, one at a time. She put my cup in front of me. "Tea is supposed to be so good for you. I read an article about it just the other day."

"Tea warms the soul," Garret said, and he smiled at me.

The smile gave me the creeps in an odd way. He isn't a creepy man, he's almost elflike, but his smile really got at me. I felt the way I'd feel when I'd go to the doctor for my yearly checkup, and he'd smile at me when he asked me to say ahh, as if Garret believed he was only trying to help, yet somehow, he was causing pain.

The three of sat there and sipped our tea in silence. My mother and Garret smiled at each other across the table, and I started to feel sick.

I could tell she was in love with him just by the way she smiled.

I told Tommy about Garret at lunch the Monday after I met him. "I can't believe she invited him over there," Tommy said, shaking his head. "If my mother ever . . ." He didn't continue, as if the thought of having to have tea with his mother and Irwin was something too painful to put into words.

"I have to do something," I said.

Tommy nodded. "When my parents used to get in fights, my father used to send my mother flowers. Maybe you could get your father to do that."

I shook my head. There was no way my father was going to send her flowers; I could see it in his eyes, the way he'd already given up on her. But what Tommy said gave me another idea.

The next Saturday I went to my mother's armed with my lunch money from the entire week. I'd been sharing

Tommy's lunches every day and saving the money my father gave me for something far more important.

After I got out of the car and walked into the building, I waited for a few minutes, until I was sure my father had driven away, and then I went back outside and walked one block down to the minimart.

It was really the first time I'd been out alone since Becky disappeared, and the thought was both exhilarating and frightening; anyone could take me, snatch me right there off the street.

With the money I'd saved up, I had enough to buy my mother a dozen red carnations, and as I carried them up to the door of her apartment, I already had it planned out in my head, the lie I would tell her. "These are from Dad," I said as soon as she opened the door.

"Oh?" Her hands shook as she took them from me.

"They're beautiful, aren't they?" I walked inside.

She nodded. "I don't even know if I have a vase." She rummaged through her kitchen cabinets and came up with a large plastic cup. "Well, I guess this will do."

After she'd put the flowers in water, she came and sat next to me on the couch. "Dad really misses you," I said. "He talks about you all the time." This was a lie that I told myself was okay to tell her because it really was for her own good.

"Oh?" She pulled a cigarette from a pack on the table and lit it, and then she turned away from me to blow the smoke into spirals in the air. But I felt a sort of satisfaction; I could tell by the nervous way she tapped her cigarette in the ashtray that the flowers had gotten to her.

Over the next few weeks I tried to do other things, smaller things. When I got home from my mother's each Saturday, I'd tell my father how much she missed him. "She said that?" my father would ask. I'd nod, knowing it was wrong to lie to him, but I also knew if I didn't, my father would let her go.

I brought my mother flowers three weeks in a row, until the Sunday after the third week, when my father came up to my room while I was doing my homework. "Your mother called to thank me for the flowers." He stood in the doorway in the dark hallway, and when I looked up, he seemed more like a looming shadow than my father. I tried to think of what to say to him, but before I could think of anything, he said. "Just don't do it again, okay, Ab?"

I was surprised that he didn't seem angry—his voice

instead sounded broken and forlorn, so I knew just from hearing it how much he really did miss her.

Some days I thought I was the only one who remembered Becky, the only one who thought about her in the quiet, empty spaces of the evening. I knew this wasn't true, but because we didn't talk about her anymore, it sure felt that way.

Detective Kinney called periodically with updates. They'd caught a serial killer in Philadelphia who might have some answers; the police went back out to dig in Morrow's field. But each lead turned up nothing, no sign or trace of Becky.

In April my father let Hal Brewerstein go. "He's terrible," my father said to me. "He didn't know what he was doing." But I remembered the files Hal brought us, the secrets he'd revealed about my neighbors, and I couldn't help thinking that he wasn't terrible at all, that my father just needed to blame someone for something.

Detective Kinney stopped by a few more times to talk to my mother. Each time my father told him she wasn't here; only he neglected to tell him that she'd moved out.

Kinney finally caught up with my mother in her

apartment in late May, because she complained about him when I went there one weekend. "That man," she said, "that darn detective. He doesn't know anything." She seemed especially shaky, suddenly subject to all the evils of the world living alone in her horrible apartment.

"You should come home," I told her, though I knew that nothing I could say or do was going to bring her home.

"Oh, Abby." She gave me a half hug with her one arm that she wasn't using to smoke. "Someday you'll understand."

But I don't think I ever will understand why she left my father.

Chapter 26

BY JUNE MY quietly abnormal life felt like a routine. I tried not to think about the way things had been a year earlier, when the four of us had gone to the beach. It felt like so long ago, like something that had happened to me in another lifetime.

Once school was out, I spent most days with Tommy and Mrs. Ramirez. My mother took a part-time job as a waitress at that diner she'd talked about. Some days, when she wasn't working, I spent the day with her. But most days I was with Tommy.

Tommy and I were friends but not the kind of friends Jocelyn and I had been, the kind who told each other everything. Mostly we had a quiet friendship, where we would do things without talking much. And then occasionally there were moments like the day we kissed in the snow, when suddenly there'd be an instant of something else passing between us. Tommy would squeeze my hand or reach up and brush a piece of hair away from my cheek or kiss me again, as he did right after school let out for the summer and Mrs. Ramirez let us go swimming in my backyard without her.

Kissing in the pool, I felt oddly weightless, and the whole experience seemed unreal, almost as if it had happened in a dream. It didn't feel like the same pool that Becky and I had swum in the summer before.

At night I lay in bed and thought about Tommy. Sometimes I would lie there and close my eyes and think about Tommy kissing me and what it might be like if he French-kissed me, how his tongue might feel against mine. Then I'd start to imagine if Tommy had ever wondered the same thing, if he wanted to kiss me that way.

Jocelyn and I had talked about it the year before, and we'd decided that French kissing was disgusting, yet the thought of it was different now. It felt somehow thrilling. When I'd think about Tommy this way, though, it would pain me to look him in the eye the next day. Or I'd stare at him too closely sometimes, watch the way his eyebrows arched when he laughed. His hair had grown back in, but he'd gotten it cut a few times over the spring, so it was still a lot shorter than when I first met him. I kind of liked it the way it was in the summer, short enough to still look cute. I could see his entire face without it looking too shocking, the way it did with the buzz cut.

The relationship between my father and me also changed into something new, something completely different. Last summer I was a child, the one who fought with her sister, who whined, who was punished and sent to her room. This summer I became something like his equal, cooking dinner for us some nights, cleaning up the house, washing our clothes. We too hardly talked, but when we did, I noticed my father treated me more like an adult. He spoke in softer tones. He asked my opinion on things. Sometimes I wondered if he mistook me for my mother or for some strange blurry combination of all three of us—me, my mother, and Becky.

It was strange to hear my father talk to me about mortgage payments and car repairs. "Car needs new tires," he would say.

And I nodded like I understood. But inside, I was

thinking, *So what? Who cares?*

After dinner we swam in the pool sometimes before bed, but it was so quiet that I didn't like to do it. Every time I got in or I looked at the inner tubes, I thought about Becky swimming toward me, wanting the pink one so badly. I'd feel guilty, and I'd think, *Why didn't I just let her have it?* What was the big deal anyway? She could've had this one thing; it wouldn't have been so much to give.

My father swam laps at night; he'd move quickly across the pool, so he reminded me of an eel, the way he slid through water as if it were nothing. Some nights he'd swim for over an hour, and I'd get out of the pool and just sit there in what used to be my mother's chair and watch him.

When he was finished, he'd lean over the side, out of breath, and say, "Get me a towel, Ab." And I'd have to run to the deep end of the pool with the towel for him, a towel that I'd washed myself earlier in the day and would wash again a few days later. There was something about being in charge of the washing machine that made me feel grown up.

One day in the middle of June, Tommy ran over to my house to tell me what his grandmother just heard when she was getting her hair done: Katie Rainey had disappeared from her bedroom the night before. Katie Rainey, the almost popular girl, whose sister had taken over my spot at the lunch table, was gone, vanished, just like Becky.

I shook my head over and over again because I couldn't believe it. There was another family; there was someone else. And then I started to feel a little ashamed for what I felt creeping up my body; was it joy? The feeling startled me so much that I was speechless.

"The police are looking for her right now," Tommy said.

The police. I began to feel a smug sense of satisfaction when I thought about Kinney's having to admit that my parents had had nothing to do with Becky's disappearance after all. I imagined his big nose wrinkled up with dismay, with the realization that he had been wrong, that it was his fault Becky hadn't been found yet.

For the first time in months I considered that Becky could be alive. I wondered if Katie was with her, if they were together. Would Katie remind her of me? After all, we were the same age, and we used to run with the same crowd at school.

With Katie's disappearance there were new clues, new leads. Kinney came back to our house for the first time in months, and he spoke in hushed tones to my father in the kitchen while I tried my best to listen in. I heard that neighbors had spotted a blue truck, that some of Katie's clothes were missing, that the screen was gone from her bedroom window.

"It's terrible," my father said to me after Kinney left. "Just terrible." His face was twisted funny, and he pulled on his mustache. I imagined that suddenly he could feel it all again, the pain of realizing Becky was gone, like a knife twisting over and over in his stomach.

A few hours later I heard my father talking on the phone to someone I assumed was Katie's father. "Really," he said. "If there is anything I can do. Anything at all."

While the police searched for Katie, both my parents lit up just a little bit. My father decided for the first time since my mother had left that it was time to clean the house, and he moved out all the furniture and had me do the dusting and vacuuming. My mother had a little makeup on when I went to visit her at her apartment, and for the first time in a long time she wasn't smoking. "Oh, those poor people," she said to me, sucking in her breath as she said it, but I wondered if like me, she felt hope, a sense that everything could be all right again.

One evening about two weeks after Katie had disappeared, my father called me into the kitchen. "Look," he said, pointing out the window. "Look over there. Do you see that?"

I saw something moving between Morrow's field and our yard, only I couldn't make out its shape. "I think it's a deer," I said.

"No." He shook his head. "It's a person. There's a person in our yard."

I felt something catch in the back of my throat and then the brisk pounding of my heart. For an instant I thought I could believe him, that it could be Becky, back from a year-long trip, unharmed and no worse for wear.

I followed him out the back door across the yard. He ran so quickly that I almost couldn't keep up with him. "Hello," he called. "Anybody there?"

Then I heard a bark, and I stopped right where I was. The dog came out a little, and I could see her. She was medium size with longish fur that was matted down probably from weeks of being on her own. My father sat down in the grass and put his head in his hands. The dog rolled over onto her back and put her paws in the air.

"Look. She likes you," I said.

"Goddamn dog," he said.

"She looks sweet." I walked up to her and let her sniff my hand. Becky and I had always wanted a pet, but our parents never let us. My mother was allergic to cats, and my father thought that dogs were too much work. When we were younger, we'd dreamed of having something furry and cuddly we could play with. "Can we keep her?" I said.

"What, Ab?"

"The dog. We should keep the dog."

He shook his head. "She's a stray."

"Look how thin she is." You could see the outline of her ribs across her chest. "I'll take care of her. I'll do all the work and everything. You won't even know she's here." I suddenly wanted the dog so badly, more than I wanted anything else.

"I don't know, Ab."

From my father, this was a yes, so I hugged him. "You won't regret it," I told him.

"We'll have to take her to a vet. She could have rabies."

When I thought of rabies, I thought about raccoons foaming at the mouth, not about skinny, needy dogs. "She's fine," I said. "She doesn't have rabies."

"Still," he said. "We'll put her in the basement until then. I don't want her walking around the house."

I was so thrilled that he was letting me keep the dog that I didn't care. I thought about what Becky would think if she could see me. I knew she'd be insanely jealous, crazy over the fact that we hadn't been allowed to have a dog when she lived here.

I put the dog in the basement, and once I started petting her and gave her some leftover hamburger from dinner, she came over and snuggled up with me. It was such a nice closeness, so simple. She already loved me, and I'd given her almost nothing.

The dog became as much Tommy's as she was mine. He too had never been allowed a pet, so he was thrilled when he saw her. He went with me to walk her every day (I, of course, wasn't allowed to go alone), and he liked to come over just to sit with her. He was even the one who helped me come up with her name, Tabby, a combination of Tommy and Abby. She was just this kind creature who wanted nothing more than to love us, even when no one else did.

Katie Rainey was gone nearly a month before the police found her. Kinney didn't call my father to tell him what had happened. One evening, as my father and I watched the news during dinner, Katie came in as a breaking story. She was found safely in New York City with her boyfriend. As it turns out, she'd run away with him, intentionally left her family behind.

My father's face drained of color as the newscaster recounted the details. It took him a minute before he said it. "Well, thank goodness she's safe."

I couldn't answer him; I didn't want to say out loud what I knew we both were thinking. Everything was still ruined; Becky wasn't coming back.

Chapter 27

ONE YEAR TO the day that Becky disappeared, my father stayed home from work. He lit candles in the kitchen and played Becky's favorite Christmas songs on his record player. It was weird because it kind of felt like a memorial service.

I sat with him in the kitchen for a while and thought about the fact that I could almost forget the sound of Becky's voice echoing through the upstairs hallway, could forget that something like that had ever existed.

For the anniversary, as my mother called it, she and Garret planted flowers in a public garden near her apartment. She called and invited me to go with them, but I told her I thought I shouldn't, that someone needed to stay with my father.

"Of course, sweetie," she said. "I understand." But I knew she really didn't. Her voice had this sad, hectic lilt to it, so I could tell she was really hyper but on the verge of being depressed.

"It's just that you have Garret," I told her. "Dad has no one."

"You don't need make me feel guilty, Ab. I'm not the enemy here."

"I know," I said. I hadn't been trying to make her feel guilty necessarily, though I did think she deserved it.

"How's he doing?" she asked.

"Not good. He's lighting candles in the kitchen."

"Your father is lighting candles?"

"Yeah."

"He keeps it all bottled up," she said. "He never talks about anything."

"He talks." But I knew this wasn't true. I just felt the need to defend my father, to make my mother see that he was better than Garret.

"He should see Dr. Shreiker. He's been doing wonders for me."

"He's fine," I said. "He'll be fine." I didn't think my father would ever see a therapist. It wasn't his thing. He was good at putting on a sane outer appearance, even if he was going crazy inside.

"He's always too darn fine." We were both silent for a minute. "I'm sorry. I shouldn't have said that about him. Don't tell him I said that."

"Okay." It was a promise I meant to keep.

"You take care of him then, Ab. I'll talk to you soon."

I didn't ask my mother what kind of flowers she and Garret planned on planting, though for some reason I guessed it would be roses. I thought roses were the perfect flowers for Becky, thorny and beautiful all at once, their deep red color so vibrant that when you walked by they would assault you. That was Becky.

I guess it wasn't fair of my mother to ask me to take care of my father. It should've been the other way around; they should've been taking care of me. But I was past being angry about this, and I just started to accept my role as another fact, another normal part of my life.

"What did your mother want?" my father asked when I went back down to the kitchen.

"Nothing," I lied.

"What's she doing today?"

"Planting flowers," I said, intentionally leaving out

the part about Garret.

"Flowers," he said. "Your mother always loved flowers." I thought he was going to bring up the carnations I'd given her, and for a moment I felt embarrassed, but he didn't mention it, and he had this sort of dreamy faraway look in his eyes.

Years ago my mother had had a garden in the backyard in a corner behind the pool. She planted all kinds of flowers—roses and azaleas and marigolds. In the spring her little garden would bloom up so nice—oranges, yellows, reds, pinks. It gave our yard a whole different look, made it something special.

But the spring after Grandma Jacobson died, she stopped taking care of it, and all the flowers died, shriveled into brown eyesores in the back of our yard. Sometimes when I look out there, I miss the flowers so much it surprises me, this deep aching sadness for them.

"It doesn't seem like only a year, does it?" my father said. I shook my head. It felt like a lifetime, an entirely different universe. "She's not coming back, is she?"

At first I thought he meant my mother, but then I realized he was talking about Becky. "I don't know," I said. "I don't think so."

"You're all I've got left, Ab." He reached out for my hand and squeezed it.

For some reason this frightened me. It made me feel too fragile, as if I too could disappear at any moment.

A few hours later my father blew out the candles and went outside to sit on the patio. "There's something about being out there," he said. "I feel closer to her."

I knew my father's closeness to Becky was imaginary, but sitting out there made him feel better, so I pretended not to notice. "That's a good idea," I told him. "I'm going to take Tabby for a walk."

I took Tabby next door to pick up Tommy, and the three of us walked around the neighborhood. "My grandma told me," Tommy said, "about today."

"It's no big deal," I said, though suddenly I felt like crying. It was strange, the way I could be so calm in front of my parents, but when I talked to Tommy, I wanted to break.

"My father left on a Thursday," Tommy said, "sometime in August. I don't remember the exact date, though. I didn't think about it at the time."

I nodded and handed him Tabby's leash. She'd been pulling me to go faster, and I didn't feel like keeping up. "Here, you take her."

"I didn't think I would have to remember it a year later. I thought he'd be back in a few days."

"It doesn't seem real," I said. "This stuff happens in books, not in real life." Tabby barked and surged ahead, pulling Tommy with her. I had to take big strides just to keep up.

"What is it, Tabby? What is it, girl?" Tabby rarely barked. I knew this was her defense mechanism, something she did if she was frightened.

"Maybe she saw a bird," I said, "or a rabbit." I'm not sure what she saw, but she started running faster, pulling Tommy and me behind her. She ran and ran until we got to the large open space of Morrow's field, and then she stopped and started sniffing the air. "She smells something," I said. Tommy was breathing heavy, and he had to hang his head down just to catch his breath.

For a moment I wondered if Tabby was an amazing dog, some sort of superhero that would stop right there and find Becky. I imagined her digging up something horrible like a bone, or sniffing out Becky's scent, or taking us to the spot where she was buried. But she wasn't Lassie. And after a few minutes of sniffing, Tabby lay on the grass and started panting, out of breath from her run. "We should take her back and get her some water," I said.

"Let's sit down first." Tommy sat on the ground next to Tabby, and I sat next to them. "There's a whole world out here," Tommy said, "just behind the neighborhood." I thought of the first time I'd taken Tommy to Morrow's field, and I thought about the way he'd kissed me and made me feel something for the first time in the longest time.

I reached over for his hand because I needed something solid to hold on to. And he let me sit there and hold it for just a few minutes. There was something peaceful about the whole thing, sitting like that in the sun with Tommy and Tabby, and I felt this moment of warmth, the sudden feeling that everything would be okay.

After a few minutes of quiet, Tabby started sniffing the air again and barking, and she jumped up and started running back toward my house. "What's wrong with her today?" I said.

"Dogs know. They can sense when things aren't right."

Tommy and I ran after her, and I wondered if what he said was true, if Tabby knew that there was something different about this day.

Once we got through the clearing and entered my yard,

I saw what Tabby had been barking at. There was smoke coming from our back patio. My father was sitting on my mother's smoking chair, a bowl sitting in front of him with its contents on fire and smoking.

"What the heck?" Tommy said. "What's he doing?"

I shook my head and ran toward my father. Tabby was still barking and running around in circles by my feet now.

"Jesus," my father said. "Get that mutt to stop yapping, will you?"

Tommy and I exchanged glances. I could tell he was thinking what I was, that Tabby might be a mixed breed, but she was no mutt. Still, Tommy and I stood back and watched as my father threw pictures into the flaming bowl.

"What are you doing, Dad?" I finally said.

"Cleaning. Getting rid of things."

I went closer and saw he had a shoe box of pictures next to him; most of the pictures were of Becky and me, and then some of him and my mother. I recognized the box. My mother had kept it in their bedroom, and she'd always said she was going to make it into a scrapbook; only she never did. It was one of those things she never got around to, like signing Becky up for voice lessons. My first reaction was to be surprised that she hadn't taken these pictures with her. Then

I realized what my father was doing, destroying my whole life, my history. "Stop it." I grabbed the box from him. "Stop."

"Ab, give those back."

I shook my head. "I'm not letting you burn these. I want them."

"You don't tell me what to do," he said. "If I want to burn them. I'll burn them."

"Mr. Reed," Tommy said. His voice sounded higher than usual, and it cracked on my father's name.

"Tommy, stay out of this. Why don't you go home? And take that stupid dog with you."

But Tommy didn't move, and neither did Tabby. She just kept barking. I think both Tommy and I were frozen for a moment. But I knew I didn't want my father to burn those pictures, so before he could take the box back from me, I turned around and started running as fast as I could, back toward Morrow's field. I wasn't sure where I was going, only that I had to get away from him, that I couldn't let him take anything else from me.

"Abby," I heard my father yell after me. "Abby, get back here. Oh, for Christ's sake." But I didn't turn around or slow down or anything. I just ran as fast as I could with the pictures, through the field to the other side, to the neighborhood on the other side of it. I must've run a half mile before I stopped to catch my breath, and then, as I stopped to breathe, I realized I was crying. I almost couldn't distinguish between the sweat and the tears on my face because they both were there, blending together, and I could feel them both, but strangely, I also felt nothing.

Before I knew it, Tommy ran up behind me. "You can really run for a girl." He was out of breath and panting the way Tabby did when she needed water.

"Where's Tabby?"

"I put her in your house."

"Why did you do that?" I felt myself getting hysterical, thinking that if my father could burn pictures, could destroy an entire life, he would think nothing of hurting a dog.

"She's fine," Tommy said. "She'll be fine."

He put his hand on my shoulder. "You can come home with me. My grandma is cooking menudo. We can look at your pictures."

I didn't say anything, but when he reached his hand out, I took it.

Mrs. Ramirez didn't ask why I was staying for dinner or why I had a box of pictures with me or even why I'd been crying.

I heard her go into the other room to call my father and tell him I was there, but I also heard her say, "Let her stay, Jim. Maybe some menudo do her good."

"Let's go upstairs and look at the pictures," Tommy said. I followed him blindly up to his room.

We sat on Tommy's bed, and I finally let go of the box. He started taking out pictures and asking me questions: "Who's this?" and "What are you doing here?" and so on.

I told him all about Grandma Jacobson, about her sapphire hearts and her terrible cancer. We looked at pictures of my parents when they were young, when they both looked so happy and they were holding on to each other in a park and smiling. And then we looked at pictures of me and Becky—us as babies, us as toddlers, us dressed up for Christmas in these little red velvet matching dresses, us at Thanksgiving with bright orange bows in our hair.

"She looks different than she does in the other picture." I knew he was referring to Becky's school picture, the one that still hung on bulletin boards and telephone poles around Pinesboro. "She looks more alive here. You can see how much energy she had. That other picture makes her look flat."

"Who ever looks good in their school picture?"

He nodded. "I guess they're just supposed to be for parents and grandparents to gush over or whatever."

"Not for this."

He looked at me, and his eyes were so expressive that I could tell there were so many things he wanted to say but didn't know how. I could see everything he was feeling: pain for me, compassion, longing, the need to fix something that was so broken it was unfixable. "Did you ever think about its being you?"

I've thought about it a million times. What if I'd been the one to disappear instead of Becky? What would've happened to my family then? I wonder if we would've broken in the same way or if somehow Becky's spark would've fixed things in a way my quietness couldn't. But I didn't feel comfortable telling Tommy any of this, so I just shrugged and said, "Not really, no. I try not to."

"I'm glad you're here," he said. He could've meant right here, right in this moment, in his bedroom. But I suspected he was saying that he was glad I wasn't the one who'd gone missing. I tried to imagine if he would've been friends with Becky had I been the one to disappear, and I just couldn't see it.

Tommy stood up and locked his bedroom door, and

then he sat back down on the bed next to me and started to put the pictures back in the box. I knew as soon as I saw him lock the door that he was going to start kissing me, and I wanted him to so much.

I don't know why, but I started crying again. It was different now, though. It was more like relief, the sudden feeling of safety, the deep pit of missing Becky. I was crying silently, and I felt the tears running down my cheeks; I didn't move to wipe them away. But Tommy did. He reached up and touched my face with his thumb, gently pushing away the tears. "Don't cry, Abby," he whispered.

"I don't want to." But I couldn't stop myself.

"I want to kiss you," he whispered, almost as if he were asking me a question.

I nodded, to let him know I wanted to kiss him too. And then we were kissing and not just a quick kiss like we had those few other times. No, this was slow and long, and it lasted for probably five minutes. And it was the most amazing thing I'd ever felt.

I felt his lips moving over mine, his tongue pushing slowly into my mouth, and it all felt perfect and warm and so nice. I knew it wasn't the same thing, but I thought it felt the way sex was supposed to, like there was this whole new completeness that I hadn't even known existed before that.

When Mrs. Ramirez knocked on the door, we both jumped and as a reflex moved to opposite sides of the bed. "Dinner, kids," she called.

"We'll be there in a minute," Tommy said. I instantly thought she would know what we'd been doing. His voice had cracked, and he'd sounded as if he were choking for air. But if she knew, she didn't let on, because I heard her turn around and walk back down the stairs.

I was suddenly embarrassed, and I didn't know how to look at him. He reached over and squeezed my hand. "I love you," he whispered.

"I love you too."

It was something I knew the adults around us would never understand or believe. But I believed it when he said it. I knew he meant it.

It turns out that menudo is really cow stomach, something I didn't know until after I had some. Then I started to feel sick, but luckily Mrs. Ramirez wasn't offended. She was convinced that the day had taken its toll on me. "Maybe you go home and go sleep," she said.

But I shook my head. I wasn't ready to face my father.

For a few moments up in Tommy's bedroom I had allowed myself this fantasy that I was loved, that life could be something amazing. I wasn't ready to let that go.

"It been hard year." Mrs. Ramirez shook her head. She was talking more to herself than to either me or Tommy, so we both kept quiet. "May God pray for us." She bowed her head and started whispering things under her breath. I looked at Tommy, but he just shrugged.

"We're going to go watch TV, Grandma." She waved at us to go but didn't miss a beat with her prayers.

"Does she do that a lot?" I asked him, remembering the time in my living room when she tried to get me to pray for Becky.

"Sometimes. On and off. Like she's religious when she feels like it."

"Does it work then if you don't do it all the time?"

He shrugged. "I don't know. I don't believe it anyways."

"Neither do I."

"It's like if praying worked, then why do bad things even happen?"

We went back up to Tommy's room, and I put the rest of my pictures back in the box. "You can leave these here if you want," Tommy said. "I'll take care of them for you."

"Thanks." I knew he would.

"I'll keep them on the high shelf in my closet. No one looks up there. Grandma can't even reach that high. They'll be safe."

I handed him the box. "I know. I know they will be."

"What are you going to say to your father?"

"Nothing. Probably we'll forget the whole thing ever happened."

"You won't forget," he said.

I knew he was right, but I didn't want to admit it. I felt myself starting to hate my father and my mother as well. I knew my anger toward them was wrong, but I couldn't help it. They both were destroying my life in their own way.

He took the box of pictures and pushed it up onto the high shelf. "There," he said.

"Thanks." And I didn't just mean for the pictures. I meant for everything, for the kiss.

Tommy came back and sat down next to me on the bed. "Do you know if my father hadn't left and your sister hadn't disappeared, we probably never would've met."

"Even if we had," I said, "it wouldn't have been the same." If Becky had still been here, Tommy would've been my obligation, someone I was forced to be kind to because my mother made me, someone whom Jocelyn and I would've secretly made fun of. I felt kind of bad just thinking about it.

"My mother always says that everything happens for a reason. It's such a stupid thing to say, though, you know?"

I nodded. "My grandma Jacobson used to say that all the time. I always thought it was something that old people said to make themselves feel better."

"Does it make you feel better to think that?"

I shook my head. "No, not really. You?"

"Nah. I guess not." Tommy leaned over and hugged me, holding me so close to him that I could feel his breath against my neck. We sat there and hugged each other for a while, neither one of us saying a word. We didn't have to.

When I got home, my father was sitting in the living room watching TV, Tabby curled up at his feet.

"She's a good dog," he said when I walked in.

I nodded. "I know."

"We should've gotten a dog years ago."

I didn't point out that Becky and I once begged him for a dog for what seemed like weeks after one of her friends from school had gotten a terrier puppy and brought it in for show-and-tell. I didn't remind him that he had a theory about children and dogs, that the two didn't belong together because children just weren't responsible. Everything was different now; it was a whole new world.

Chapter 28

THE SECOND FALL when school began again, I was just Abigail Reed. People had other things to talk about. Katie Rainey was an instant celebrity, being that she had both successfully run away and had a boyfriend who was old enough to drive. James Harper had lost his middle toe over the summer after getting his foot caught under a lawn mower. He'd spent weeks in the hospital and lost a lot of blood, and apparently it was touch and go for a while. But he was there, on crutches (and missing a toe), for the first day of school. I was old news.

Tommy began the year at the high school, so it was lonely at lunch. He turned fifteen two weeks before school started, and Mrs. Ramirez gave him a bike and a helmet for his birthday. He rode the bike to school most mornings, and he was supposed to walk it home with me, but often I ended up walking by myself as he sped away on the bike with two new boys he met at the high school. It was as if he'd already forgotten our summer, and I suddenly felt more angry with him than I did with my parents.

On my fourteenth birthday my mother came over to the house for dinner. It was the first time the three of us had eaten together in months, and quite possibly the first time my parents had spoken to each other since the spring. It was my mother's idea. She called me the week before and told me to tell my father she was coming. "Nothing fancy," she said. "But I thought it would be nice for you, sweetie."

My father picked up a pizza on the way home and opened a bottle of red wine that he and my mother shared. "To Abigail." My father lifted his glass and touched it to my mother's. There was this awkward moment of silence where I waited for my mother to add *and Becky too*, but she said nothing. She smiled at me. "Happy birthday, Ab," my father said.

"You're getting so old," my mother said. "I can't believe it. It seems like just yesterday when you were born." She shook her head.

I didn't feel right celebrating my birthday. It wasn't like the year before, when we all were just waiting for Becky to come home. This year we knew she wasn't, so we pretended that she had never existed at all, that she wouldn't be turning twelve the next day. I wished that we'd just ignored my birthday too, that we'd pretended it hadn't even happened. I felt this enormous weight of guilt hanging in my chest; it was a suffocating feeling, something that made me want to gag on my pizza or to stop breathing altogether. But I ate because I didn't want to upset either of my parents.

I could tell my father was excited to have my mother at dinner. He kept staring at her and offering her more food and wine, which she took. I think they both got a little drunk, because by the time we'd finished dinner, my parents' cheeks were rosy and they were laughing. When my father reached out his hand for my mother, she took it. Then she shook his hand and said, "Oh, Jim, really." And she giggled. I felt a sudden surge of hope. Maybe my mother had gotten her depression out of her system. Maybe she would move back in. Maybe even without Becky we could be complete again, something real, a family.

But my mother let go of my father's hand as quickly as she'd grabbed it and started gulping her wine, and my father, looking suddenly wounded, turned away so he didn't have to meet my eyes.

Tommy and Mrs. Ramirez showed up at the door with fourteen pink balloons just before we were ready for cake. "Happy birthday, Ah-bee-hail." Mrs. Ramirez kissed me on the cheek.

"Here." Tommy handed me the balloons. "Happy birthday." I nodded but tried not to make eye contact with him.

My father had invited them without telling me, which made me feel a little annoyed. Things had been so strange with Tommy and me since school started that when I saw him standing there, I felt a little sick to my stomach. I was angry with him for ignoring me.

"Ooh. Everybody here today." Mrs. Ramirez walked in and gave my mother a hug. "Long time no see." My mother didn't answer her, but she accepted the hug.

"Where's Tabby?" Tommy asked. He hadn't been over since school started, and I'd been walking Tabby by myself lately, though my father thought I was still walking her with Tommy.

"She's in the basement." I nodded toward the door. "Go ahead. She'll be happy to see you." I didn't mean to say it accusingly to make him feel guilty or anything, but it kind of came out that way.

"Oh, bring her upstairs," my mother said. "I've been dying to meet this infamous Tabby. I can't believe your father let you keep that dog. Really, Jim, you surprise me."

My father shrugged. "I'll get the cake."

Tommy brought Tabby upstairs, and then we all sat at the table. Everyone sang "Happy Birthday" to me. It was strange; I felt like I was watching the whole thing in slow motion, like it was one big cartoon or something. It didn't seem real that all these people were here for me and that they were singing. When the singing stopped, I blew out the candles, but I didn't make a wish. I no longer believed in wishes.

After we had cake, I asked Tommy if he wanted to take Tabby out for a walk, partly because being in the house with everyone there was starting to make me feel suffocated and partly because I really wanted to see him alone.

We took Tabby around the block and walked in silence for a few minutes, but when Tabby stopped to sniff a tree, I looked Tommy square in the eye and said what I was really thinking. "Why have you been ignoring me?"

He shoved his hands into his pocket and stomped his feet a little, as if trying to stay warm, but it was still mild outside, so I think he was really just nervous. “I haven’t,” he said. “I don’t mean to.” He took a hand out of his pocket and put it on my shoulder, a touch that suddenly felt warm and reassuring, and I didn’t pull away even though I was still annoyed with him.

“I miss you at lunch,” I said.

He nodded. “I miss you too.”

“I wish I were in high school.”

“I know.”

“Will you wait for me after school tomorrow?”

“Okay,” he said. “But I don’t know if I can every day. It’s just . . .”

I felt bad for being so jealous that Tommy had other friends, because I felt like a terrible person for wanting him to be as lonely as I was. “Well, it’s okay if you can’t.”

But the next day when I got out of school, he was there, waiting for me, and we walked home together.

Chapter 29

MAYBE IT'S THE snow that changes everything, the transformation of the world from green to white, from fresh to frozen. It was snowing again when Tommy and I went back to Morrow's field. Our last real day together.

We had off from school because of the snow, and Tommy knocked on my front door in the morning. "My grandmother wanted me out of the house," he said, almost apologetically. "We could go sledding if you want."

I was still angry with Tommy for being older than I was, for having a life that was separate from mine. After our talk on my birthday, he waited for me some days after school. But I hadn't seen him waiting for the past two weeks, so I was a little annoyed with him when he showed up on my porch. I still thought about that day in the summer when he told me he loved me, so deep down I wasn't really mad at him, but I didn't know what to expect from him anymore. "I don't know. It's kind of cold outside."

"Well, whatever. We can watch TV then."

I wondered what had happened to his high school friends, but I didn't want to ask. Truthfully I was tired of being alone. "Come on in. Let me get my boots on."

Tommy had grown taller over the past few months, and he looked a little more muscular. He suddenly seemed more grown up, and he had these large broad shoulders. His hair was a little longer, so it looked the way it had when I first met him, but it didn't look shaggy anymore. It was the first time I could really picture Tommy as a man, somebody's father or husband or whatever, and the thought thrilled me a little.

"How's school?" I asked him while I rummaged through the closet for my boots.

"Its okay. It's good, I guess."

"Hmm." I found my boots in the back, right next to Becky's, and I hesitated for a moment before pulling them out. I wondered if they would fit her now, how much her feet could've grown in a year and a half.

"I got an A on my English paper last week. And I'm doing pretty good in all my classes."

I took my boots into the foyer and sat down to yank them on. "Well, that's good, I guess."

"Yeah. I like it a whole lot better than last year."

"Gee, thanks a lot."

"You know I didn't mean it like that."

"Well, I don't know how you meant it." I felt myself getting jealous. It was the way I'd feel when Becky would get all the attention, when I'd feel my parents loved her more than they loved me. Tommy liked high school better than he liked the time he'd spent with me last year.

He sat down on the floor next to me. "I do miss you."

"Whatever."

"No, I mean it."

"It's not a big deal." I stood up. "Let's go outside."

Out in Morrow's field it could've been any other winter day in any other year. People were playing and throwing snowballs and building snowmen, and everyone was laughing. I couldn't stop thinking about Becky. It was worse than the year before, when it was quiet, like a shrine. To me, this all felt wrong, and I thought about God striking all of us down with a big bolt of lightning or something. Everybody had already forgotten.

"It's too crowded here," Tommy said, as if he could read my mind. "Let's just take a walk instead." I let him take my hand and lead me around the block, so we just walked together in the snow. Being out in the open like that for the first time made me feel like we were a couple, like something solid that belonged joined together.

"I'm so sick of this place," I said. All the houses in our neighborhood looked perfect, little icicles hanging off the undersides of the roof and all that, snow covering the front lawns.

"Everything is freezing," Tommy said. "Everything dies in the winter." He squeezed my hand, and I felt it tingling, even through the thicknesses of our gloves.

After Tommy and I got too cold from walking, we went back to my house and made hot chocolate. I made it with milk, on the stove, the way my mother used to do for Becky and me in the winter, and I sprinkled cinnamon on top. I felt old doing this, cooking in the kitchen with Tommy watching me. I felt his eyes on me, following me as I walked back and forth between the stove and the refrigerator.

We sipped our drinks in silence at the kitchen table, but we stared at each other the whole time. Finally Tommy said, "I'm sorry we didn't find her."

I shook my head. "Don't be sorry. It's not your fault."

"I wanted to give that to you," he said. It sounded so odd, yet it was the sweetest thing anyone ever said to me, so it made what he said next feel just right. "Can I kiss you again, Abigail?"

I knew that to someone else, it might have seemed like Tommy was just using me or something, but I knew he wasn't. We had this undeniable connection when we were alone together that made everything else in the world disappear: Tommy's high school friends, my parents, Becky. Every time he wanted to kiss me, I wanted him to, and not because I was lonely or depressed or needed the attention or whatever, but because I genuinely wanted him to.

I stood up and held out my hand and led him into the family room. We sat on the couch together, just staring at each other for a minute, and then Tommy reached up and put his hand on my cheek. "You're cold still," he said.

"I'm okay." But really I was freezing, unable to warm up. He started kissing my cheeks, slowly, just small kisses that he dotted around my face. Each kiss was warming, amazing.

Then I tilted my head so he could kiss my lips again. We just sat there and kissed for probably twenty minutes, and the whole time, I let myself think of nothing else but him kissing me.

"Let's lie down," Tommy whispered, and I let myself lean back and relax. He was lying on top of me, and I felt his entire body, the warmth of it. I felt my heart pounding in my chest, but I wasn't afraid. I wanted to kiss Tommy. I wanted more.

He put his hand on my stomach and then started moving it up slowly. "Can I?" he said. "Do you want me to?"

I nodded. I was afraid to speak. I thought that if I did, the perfect moment would collapse. He put his hand under my shirt and then on my breast, softly at first. He cupped my left breast with his hand, and just let his hand sit there a minute. I don't think he knew what he was supposed to do next, but I didn't know either, so I just let him keep his hand there while we were kissing. "Can I take your shirt off?" he whispered.

I nodded again and sat up so he could lift my shirt over my head. He traced the outline of my bra with his finger and then reached behind me to unhook it. He fumbled a little; he couldn't get it undone, so I reached back and did it for him. He took my bra and put it on the floor, and then he sat up and just looked at me for a minute. I should've been cold, sitting there with my shirt off, but I wasn't. I was completely warm. "You're beautiful, Abigail."

No one had ever told me I was beautiful before, not even my parents, really. I was always the special one, the smart one, and Becky was the beauty. I know it's true; mousy, frizzy hair won't win me any beauty contests. But Tommy sounded so sincere that I knew he meant it, and I loved him for that.

I started kissing Tommy again, and he touched my breasts.

I was so involved in Tommy that I didn't hear the front door open; I didn't even hear my father's footsteps as he approached us. In fact I didn't even know he was there until I heard him say, "Jesus Christ, Ab." And then suddenly Tommy sat up, and I started grabbing for my shirt, but I couldn't find it. "Ab," my father whispered. I knew he was there, but I couldn't turn around. I didn't want to look at him. "You little bastard," he said to Tommy. "What the hell do you think you're doing?"

I finally found my shirt and slipped it back over my head. I knew that I needed to save Tommy. "Go home," I said to him. "I'll talk to you later."

"Abby." He turned to look at me, and I saw this incredible sadness, this weight of knowing we'd just done something we could never take back. Everything would be different now; we'd lost our bubble, our little private world that protected us from everything else.

"Get the hell out of my house," my father yelled at him. "Jesus Christ."

Tommy got off the couch and ran to the front door. He forgot his boots, but I didn't want to call after him.

"Dad," I said, "it's not what you think."

"Abigail." He sat down in his chair in the corner, but we didn't look at each other. "Is this because your mother left? We tried to raise you right, do the best we could. This is because you don't have your mother, isn't it?"

"You make it sound like I committed a crime," I said. I wasn't sorry for anything, and I didn't think it was wrong. I was fourteen; I made out with a boy on our couch. It wasn't the end of the world.

"Abigail," he said, "just go up to your room. I can't look at you right now."

"Dad, I—"

"Just go, Ab. "

So I went upstairs and sat on my bed, and I thought about Tommy kissing me and what might have happened if my father hadn't walked in.

I can only imagine what happened next, when Tommy went home:

Tommy walked across the snowy lawn in his socks. By the time he got to his front door, his feet were soaking wet and freezing. He was shivering, and so cold, and thinking about how he'd left me there with my father. And he was still picturing my breasts, how soft they were, so much softer than he'd imagined.

As he walked up to the front door, it finally dawned on him that he'd left his boots at my house, and he tried to think of what he would tell his grandmother, how he could've left his boots, for Christ's sake. He worried about what my father would tell her. Then he decided to stand out on the snowy porch for just another minute, soak it all in. He took a deep breath and realized how much he loved the snow, how much he would miss it when she sent him back to Florida. But he realized he needed to face things, to accept the consequences. He took a deep breath and then stepped inside.

The house was strangely quiet except for this odd whirring sound, the noise of a mixer, going on and on and on. "Grandma," he called out, "I'm home." She didn't answer. "Grandma," he said, louder this time. Nothing. But maybe she couldn't hear him over the sound of the mixer. So he left his wet socks in the foyer and walked to the kitchen. The first thing he noticed was the mixer. She'd left it on and in the bowl. So forgetful. He walked to turn it off, and on the way he almost tripped over her. She was lying on the kitchen floor, not moving.

He screamed and jumped back, and he thought she was dead. *I've killed her*, he thought. *The God she believes in is punishing me.*

My father and I both heard the sound of the ambulance. At first I thought it was coming to our house, and I ran down to see if my father was all right. My first thought was that my father had done something terrible to himself, that I'd ruined him, pushed him over the edge.

"It's next door," he said when he saw me. And we both ran out to the porch to see. For a moment I thought that Tommy was hurt, that he'd told Mrs. Ramirez what had happened and she'd gone after him with her carving knife.

But I saw Tommy run outside to talk to the EMTs, and that was when my father ran across the lawn.

"What's going on here?" he said to Tommy. They eyed each other for a minute, and I could tell Tommy was unsure if he should even be talking to my father, but then my father shook his shoulders a little. "Son, what happened?"

"I don't know," he said. "I just found her like this."

A few minutes later they carried Mrs. Ramirez out on a stretcher, and she looked dead. She had these tubes hanging out of her nose, and she wasn't moving. It was worse than seeing Grandma Jacobson with cancer or imagining Becky buried in Morrow's field, because it was real and right in front of me. I was so stunned to see it that I had to look away. "I'll drive you to the hospital," my father said to Tommy. To me he said, "Ab, go call your mother and tell her you're staying with her tonight."

I was so numb that I just nodded and didn't even argue with him. I guess I should've wanted to go with them, to comfort Tommy or something, but I didn't want to. I wanted to be as far away from there as possible.

I don't know what my father and Tommy said to each other on the way to the hospital or while they sat there and waited.

That's something I don't even want to try to imagine because it's too weird to think of it.

What I do know for sure: Mrs. Ramirez had a massive heart attack while she stood in her kitchen making brownies. Had Tommy not found her when he did, she might have died. Apparently she'd been having chest pains for weeks, but she'd been ignoring them, passing them off as indigestion. The heart attack forced her to look at things: She had a weak heart, and unless she started taking it easy, she was going to die.

I spent the night at my mother's apartment, the first and only time I slept over there. I'm not sure how much my father told her or exactly what he said, but as she sat next to me on the couch, tapping her cigarette nervously on the ashtray, she tried to talk to me about sex. She didn't tell me anything I didn't already know. I'd heard it all in school, in sixth-grade health class. Only when my mother said it, she turned bright red and put a funny emphasis on certain words, like "condom."

I told my mother that I wasn't ready to have sex, and when I was, I wouldn't be stupid about it. This basically shut her up. "Well, I know, Abby. Of course," she said. "It's just your father . . ."

“He was exaggerating,” I said. I wanted to change the subject in the worst way, so I said, “I don’t know what Dad was doing home in the middle of the afternoon anyway.”

“Oh,” she said. “He must’ve had his appointment with Dr. Shreiker.” It surprised me that she knew something about my father that I didn’t, which indicated to me that they were still talking, even when I wasn’t around. “They’ve been letting him have the time off work once a week,” she said. “He needs it.” I couldn’t imagine my father talking to a therapist. But I could tell the whole thing made my mother happy, so maybe, in some strange way, he thought he was doing it for her.

Chapter 30

AFTER MRS. RAMIREZ had her heart attack, Tommy's mother drove up from Florida. I watched from my bedroom window as she arrived. I saw the car with Florida plates drive slowly up our snowy street, and I knew immediately who it was. I felt myself cringe for Tommy, for the way his whole world had suddenly been shattered, again.

I watched her get out of the car. She was Mrs. Ramirez's height but a lot skinnier and younger-looking. She had long, thick black hair that she'd pulled up on top of her head for the ride. I watched as she pulled her suitcase out of the trunk, but then she disappeared from my view, so I couldn't witness her reunion with Tommy firsthand.

My father kept me updated on Mrs. Ramirez's condition,

and a week and a half after she had her heart attack, and a day after Tommy's mother arrived, he told me she was coming home from the hospital. "We'll go visit her at home tomorrow," he said.

I had no idea where Tommy had been staying while Mrs. Ramirez was in the hospital. I didn't think he'd been over there, in her house, all alone, but I hadn't seen him since the week before, not hanging around after school or anything, so either he was avoiding me or he hadn't been going to school for the past week. I wanted to believe it was the second choice; I didn't think he would ignore me anymore.

It felt strange walking over to Mrs. Ramirez's house with my father the next evening. The ground was still covered in snow, and the only sound as the two of us walked was the crunch of our boots. "Stay where I can see you, Ab," he said as we walked up to the front door.

I couldn't help rolling my eyes. "I will."

"I mean it."

Mrs. Ramirez's daughter answered the door. "Oh, you must be Abby," she said when she opened the door. "My mother has told me all about you. Please come in." She shook my father's hand as we walked in. "Mr. Reed, I can't thank you enough for everything you've done for my mother."

"Jim, please."

"Jim, then. Okay. You've been a godsend." I wasn't exactly sure what my father had done for Mrs. Ramirez, aside from visiting her in the hospital a few times, but I suspected there must be something else for her daughter to seem so thankful.

Mrs. Ramirez was lying on the couch with an afghan covering her legs. She looked older than she had two weeks ago, tired. Tommy sat on the love seat, watching TV with her. He looked up and caught my eye as we walked into the room, but then he turned away, quickly. My father put his hand on my shoulder, something that may have looked like a nice gesture to everyone else but to me felt like a restraint, something holding me back from everything.

"How are you feeling, Rosalie?" My father bent down so she didn't have to turn her head.

"Eh, *así así.* I've been better." My father squeezed her hand and stood back up.

"I have some cookies in the kitchen," Tommy's mother said, "if you'd like some."

"We don't want you to go to any trouble."

Tommy's mother smiled. "No trouble at all, Jim." She

may have been taken in by my father's politeness, but I wasn't, and I doubted Tommy was either. I could still hear his voice yelling that Tommy was a bastard.

It was strange the way we just sort of stood around there. "Why don't you have a seat?" Tommy's mother said when she came back in with the cookies. My father sat down in the chair right next to where we were standing, and I had nowhere else to go but to the love seat, next to Tommy. When I sat down, Tommy looked away from me. I think he was afraid to watch me, to catch my eye in front of my father.

Tommy's mother put the plate of cookies down on the coffee table, but no one reached for them. She sat on the couch with Mrs. Ramirez and rubbed her feet. "How are you doing, Mom? Is it too cold in here?"

Mrs. Ramirez shook her head. "No. I okay."

"My mother has hated the cold for so long." She sounded like she was apologizing, the way she said it.

My father nodded. "Who doesn't?"

"So she'll be much happier in Florida, won't you, Mom?"

It took a minute for what she said to really sink in. Then I felt it settling deep in my chest, my heart. Tommy was going back to Florida.

"A little bit of sunshine, Rosalie, and you'll be as good as new."

She shook her head and chuckled. "Oh, I don't know."

"Sure you will, Mom."

I tried to sneak a glance at Tommy, but he still wasn't looking at me. If I hadn't been so sure that my father was watching my every move, I would've kicked him or pinched his leg or something. I had this sudden, overwhelming sense of devastation. This loss would be different from Becky, because I knew where Tommy was and where he was going, but I also knew it was far, far enough that I might never see him again.

When I saw my mother on Saturday, she mentioned to me that it had been my father's idea for Mrs. Ramirez to move to Florida. He'd come up with it in the hospital, right after he'd called Tommy's mother to tell her what was going on. He'd even offered to pay for Mrs. Ramirez's move, and he promised to clean up her house and get it on the market. It made him seem like a generous guy, so warmhearted.

My mother's hand shook as she tapped the cigarette in the ashtray. "Your father, always trying to take care of people." But she wouldn't even look at me as she said it, so we both knew that wasn't why he did it.

Tommy went back to school for a few weeks before they left, but I didn't really see him until the day before. I walked out of school, and I saw him across the street on his bike with his high school friends, but I walked over there anyway because I knew I had to talk to him. As soon as I got up close, his other friends waved and took off, and then there I was, standing next to him on the sidewalk. He leaned against his bike, looking awkward, but still sort of cool in a way.

"Hey," he said, "I was gonna wait for you. I'm sorry I haven't seen you in a while. My mother made me promise to come right home after school."

"Oh." I felt myself blushing. I wondered what my father had told her. But I was also glad that he said he was going to wait, that if I hadn't approached him, he would've found me.

"We're leaving tomorrow," he said. I nodded. I knew he was leaving soon. I could see them from my bedroom window, and I'd watched Tommy and his mother take bundles of trash to the curb. I wondered how Mrs. Ramirez felt about their throwing away the remains of her life. She'd always said she'd wanted to move to Florida someday, but I doubted she'd imagined it this way. "I didn't want to leave without saying good-bye."

"Thanks," I said, but I turned my head a little so I didn't have to look at him. I didn't want to see everything in his eyes. I didn't want to know that he was hurt or angry or, worse, excited about going back to Florida.

"We could walk home together if you want."

"Okay."

Tommy held his bike to his left side, and I walked on his right. We couldn't hold hands or anything because he was using both hands to walk the bike. I don't think we would've held hands anyway, though. "So, will you miss Pinesboro?"

"I'm not sure," he said. "Some of it, I guess."

"No more snow," I said.

"No more snow." He sighed, but I couldn't tell if it was really the snow he'd miss or me.

"Your grandmother going to be okay?"

"I don't know. I guess so." We walked for a little while in silence, both of us staring straight ahead. It's not that I didn't have anything I wanted to say to him, because I did. There was so much that I was afraid of saying it. "Maybe you could come to Florida sometime, to visit."

"Yeah, sure. Maybe." But we both knew I never would. "We can write to each other." But we knew we wouldn't do that either.

We walked into our development, and I found myself going slower. I didn't want the walk to end, didn't want this to be the last time I ever saw Tommy. It was so strange saying good-bye to someone and not knowing what to say. I wondered what I would've said to Becky if I'd gotten to say good-bye to her. But I wasn't sure about that either. I might've told her that I loved her, that I hoped she was happy wherever she was.

I looked at him carefully and tried to memorize his face. I realized suddenly that I didn't even have a picture of him, not even a school one. I would have to rely on my memory to recall his eyes, the smooth shape of his face, the way he smiled, the sound of his voice when he said my name.

"I have something for you," Tommy said, so I knew he'd been telling the truth—he really had planned on waiting for me. He stopped walking for a minute and took a book out of his bag. "They're Shakespeare's sonnets. I thought you'd like them."

I felt overwhelmed that Tommy had gotten me a gift, the first gift I ever got from a boy. "Thanks." I took the book from him. "You didn't have to get me anything."

"I wanted you to have something so you wouldn't forget me."

"I don't have anything for you." But I suddenly wished I had, for the reason Tommy had gotten me something. I wanted him to have something to remember me by. I'm not sure why I thought to give him my necklace, but it seemed like the only reasonable thing to give him. I put down my bag so I could unclasp it, and then I held it out to him. "Here."

"I can't take your necklace," he said.

I nodded. "I want you to have it." I thought about what my grandma Jacobson had said when she'd first given it to us. "My heart."

Tommy closed his fist around the necklace, as if he could feel it beating, feel its pain. "Are you sure?"

"Take it."

We started walking again, and then we rounded the corner and could see both our houses right up the street. Though we walked slowly, there wasn't much farther to go. When we got to my house, we stopped, and we just stood there not saying anything.

It was the end of us, right there in the street, and we

both knew it. But neither one of us knew how to say goodbye. "Have a safe trip," I finally said.

He opened his fist to show me the necklace, then squeezed it shut again and closed his eyes. It's the last real memory I have of Tommy, standing there in front of my house, holding on to his bike with one hand, my heart with the other.

In the book of sonnets, Tommy had circled No. 116 in red ink and written at the top, "To Abigail":

Let me not to the marriage of true minds
Admit impediments. Love is not love
Which alters when it alteration finds,
Or bends with the remover to remove:
O, no! it is an ever-fixed mark,
That looks on tempests and is never shaken;
It is the star to every wandering bark,
Whose worth's unknown, although his height be taken.
Love's not Time's fool, though rosy lips and cheeks
Within his bending sickle's compass come;
Love alters not with his brief hours and weeks,
But bears it out even to the edge of doom.

If this be error and upon me proved,
I never writ, nor no man ever loved.

When I first read it, the poem seemed like an odd thing for Tommy to have circled. I don't think Tommy really meant it as a sign that he would always love me, that he would be waiting for me one day, that our love would last forever. Or maybe he did.

We had been to the edge of doom, all of us, me and Tommy, my parents, even Mrs. Ramirez. And our love became all twisted up in funny ways. My parents' love didn't survive. It had broken over this edge. My mother had fallen to the bottom; my father was hanging ever so carefully at the top. I thought that my love for Tommy might survive, though even as I thought it, I knew it was foolish. Deep down I knew our lives would continue on separately.

But as I understood it, Tommy and I had sat at the edge of doom together, and somehow this was what made us learn to love each other. I decided that the poem was Tommy's heart. And when I wanted to remember it, all I had to do was open the book.

The next morning I watched from my bedroom window as Tommy and his mother packed up the car. They filled the trunk with boxes and suitcases and tied his bike to the back. Before Tommy got into the car, he turned and looked up at my window. I'm not sure if he could see me sitting there or not. It's hard to say with the glare from the sun and the distance. But I felt we were staring at each other for a moment before he turned and got in.

I sat at the window and looked outside long after they drove away. I couldn't believe how quiet it was, how empty the world outside appeared.

Chapter 31

SIX MONTHS AFTER Tommy left, my mother gave up her apartment and moved in with Garret. They bought a little house not too far from Sycamore Street, close enough for me to walk to. Though I don't like it, I've started to realize I'm going to have to try to forgive Garret for taking my mother. In some ways, I guess he tried to save her from herself.

After she moved, my mother told me she quit smoking, but I still smell it on her sometimes, the smoke poorly concealed by too much gardenia perfume, a smell so sickeningly sweet that it makes me nauseated.

About a week after my mother moved in with Garret, I watched Mrs. Peterson move out. I saw her out the front window, her beautiful face splotchy and red from crying. The next day the other woman moved in. She was tall with short black hair, and she had an autistic daughter with the palest ivory skin and darkest black hair I'd ever seen, the girl Tommy must've seen in the window the snowy day we sledded down the hill. It struck me, the way families fell apart so easily, as if the ties that bound them together could come loose with even the slightest pull.

In the fall I started high school. The school combined three junior highs, so there were plenty of people there who didn't know me. Though Jocelyn was still in my homeroom, for the first time there was another girl alphabetically in between us, Kathy Redman, a girl who had no idea that I was Becky's sister. She and I both joined the school newspaper, and we became friends. We sat together at lunch, and my father even let me go to a football game with her on a Friday night the weekend of my fifteenth birthday, though he did insist on sitting up in the bleachers a few rows behind us.

I started to understand what Tommy had felt at the high school, the idea that in a brand-new place where everyone was starting over, you could become someone else. And for the first time since Becky had disappeared, I didn't mind going to school. This feeling, this incredible weightlessness of starting over, lasted for about six weeks, until one day in the middle of October when I was called out of my honors English class to go to the office.

"They've found her."

His words are an ending, a relief and a heartbreak all at once, because I know that everything that happened over the last two years, everything that has led me right here, right to this moment, is finally over.

I can tell you that my father's words are a surprise, but that isn't entirely true. Though I had started to move on in high school, I was still waiting for something. I could still remember the echo of my mother's words, her thin voice faltering just a little bit. *Little girls. Little girls don't just disappear.*

My father signs me out of school and takes me home before he tells me all the details. I'm glad that I don't have to hear it standing there in the hall of my high school, because I have the image of myself falling down, collapsing onto the floor in front of everybody, setting myself up for another three years of being an outsider.

My father sits me down on the couch and gets me a glass of lemonade before he starts talking, and the gap between those words, "They've found her," and what he tells me afterward seems like forever. I think about the last two years the whole time, in that empty space, the way Becky looked the last night in the pool, her sapphire heart buried in the mud, Kinney's accusatory stare, the red glow of my mother's cigarette as she smoked at our kitchen table.

When my father finally starts to talk, his voice is so soft, so even that it almost doesn't sound like he's telling me something horrible.

Becky's body was discovered in a backyard in Harry Baker's neighborhood, just behind Morrow's field, so close to where the police were looking, yet so far away. The man who'd taken her lived six houses down from Harry and, according to my father, had been at the last barbecue we went to at Harry's house. I wonder if Becky had talked to him that night after I left or if he'd watched her from a distance, stalked her even.

The man's name was Jack Turner, and he died of a sudden heart attack just around the time Tommy left for Florida. It's possible Becky might never have been found, that his horrible secret would've died with him, if the people who bought his house at an estate sale hadn't decided to put in a pool. It was the pool contractor who found her nearly as soon as he started digging up the backyard.

My father admits that he has known about the body for two months, but it was just this morning that he found out for sure. Kinney called him at work to let him know it was a definite DNA match. "Why didn't you tell me?" I ask him.

He shakes his head. "You didn't need to know if it wasn't her."

For once I don't feel annoyed by his need to protect me.

We have Becky's funeral on a snowy day in December, nearly two and half years after she disappeared. It takes us two months to get the body back from the police, two months for them to determine that they are not exactly sure how or when she died or if she'd been molested. I am glad for that, because I think it might be better not to know.

Standing in the cold cemetery, my mother reminds me of an ice sculpture, perfectly still and frozen. She has her hair pulled back, and I notice how it has started to get a little gray. Garret holds on to her the whole time, and it looks like he's holding her up, keeping her from crawling into the icy ground with Becky. Even when I hug her, she doesn't respond, doesn't curl into me in the slightest. "She's not well," Garret whispers, and I nod.

My father dresses in a dark suit and tie, with a long black overcoat and black hat. His handsomeness surprises me. He's the one I stand next to, the one I hold on to.

"Are you all right?" my father whispers.

"Yes," I whisper back. "She's dead. She's dead, dead, dead."

He nods. Maybe he already understands what I am just beginning to realize. There is an ending. Finally there is an ending.

A few weeks after Becky's funeral I receive a package in the mail from Tommy. I didn't expect ever to hear from him again, so the package is a nice surprise. I hastily pull off the wrapping, and I see it, the old shoe box. I let out a little cry. My pictures.

Tommy wrote a note and taped it to the box:

I heard about Becky. I'm so sorry. I forgot to give these back before I left, but I kept *them safe just like I promised. Hope they bring back good memories.*

Tommy

I open the lid. Suddenly there we are, me and Becky as children, in our matching pink bathing suits with our feet hanging in the pool. The blond girl with pigtails, slightly different from how I've made her in my memories. She's missing teeth in the one picture, and her hair is lighter than I've come to picture it. And then there's me, the frizzy mop of brown hair, my head hanging off to the side, annoyed at having to pose for one more of my mother's pictures.

The pictures from Tommy are a gift, a childhood in a box, something to take out and look at when all I can think about are the two years that followed, the two years of which there are no pictures.

When I go back to school after Christmas, people suddenly seem to remember, to know me again as the sister of the missing girl. Kathy still eats lunch with me, but she's become close to some other girls on the paper who make me feel a little uncomfortable, their stares sometimes piercing me as if I were some kind of scientific specimen.

But there is one person who doesn't stare, the new boy who has moved to our school from upstate New York and has never even heard of Becky. He's tall, and he has this thick, wavy brown hair. He wears tiny glasses, and when I first see him the day he comes in to join the paper, I immediately think his glasses make him look very smart in a handsome sort of way.

On his second day at the paper, he comes over and sits down next to me. For a minute I look around thinking that it's someone else he came to talk to, but I'm the only one there. "I'm Richard Rucker," he says.

"Abby Reed." I search his face for an indication that he recognizes the name, that he knows I am Becky's sister, but I see nothing there.

Richard and I become friends, and we talk on the phone, sometimes for hours. He asks me to go to the junior prom with him, an idea that doesn't thrill my father since I'm only a sophomore still, but he reluctantly says I can go after I tell him how excited my mother is about the whole thing. She is so excited, in fact, that she actually takes me to the mall to shop for a dress. In the dressing room she's lit up and laughing, and when she sees me in the dress I end up buying, a red strapless one that flows out at the bottom, she has tears in her eyes. She holds her hand up to her mouth and gasps, "My little girl is all grown up."

When Richard comes to pick me up, my mother and Garret come over to the house to see me off. My mother is smiling, and Garret is laughing, and he looks more relaxed than I've ever seen him. My father takes out the camera, and I realize it's something I haven't seen since before Becky disappeared.

This is the first time Richard meets my parents, and I'm surprised by the easy way my father shakes his hand. My mother gives him a big hug. "Don't you look so handsome," she says, and though I feel myself getting embarrassed for him, her comment pleases me.

The prom is magical, the high school gym disguised so well by balloons and streamers and painted backdrops that it doesn't feel like our high school at all. Richard and I dance almost the whole time, fast fun songs and slow songs where I lean in close to him, where I feel the warmth of his body against mine. We kiss on the dance floor, in the middle of a slow song, and for the first time I feel like I'm in a fairy tale, a happy story, not a sad one.

I can walk to the cemetery from my house, and a few weeks after the prom I make a deal with my father so that he lets me go alone as long as I get home before dark. I realize how strange it is that it's Becky who made him so overprotective of me and then Becky who allows him to start letting go.

Sitting there alone, on the warm April grass, I feel this strange new sense of freedom. It is refreshingly quiet in the cemetery, and I sit there and think about Becky, about all the times we fought, and then I see her so clearly that last night in the pool, her head bobbing above the water. After a few minutes I feel like I should say something, that I should talk to her, that maybe she will actually be able to hear me.

Once I start talking, I can't stop, and I tell her things that I haven't told anyone else: everything that happened with me and Tommy and how it feels to kiss Richard. By the time I'm done talking, I realize it's almost dark, and I know I will have to run home to keep my promise to my father. But I tell her that I'll be back soon, that I will have other things to tell her.

And I know I will be back to tell her these things because I imagine as the two of us got older, we would've become friends, we would've loved being sisters, just the way my mother always said we would.

Acknowledgments

I AM ENORMOUSLY indebted to my agent, Jessica Regel, at the Jean V. Naggar Literary Agency, for her enduring belief in me, her infinite patience, and her wisdom. Thank you to my editor, Jill Santopolo, for falling in love with this book and for giving me the guidance to make it work. I am also tremendously grateful to Laura Geringer and everyone else at HarperCollins who has worked so hard on my behalf.

Many thanks to all the teachers who showed me the power of the written word and encouraged me to keep going, most notably: Mrs. "I," Andrea "La" Lamberth, Charlotte Holmes, and Aurelie Sheehan.

For their encouragement and support, thank you to my friends and fellow writers Ann Stewart Hendry and Meghan

Tifft. Thank you to Monica Hoffman Tufo—a wonderful friend in junior high school and still today

My deepest thanks to my parents, Alan and Ronna Cantor, for teaching me that anything is possible and for being the most enthusiastic readers. Thank you to my June sister, Rachel Cantor, for her friendship. And thank you to my two beautiful children for being a constant source of inspiration and joy.

Most especially, thank you to my extraordinary husband, Gregg Goldner, who is always my best friend and best reader. Without his love and support, this book never would have existed.